UNINTENDED CONSEQUENCES

A SOPHIE STAR SERIES BOOK TWO

L. J. WEBB

UNINTENDED CONSEQUENCES
BY L. J. WEBB

eBook ISBN **978-1-7330939-2-7**
Paperback ISBN **978-1-7330939-3-4**

Library of Congress Control Number: 2020906811

TABLE OF CONTENTS

For I know the thoughts that I think toward you, says the LORD, thoughts of peace and not of evil, to give you a future and a hope. Jeremiah 29:11

CHAPTER ONE

At approximately 7 pm, three men in a Zodiac Milpro, motored onto the shore of Wonsan, North Korea. They came ashore about 3 miles from their target location. The men dressed in shozoku, katanas strapped to their back, pulled the craft to shore, and tied it to a tree. The leader grabbed the rope from the craft and placed it over his head and around his shoulder. Without a word, they jogged to the offices of Yon Brothers Enterprise in the industrial area.

As the leading counterfeiters in the world, with the best quality in the business, they sell more counterfeit US $100 bills than any other country. Peru is fighting for first place with its Superdollar. The US government is struggling to keep these bills from circulation.

The notoriously unreliable electrical grid of North Korea caused the blackout. The intruders traversed the rugged terrain by using night vision goggles, virtually invisible. The men paused at the edge of a copse of trees next to the industrial area. They spotted Yon Enterprises.

To the east was a manufacturing plant and to the west a warehouse. Sixteen wheelers sat dark, abandoned, waiting to be loaded in the morning. All was dark except Yon Brothers. The men could hear the generator from where they stood. A reward for funneling millions of dollars into the Supreme

Leaders obsession; the missile program. Their support afforded the Yon's many luxuries.

They crossed the road at the darkest point. Seeing the two guards, they avoided approaching the front entrance. The men moved to the back of the building, looking for another entry point. A window on the second floor was slightly ajar. Using themselves as a ladder, they stood on each other's shoulders, allowing the last man to open the window. He then dropped a rope down to the others after tying the end around his waist.

The three men moved ninjutsu, looking for the room where the partners held their weekly meeting. They stopped on the third floor when they heard men's voices. Accomplishing the mission in less than three minutes, they sent proof in picture form to Izumi, who ordered the hit. Then they were out in the cover of darkness again, heading back to their vessel. All of it done without a word said between them.

Yon had packed his bag and headed back to his mandatory appearance at Appa's weekly business meeting. It would draw too much attention to not show up. Yon walked to the third floor and headed to the conference room. When he opened the door, the smell hit him. He saw the scene before him and threw up. Against the opposite wall were the heads of his Appa and uncles. Their bodies left where they dropped on the other side of the room. Yon's legs collapsed under him. He crab-walked backward until his back hit the wall. He couldn't suck in air.

"APPA!" He cried. "Oh, Appa, I never intended for this to happen."

CHAPTER TWO
TWO MONTHS EARLIER

Houston couldn't believe his honeymoon was over. Sophie was settling in her seat, looking through her purse. He was putting their carry-ons in the overhead compartment. It had been over a year since Houston fell in love with his wife. He met her while working for the DEA.

Sophie came in with a proposal to take down one of the most notorious drug empires in the country. She convinced the powers that be that indeed she could dismantle the drug empire of Nikko Morano. She knew how because she was the one who had made Nikko's enterprise nearly impenetrable. Though the mission was successful, Nikko kidnapped Sophie while on bond awaiting prosecution. He had been obsessed with her and planned on leaving the country, forcing her to go with him.

Houston and his partner Alfonso Rodrigues, known to friends simply as Fons, were undercover. They were working with Nikko's brother, Thomas. Chasing Nikko through several states trying to rescue her. It ended badly. Nikko died when SWAT was called to the scene playing out between the brothers on a New Orleans wharf.

The plane took off just as the sun was setting. Houston had purchased first-class tickets; he liked spoiling his bride. The lights were low and the noise had died down. Sophie snuggled up to his arm, her head on one of those tiny airplane pillows, her legs curled up on her seat.

It took several months for his custom-designed ring to come in. A flawless 4 carat Princess cut diamond. Set in a platinum wedding band with 12-quarter carat baguettes. Inside of the ring was the inscription, 'my one and only princess'.

The night before the wedding, he had her signed onto everything he owned. He showed her his net value; he was wealthy due to the investment he made in his father's wildcatting operation.

Houston knew she didn't need his money. She had her own, most of it coming from the reward by the DOJ. She received a percentage of the assets taken in the raid on the Morano empire. She reciprocated by adding him to her offshore accounts. They decided to stay in her penthouse near central park. He knew she loved her home and it was twice the size of his house.

The wedding was in Trenton, New Jersey, at the church Sophie and he attended. Houston's family also attended the church and lived close by. The reception was outside on his parent's property.

Houston recalled the fun they all had, but the wedding itself was a blur. He stood in his tux next to his partner and best man Fons, worried she would change her mind at the last minute. He didn't even breathe until he saw her come down the aisle on his father's arm. Sophie was exquisite in her designer gown. Her perfect curves emphasized by the shape of the dress. She chose a Mantilla and a jeweled comb instead of a veil. Her auburn hair was up with soft tendrils framing her beautiful face and hazel eyes. That's what he remembered; the rest was a blur, except for the moment the Pastor said, "you may kiss the bride," which Houston did with great enthusiasm. He finally ended the kiss when the guest started to laugh.

Houston hoped for an intimate and cozy ceremony. That hope was lost when many high-ranking government and law enforcement officials requested an invitation.

The first leg of the honeymoon was a week in Paris in a condo only a block away from the Eiffel Tower. After site-seeing, shopping, eating all day and late into the night. They would sit on the balcony and watch the light show on the Eiffel Tower. The days they spent walking hand in hand down the vendor laden streets were some of the best times of his life. The next week they drove up the Corniche de l'Esterel stopping whenever they felt like it. Finally, before flying back home from Paris, they spent a week on a yacht cruising the Ligurian Sea. The intimacy they now shared brought their love to a whole new dimension.

Now they were on their way home, and he wanted to make sure he'd never forget all the promises he made her. He took her left hand from his arm and brought it to his lips, kissed her palm, and looked at the wedding ring on her finger.

Sophie wasn't sure how long she had slept. But now she was in that in-between place and heard Houston whisper.

"Sophie Star-Townsend, God created you with me in mind."

Sophie surprised him by saying back to him, "Mr. Houston Townsend, God created you with me in mind."

Houston turned in his chair to face her and they kissed. She felt his passion and hoped his love for her would never grow cold.

She settled back into her seat and pulled up the shade over the small airplane window. It was still dark, but she could see stars and the light from some city in the distance.

Sophie looked at her beautiful wedding ring. She couldn't help thinking of the proposal. Even though she knew it was coming, she was surprised at the creative way Houston had done it. He got box tickets at the ballet, and during intermission, in his tux, he got down on one knee and proposed. With happy tears ruining her flawless makeup, she bent down, kissed him, and said yes.

Sophie loved everything about the honeymoon. She tried to push down the feeling that someone had been watching her. She felt it first in Paris. It got worse when she called down to the management to thank them for the champagne they sent up. It was a surprise to find they hadn't sent it. They poured it down the drain since neither of them drink. Sophie wanted to believe it was paranoia, an after effect of what she went through with Nikko. But she felt it again when they were at the airport; she wondered if the person was on the plane with them. Telling Houston was out of the question. He would immediately set up a 24/7 security detail. Sophie had to live with that kind of protection while she was working with the task force. She promised herself never again would she allow it. She loved that Houston was protective of her, but she couldn't go through it again. And, after all, she could be imagining it.

CHAPTER THREE

Houston had been back at work for two weeks. He had already moved his things from his home into the 'his' walk-in closet in the master bedroom. His mind still on his honeymoon.

Rodriguez broke his train of thought, "when are you going to get that stupid grin off your face, buddy."

He laughed, "you're going to have to get used to it because it's permanent."

"You remember before we joined the DEA we had put our applications in at the US Marshals. Do you ever wonder about trying again?" Rodriguez asked.

"After tracking Nikko and working protective detail, I have to say I prefer it to this. We didn't take the job because they couldn't offer us New York at the time, right?" Houston shifted some files aside.

"Yeah, and now with Sophie, I'm sure you don't want to move her away from her comfort zone right now." Rodriguez's facial expression showed disappointment.

"We can always apply again and see what happens." Houston looked up at Rodriguez with a smile.

"We can apply online. Since Hampton got his promotion to Division Chief he'll be leaving soon, so this is the perfect time to move on." Houston nodded his head in agreement.

"The big wigs have been keeping the boss busy lately. It must still have to do with the Morano wrongful death litigation. I heard it would likely get thrown out of court, like all the other litigation the Morano's threw at the DEA." Houston speculated.

"We'll catch up with him tomorrow. My report is done on that last street dealer's interview; how about you?"

"I'm ready too." Houston got up, and they walked out together. Chief Hampton wasn't the only one who got a promotion. Everyone that was part of the task force got bumped up. Houston and Fons were now Senior Agents with a significant bump in pay.

Approaching the condo, Houston noticed it smelled like something was burning. He rushed to open the door. There was Sophie, sitting at the kitchen table, Bully's head in her lap, tears streaming down her cheeks. The picture in front of him explained it all. It was hard not to laugh at that sad but humorous scene. She had burned the dinner she tried to prepare for him. He went over to her, sat down, and took her hand.

"Sophie, honey, what's the matter?" He asked, already knowing the answer.

"Houston, you are the perfect husband, you take such good care of everything. I want to be a perfect wife for you." She half sobbed the response. He lifted her to her feet and wrapped his arms around her.

"You are the perfect wife. You're smart, funny, kind. You make me the happiest man on earth, what else could I possibly ask for?" Houston wisely answered and kissed her forehead.

"Dinner." Sophie looked up at him, "you need to eat."

Houston couldn't hold in the laugh this time, "what happened." She turned to the kitchen.

"After I put the casserole in, I went to work on the computer and didn't hear the timer."

He noticed the other casseroles on the counter. "How many times did you try to make this?"

"The first time I left something out. I was following the recipe, but then my mind wandered. I've been working on an idea to expand my networking on the computer. It tasted horrible. The second time I left the flour out when the phone rang; that one was all soupy. Your mom wanted to know if we could come Saturday night for your sister's birthday. Anyway, I thought I'd try one more time."

Houston tried to control a laugh that was desperately trying to come out but he didn't dare. Sometimes he felt like he lived in a Lucille Ball episode. He opened the refrigerator.

"Look we have steaks, how about I put them on the grill, and you can make a salad?" He negotiated.

"I need to clean up this mess and what are we going to do about meals? You knew how much I hate to cook when you married me." Sophie sat down again flustered.

"Yes, and I married you anyway," he laughed. Sophie was not amused. "Let's figure this out. You make a great breakfast. We can both handle a simple lunch, and for dinner, I'll grill a couple of nights a week. We eat at mom's on Sunday, and we eat out at least once a week." He was gaining momentum.

"That still leaves three dinners not accounted for." She pouted, looking over the mess in the kitchen.

"We'll hire a chef to come in once a week and prepare three meals for us; then we can cook them as we need them." He decided.

"Like costly TV dinners?" She asked, a gleam of hope in her eyes.

"Well, sort of, they just won't be frozen."

9

She looked up at him, "that's not a bad idea, but I insist on paying for the chef." She moved to the first casserole and started scraping it into the garbage disposal.

"Sweetheart, no, let your account be. I'll cover it out of the household expense.

Agent Hoyt from the communications department of the FBI knocked on the open Deputy Directors door, then entered the office.

"Deputy Director Cosby, I got a heads up from the Secret Service Director Adam Bean. They have been tracking calls going into North Korea from this area. He wants to talk to you about it."

"Thank you, does he want a face to face or will the phone do?"

"A face to face, ASAP, sir," he waited for a reply.

"Understood."

The next day Rodriguez and Houston were waiting for a chance to talk to Chief Hampton; he wasn't in his office.

Houston walked up to Sara, his secretary, at her desk and asked where he was. She pointed to the conference room.

They nodded and headed for their desks. Houston recounted to Fons the tale of Sophie's kitchen disaster and they both got a chuckle out of it.

"I don't understand how the smartest woman I've ever met can't cook." Houston laughed.

"If that's the worst dilemma you ever face, you're a lucky man." Rodriguez harassed him.

"Don't I know it."

"Townsend, Rodriguez, in here." They lifted their heads when they heard the Chief call their names.

They walked into the conference room. Sitting with Chief Hampton was now Deputy Director Cosby from the FBI. Cosby was heavier than before and his bald spot was gaining ground. Houston wondered why he didn't shave his head.

"Have a seat," Hampton directed.

"Thank you, sir," Houston replied while they took a seat.

Deputy Director Cosby stood up, directing his attention to them.

"Gentlemen, I have had this idea since the Morano takedown. Our agencies assemble a task force every time an issue comes up that crosses more than one agency. What we need is a task force ready on a moment's notice. One that consistently works together.

"Nikko Morano was killed by SWAT because they didn't have all the information they needed. That has cost the government months and months of litigation. The family attorneys are still filing petitions. It's costly and time-consuming." He looked straight at Houston, "don't get me wrong, SWAT did what they are trained to do. The flaw came in their lack of knowledge of the players."

Houston nodded, remembering the scene on the pier that ended in the death of Nikko. It could have cost Sophie her life as well. "If our task force had been there, it would have played out differently. Having a team that knows and understands each other would have made the difference." He took a moment for that statement to sink in.

"What I'm doing here today gentlemen, is offering you a place on the joint task force. The Task Force will work across every jurisdiction. FBI, CIA, DHS, DOJ, Secret Service, and DEA. It will only take cases that traverses more than one department in its scope. It also has to have a major impact on the country as a whole. When the threat is enough to call in this task force, we will be expected to take down the entire operation. The joint task force will operate out of the FBI facilities in Washington, DC. And it will have the most up to date technology and real-time capabilities. Agent Mathews is working on making sure the systems can't be hacked." He sat back down and looked at Agent Townsend. "Houston, you and Rodriquez would run the operations center and the field logistics. The strategic planner would run the live operations. A Seal team, and a SWAT or SRT unit would also be at our disposal when needed," Cosby said.

"The Morano confiscated funds are funding much of this task force. Many of the people who worked that takedown will be offered a position." This was the first time Hampton added to the conversation.

"Gentlemen, are you interested?"

Houston spoke first, "Sir, I'm very interested, but I need to think about it. When we're not on assignment with the task force, can we work out of the US Marshals office in New York?"

"Yes. You would have a desk in whatever department you wanted. Since the task force will pay your salaries, they would be getting highly trained Special Agents for free. There isn't an agency head in the country that would turn you down."

Cosby looked around, "let's take a lunch break." The men stood.

"Agent Townsend, could I speak to you a moment, please." Cosby indicated for Houston to sit down across from him.

"Agent Townsend, I have a favor to ask. I have interviewed several people for the position of head of strategic planning. None comes close to having your wife's abilities. Ms. Star reads people. I've seen her predict reactions to a given scenario with uncanny accuracy. Unlike most strategists, she simplifies things and makes everyone's safety a priority. Even the targets." Cosby took a minute to consider his wording. "I would appreciate it if you would be willing to talk to her about what we're doing. See if she might want to work with us. I thought it would be worth a try. At this point, filling that position is the only thing holding this up. If her answer is no, then I know I have to decide on one of the others."

Houston looked at him. "Sir, I have to tell you, I'm not sure I would be comfortable with the risk my wife would be taking. However, she can decide for herself. I'll approach her about it."

"That's all I can ask. Thank you." Cosby stood up to shake his hand. Houston reciprocated. Then he stopped at the door, turned and said.

"You might be careful what you wish for. You know she will want full control of the team during the action."

"I remember, but Ms. Star has the abilities we need." Cosby thanked him, and Houston left.

Houston and Rodriguez went to lunch. "What do you think, Houston?"

"It does sound like the change we were wanting, but I have a wife now, I can't make this decision without her being on board. They want me to try to recruit her too. I don't know that I like the idea of her life being in jeopardy, Fons."

"Hey, I'm not doing it without you, we're a team," Rodriguez added.

Houston looked him in the eye, "Fons, I want you to do what is best for you. I won't take this job without you. But I don't want to hold you back; this is a huge step up." Rodriguez nodded, but Houston knew he had no intention of taking this job without him.

Houston made it home a little early. Sophie came to the door, wrapped her arms around him, and kissed him. One of his favorite things about being married was having someone to greet him when he got home.

She leaned back and said, "I found a chef; her name is Carol King. She's recently out of culinary school and leans to the healthy side of cooking. But I like her anyway; she will be perfect."

"That's great Sophie, how about I cook on the grill tonight, I need to talk to you about something." She took his hand and headed to the kitchen.

"Sure, I never turn down a good meal. I'll make a salad." He went to get changed into some jeans.

Sophie had a tray with the steaks, spices, and utensils he uses ready for him to take outside for the grill. It was drizzling, but they had a good portion of the covered balcony to use. She was throwing the ball for Bully when he came out with the tray.

"Sophie, can you come sit with me while I grill, I want to tell you about a meeting I had at work today."

He went on to tell her about the new joint task force and how it would change his daily routine if he decided to take the job.

"Sophie, I can't say I'm not interested in the job. But I'm more interested and committed to you being happy with our lifestyle. Neither of us needs to work. If you don't want to move, Fons and I would reapply for a US Marshalls opening in New York and be very content with that. This task force offer comes with a big jump in pay and a higher ranking, but Fons and I are not ambitious in that way," he finished.

"Houston, I'm not a porcelain doll, moving wouldn't break me, as long as we are together. You are my comfort zone, not where we live. But I have a feeling there is more to this story." He put the steaks on the grill, hearing them sizzle.

"Cosby got his promotion. He would be the administrator of the task force; he's Deputy Director now." Houston hadn't told her that news yet. "Cosby asked me to see if you would think about joining. He made it clear that the offer to Fons and me is not contingent on you," he paused to look at her. "Only that the task force would be more efficient with you on it."

Sophie thought for a moment, "I do like the work. It's like undoing a puzzle, breaking it down into little pieces. And working with the task force was exciting, but I never sought a life in law enforcement. I was planning to take on a few wealthy accounting clients." she replied while stroking Bully's soft fur.

"What's appealing to me is that it's not a full-time gig. Fons and I will be able to work with the US Marshals but still get our bump in pay," he turned the steaks on the grill. "And you could take time off between assignments to do whatever you want," he added.

"I don't want you thinking you would be keeping me from what I want to do if you decline. If I take the job, we would get a house in DC and stay there when we needed to and stay here the rest of the time."

He didn't want to pressure her. She was quiet while they ate, which he knew meant she was thinking. They went to bed, agreeing to pray about it.

In the morning when Houston woke up to his alarm, Sophie was out of bed. Smelling breakfast, he hurried to get dressed and went to the table. She handed him a plate with bacon, eggs, and wheat toast and sat down with him.

"Aren't you going to eat with me, sweetheart?" He asked.

Sophie got up to get her plate and came back, "I've decided to talk to Cosby about the position. But I have a ton of stipulations, and if he doesn't agree; I'm out."

"Sophie, don't do this for me, please, to be honest as your husband I'm conflicted about you being in any danger."

Sophie looked at him, "Houston, you have always taken great precautions with my safety. Besides, we both learned how to trust God in situations out of our control," she reminded him. "No. If I do this, it's because God has given me instinct about people. I can tell how they will react in given situations. Fighting crime seems like the best use of that gift."

He took her hand, "I'll let him know." He was less than exuberant.

"Houston, if you rather I don't do this, I'm ok with that," she said.

He shook his head, "you're my wife, and I know how gifted you are. I also know this is dangerous even in the most controlled environment if word gets out. But, you have the right to do what you want, and I will support your decision."

"If we decide after the first assignment, it's too dangerous; we'll revisit it. Ok?" Sophie wrapped her arms around him.

"I'm ok with that," he agreed.

Houston headed to DEA headquarters. His mind racing on all the ways this was a bad idea for his wife. Finally, he whispered a prayer, "our life and times are in your hands, oh God. You gave her this intellect, and You know your plan for her. I don't want to get in the way, but please don't ever let me lose her. I don't know if I could take it. I trust you, Lord." With that, a peace came over him. He was dialing Cosby when he noticed he was in the conference room.

Cosby's head was down reading a document. He knocked on the door, "Sir, do you have a minute?"

"Of course, Agent Townsend, have you decided about joining the team."

"Not yet, sir, but my wife would like to talk to you about it," Houston said.

Cosby looked up at him, shocked, "you're kidding; she'll join the task force?"

"She said she would discuss it, but she has a *ton of stipulations*. Her words, sir."

"I know this woman will make my life miserable. If she weren't the only person for this job, I would take back the offer." Then Cosby realized who he was complaining about. "I apologize, Agent Townsend, I realize I'm talking about your wife."

Houston laughed, "you think I don't know how challenging she is going to make this for you. But you're right; she is the right person for this job."

Cosby ran a hand over his face in resignation, "can you see how soon she can get here?"

"Certainly, sir. I'll call her right now."

Houston had made arrangements with a town car company for their personal use. He vetted several of the drivers himself, with their permission. He asked that they be the only ones to pick Sophie up when needed. Sophie said she could be ready downstairs at noon, so Houston made the call for her pickup. He let Cosby know.

Sophie arrived at about 12:25 pm. Houston escorted her to the conference room. Chief Hampton and Deputy Director Cosby stood when she entered.

"Ms. Star," Houston had told him she would use her maiden name for work purposes. It was something she and Houston discussed. He agreed if they worked together, it would allow people to judge them independent of each other.

"I understand you might consider my offer to join the task force." He then directed them to sit, and he and Hampton also sat down.

"I do have some questions and some stipulations if this were to work out."

17

"Ms. Star, I know how you work, let's get to it," Cosby said with a slight smile on his face.

"I would want to work as an independent contractor. I don't want to be on any law enforcement payroll. My husband would negotiate my salary and perks. It would be on a case by case basis. I would want to be free to take consulting work from other agencies or private companies. Naturally, I would select the team who works directly with me. My preference being those who worked with us on the Morano case," she added.

"I have offered positions to most of them. But they want to know who will be in the position we offered you before they sign on. They were hopeful you would take the position." Cosby's eyes drifted to the window for a moment, trying to decide how to word his next statement. "Sophie; I hope it's alright if I use your given name?" She nodded. "I am sorry about how the Morano case ended. That's one of the reasons I want a team that can read each other in a stressful situation. It could have ended without Nikko's death if our team had been in control. They would have known to give you time, that you would have talked him down. The SWAT team did the right thing based on protocol and regulations. But they didn't know the people or the circumstances. One thing I'm looking for is someone who doesn't want anyone to die, no matter what side of the fence they're on."

Her voice choked up, "thank you for that Mr. Cosby, Nikko's death was unnecessary. It was difficult for me to reconcile."

"I understand that completely, Ms. Star."

She stood up, looked at Houston than back to Cosby. "I'm sure you have others who could do this job, so you'll need time to decide if my demands are worth the challenge to you. I will leave the decision in your hands." Cosby stood, acknowledging her as she left the room with Houston.

Houston took her out of sight of the conference room and held her close. He could see she was questioning herself, "you were brilliant in there."

"I don't know Houston; maybe this isn't such a good idea. Why would any of these people listen to me?"

He kissed her softly and held her close, "because your brilliant, and they know it."

He walked her back down to the town car and then went back to the conference room. Cosby and Hampton were discussing her demands, Rodriguez was in the room with them. Surprisingly, it was Cosby that was ready to accept her terms without any negotiation. That was 180° from his original opinion of his wife when they first worked together.

Cosby turned to Houston and said, "please let your wife know she is our first choice if she accepts; it's on her terms."

"I will sir," Houston replied.

"How soon do you want this team up and running?" Rodriguez asked.

"Our projection date is four weeks. The team will have to set up the *command center* and have everything functioning at that time. We have a situation brewing that is coming to critical mass, and we need to get to work on it."

Houston went home early and talked through the possibilities with his wife. He vocalized their final decision.

"Ok, so we sell my house."

Sophie stopped him, "I know it's your house, but may I make a suggestion?"

Houston turned to her, "it's *our* house, and what's on your mind?"

"If I recall there is a minimal mortgage on your home, I suggest you pay it off and then sell it on a contract. You can ask at least 2% higher interest than the bank. Selling it on a contract will be appealing to a first-time buyer and cause the house to sell faster. Your money will be working for you," she suggested.

"You see, that's why I married you, for your brain," he smiled and kissed her forehead.

"Yeah, just like I married you for your money."

He laughed, "you mean you didn't?" She slapped his arm.

"Anyway, we'll buy a house in DC and keep the penthouse. What do you think?"

"I would like to buy a house we both like with the money in my account. Then turn it into a duplex, that way we always have someone there watching out for the place when we're not home."

"You know I don't like using your money," Houston said furrowing his brow.

"You said we would discuss it when it came up. I want to make my money work for me. Real estate is still one of the highest yielding investments."

He thought for a moment, "you have a point. Ok, we find a house we like. You tell me the budget and how you want it to look. I will supervise and help to work on the property to get you the highest yield for your money."

"You're amazing, and remember, we agreed all real property would be in both of our names," Sophie said.

"I think you just tricked me into accepting some of your money."

"You're my husband, everything I have is yours, whether you like it or not."

CHAPTER FOUR
ONE WEEK EARLIER

Alexander Ivanov walked into his father's office. "Papa, Yon Min-Ji has offered us 50 million in counterfeit $100 bills for 20 million. His purchaser backed out saying that North Korea was under too much scrutiny. He was afraid it would get confiscated."

Vladimir looked at him sternly, "Son, we are Americans now, we don't do business with the North Koreans. We have sources in Hong Kong, Peru, and Columbia; I have no problem working with them."

"But Papa, our profit margin is not as high with them." Alex walked over to his father's desk.

Vladimir motioned for his son to sit down. "Son, I have tried to teach you everything I know. One day this will all be yours. But you don't grasp some basic principles; greed will cause you to do things that will get you in prison or dead. We can make a huge profit with our other suppliers. Being careful is why we are still here after 40 years. You must have discipline and loyalty. North Korea would wipe the US off the map if it could, any money they get goes to that purpose. How does that benefit us if we live here when they decide to do that?" His father scolded him.

"Papa, you're getting old and no longer want to take chances, but I'm young and not afraid." His father got up and moved to face him.

"Anytime you wish to challenge me, go right ahead, but if you do that, you will be on your own. I will excommunicate you from the family. Would you do that to your mother?"

"No, of course not Papa, I just want to make my mark in business."

"You are only 23, son. You have many years to do that, but if you make a foolish mistake, you will make most of your mark in prison."

Alex hugged his father and left the room; he loved his family but wasn't sure how long he was willing to wait. Yon's counterfeit money could be his chance to go out on his own. He just wasn't sure he was ready to separate from his family forever.

Alex was not happy with how the conversation went with his Papa. He turned his mind to the pretty young Korean girl, Kim Lee, who worked with Demitri. Alex had plans for her; the first step was getting her to go out with him. She had refused him several times. He wasn't used to anyone turning him down.

Houston and Sophie had finally found a young couple they trusted. The real estate contract was closing in two weeks. They found a great place in DC to renovate.

The house, an older whitewash Colonial Revival, two-story made of brick, had a wide covered front porch. Nine-foot ceilings graced the inside, with a rock fireplace, and beautiful crown molding. There was wallpaper above the wainscoting; too old to keep. The stairs to the second floor sat to the right coming in the front door. The kitchen, though outdated, was well designed. The old glass sliding door that opened to the oversized back yard needed replaced with French doors. There were two bedrooms on the main floor and three on the upper level. Other than some remodeling and cosmetic work downstairs, most of the remodeling was going to happen upstairs.

The plan was to gut the second level and make a one-bedroom apartment. The layout called for a generous kitchen and living room. They would have to create access to the upstairs from the outside and decided to add stairs and a balcony behind the double car garage and carport. Fons was helping Houston with the initial remodeling. He planned on renting the apartment when it was finished — a perfect scenario for both parties.

Dark Eyes had caught up with the newlyweds in Paris. He followed them around Europe and then to the US. He landed at Newark Liberty International Airport. Not the choice he would have made, but he understood the benefit to those who lived in Manhattan. Dark eyes initially planned on taking care of his business in New York first. He changed his plans after he watched his target for a few days. Instead Dark Eyes decided to take care of his out of state commitments first then come back to complete this job. There was no logical reason for the change of plans other than he enjoyed watching her. He went to the Delta counter and bought a ticket to Arizona. He figured he would take care of his furthest contract first and work his way back.

Dark Eyes had been gone weeks on his other business. He was glad to be back. He found a perfect spot to watch Sophie's condo. A four-tier parking garage across the street with an excellent view of her balcony. She spent a lot of time out there, tending flowers or playing with her mutt.

He watched her only a few days when he received a text forwarded to him from his answering service. A job came in that was time sensitive. He considered declining it; he didn't need the money. But as the founder of the company, he felt he needed to support the partners by keeping the coffers full. It would only take a couple of days and he could drive there and back.

Dark Eyes came back to his spot in the parking garage three days later, to find she was gone. He sat there two days watching but the place was dark. *She's never gone this long,* he reasoned, putting down the binoculars.

When he spent long hours surveilling his targets his mind wondered. Today his thoughts went back to the only woman he ever loved. She was a beautiful woman, but his best friend proposed to her before he had a chance. After that, he decided with his chosen profession, it was best to be alone. It was a conscious decision.

Dark Eyes was never lonely; he had companionship when he wanted it. But never a real relationship; he never loved any of them. He knew he was good looking, tall, fit, dark hair, dark brown eyes, a perpetual tan due to his lineage. He'd hear women refer to him as tall, dark, and handsome. But it wasn't his good looks that gave him his self-esteem. His self-esteem came from the authority he wielded and the respect shown him by others. They feared him, with good reason.

Dark Eyes wondered if watching Sophie was giving him a pseudo-relationship. He got up wondering what she was doing, and at night, she was his last thought. *You are an intriguing woman Ms. Star,* Dark Eyes thought. He had never

24

made a connection with a target before. He should have moved on a long time ago. But watching her was the highlight of his day. No matter, he needed to find her and end this.

Houston and Fons were working on the apartment upstairs when his phone rang.

"Hello?" Houston listened to the person on the other end. "Yes sir."

Fons could only hear one side of the conversation.

"I can have them all there in an hour, sir." Houston hung up. Fons waited for the information.

"Cosby wants us at the command center, ASAP."

"What's up?" Fons asked.

"I have no idea."

"I'll get Mathews to contact everyone," Rodriguez offered.

"Great, I'll get Sophie." It was Sunday night.

Sophie had finished putting up the wallpaper earlier in the day. The smell of the glue still tickled her nose. She put the last coat of paint on the floorboards. She would ask Houston to reattach them tonight when he got done upstairs.

Bully was starting to get acquainted with his new home. He loved the back yard and spent hours a day chasing rabbits, squirrels, or anything else that moved.

Sophie had felt guilty, not telling Houston about the feelings she had that someone was watching her. She was glad now that she hadn't. Sophie no longer felt watched, which convinced her she was right all along. It was just paranoia after the trauma of the last year.

Houston came downstairs and told Sophie Cosby had called them into the Command Center. She asked if he knew what was up, but he had no answer. Houston called Bully in and made sure he had water and food. He had no idea how long they would be gone.

They were out the door with Fons in fifteen minutes.

Alex called Yon Min-Ji back with his Papa's refusal of the generous offer. "Yon, I'm sorry, I would do it in a heartbeat, but if I go against my Papa, he will disown me. I don't have the funds to go out on my own yet."

"I have the same problem with my Appa; he still thinks I'm too young to take over the business. He treats me like a servant. I doubt he even plans to pass the business on to me." Yon's bitter feelings about his father were from years of being abused. "I wish there were a way we could do this deal together, without them finding out. We could split the profit. That way, we would have a seed to go out on our own," Yon said.

"I know you can't hold onto all that money, but could you hold onto 10 million for a while and I'll see what I can do?" Alex requested.

"Can you come up with 4 million?" Yon asked.

"My Papa easily has that amount, but I don't know if I can get it back to him before he found out it was missing. He would disown me."

"If I can sell the forty million in smaller increments, I can ask more for it. There is a high demand for small amounts. If I could give my Appa the 20 million he wants, no one would know I kept any of it. That would give us time to sell it." Yon was doodling dollar signs on a note pad on his desk. "I couldn't sell the extra ten over here. It would get back to my Appa, but if you buy it from me for 4 million, then you can use or resell it in the US. You would make a huge profit. Four million would go a long way to getting me out on my own. I know all of Appa's contacts."

"How much time can you give me?" Alex asked.

"As long as I sell the other 40 million, I can give you at least a month," Yon replied.

"It's a deal. Thanks, Yon, maybe we can work together on other ventures." Alex finished. They said their goodbyes and went on with their day.

"Gentlemen, we have a situation. Vladimir Ivanov's organization has been on our radar for years, for laundering money. Recently, they started moving counterfeit money. It was agreed that unless they moved more than 5 million, the new Task Force would not take over the case from SS or FBI.

"In the last three years, Ivanov has been increasing his quantity of counterfeit $100 bills yearly. He has bought from Peru, Hong Kong, Venezuela, Mexico, and Bolivia. This increase is why we were pushing to get this task force up and running.

"This morning NSA monitored a call from Ivanov's son Alexander. He is making a deal with Yon Min-Ji from North Korea. Yon has 50 million dollars in counterfeit $100 bills. Alexander wants to buy 10 million of it. Yon has potential buyers for the rest of it, but we have no leads yet on who they are. The US cannot have that quantity hit our streets at one time.

"The North Korean counterfeit bills are by far the hardest to detect. At least as good as Peru's. More importantly, we can't have the money they will get from the sale used to fund the North Korean missile program." Deputy Director Cosby finished and looked around for questions.

"Sir, how much time before the sale happens?" Rodriguez asked.

"We don't know. That's going to be your job. Then we need this task force to come up with a plan to keep the money from reaching North Korea and the counterfeit reaching the US," Cosby said.

"Sir, the command center is not fully functioning yet," Houston responded.

"Agent Townsend, I can't help what your issues are. This case is of the highest priority, straight from the Commander in Chief. You'll have to work out your issues on the fly," Cosby said. He had no patience for excuses. "This team was hand-picked for their ability to work under pressure. Now show me I chose wisely."

After Cosby and his entourage left, the team got down to business.

"Sophie, I need you to let us know what you need to get a plan in motion," Rodriguez said.

"Agent Mathews, is NSA online yet?" Sophie asked.

"Yes, the Secret Service, NSA, (*National Security Agency*), DIA, (*Defense Intelligence Agency*), are all online, FBI, DEA, and CIA are not."

"Agent Rodriguez, I need everything your men can find out about Yon Min-Ji and Alexander Ivanov. All family members, associates, you know the drill. Then give it all to Ms. Corban." Sissy Corban was a new addition to the team. Sophie liked her the minute they met.

Sophie turned to her. "Ms. Corban, can you get me all transmissions that NSA and DIA have coming in or going to Yon or any of his associates. Including phone, email, and text."

"Yes, ma'am."

"Agent Mathews, I need you to figure out who the players are from those communication. Whether they are US citizens or from any other country. And we need it ASAP," Sophie said.

When Sophie finished, Houston added, "We need to get men on Alexander. We need photos and videos of everyone he talks to and everywhere he goes. We'll get more men to help if we need to?"

"From Cosby's demeanor, it sounds like we can ask for the moon and get it," Fons replied.

"Sophie, once we have all the intel, can you organize it?" She nodded. "Matt, put NSA and DIA's intel, on the working plasmas and get the others on board ASAP," Houston ordered.

"Yes sir," Matt started heading to his computer, Sissy was already working. Sophie went to her desk to formulate a plan. She had already extracted what she could from the local DEA files on the Ivanov crime family. She needed more pieces of the puzzle. The rest of the team worked together to make sure they got access to everything they needed and the warrants to do so.

It was midnight and information was just now streaming in a way that Sophie could categorize it. Houston and the other men were still out getting HUMINT. They had been sending her pictures and videos of Alexander and his associates. She had the photos printed and was putting them on a whiteboard.

Knowing the players was crucial to her planning. She listened to the exchanges between Yon and Alex several times. Both young men were chomping at the bit to outshine their fathers. This kind of ego will work well for her as she formulated a plan.

The agents collecting intel got back at 2 am. They discussed what they had found out so far. Houston looked for Sophie and saw her talking to Sissy and Matt. He took Sophie aside and suggested she let Sissy and Matt get some sleep and tackle it again in the morning.

"It's too easy to miss something if you're tired. We don't have time to go over the material again."

He was right. Sophie sent them home and went into her office. Houston went back with the others and discussed a plan for the next day. By 3 am, he was taking his wife home for some sleep. They were all meeting back at 9 am Monday morning.

No one had time for breakfast, so Sophie called Carol to order brunch for the crew. Rodriguez volunteered to pick it up. Carol wasn't authorized to come into the Command center.

Sophie was grateful that Carol was in DC being mentored by a bakery chef.

Information was still coming in. Sophie was in the conference room, sorting it out. She called the team into the conference room. Fons was out trying to get the warrants for emails.

"I have something," Sophie pointed to the whiteboard. There were three pictures with info written underneath. "These men are the ones communicating with Yon by phone and email. We don't know what's in them yet; we need warrants to spy on US citizens."

Pointing to Wang Dequan, Sophie added, "he is second to Lee Hai out of the San Francisco Triad. The information indicates he is contacting Yon to make a deal. This," she pointed to the next picture, "is Mickey Coogan.

"It is universally believed that the Winter Hill Irish Gang disbanded, but there is still a small segment that exists. They don't call themselves Winter Hill anymore, but they still work out of Boston. He seems to be making a play to get some of Yon's money too.

"The last one, Izumi Nori, is the Saiko Komon for the Akuza crime syndicate. No one seems to know the name of the Kumicho. They are an extremely organized and fiercely loyal gang. It appears they're expanding their money laundering activities to include circulating counterfeit bills. They also want in on Yon's offering."

"That's great work, Ms. Star," Timms said, but how do we stop it.

Fons came in the conference room, waving the warrants. "By using these."

"Ms. Corban, how long will it take you to hack into their email accounts?"

Sissy got out of her chair and moved to the door, "I'll get on it now."

Sophie closed the meeting and everyone went on with their assignments. Now it was a waiting game.

A few hours later, Sissy came into Sophie's office.

"I have emails."

"Great," she took what Sissy handed her. "It's all in code. I rather expected that." She got up and went out to the media center.

"Agent Timms, can you decode these?" Sophie handed him the emails.

Agent Timms looked at them, "If I can't do it myself, I'll bring in one of the NSA's code specialists."

"Perfect. Do what you need to but do it fast."

"Yes ma'am."

Sophie turned to Fons, "I'm going to need more warrants. We need surveillance and wiretaps on Ivanov, his business, and his close associates. It needs to include communications and finances."

"I believe Deputy Director Cosby can get us what we need," Rodriguez responded. "I'll call him right away."

Houston and Sophie were in the conference room. They were dissecting the whiteboard, alone for a moment. Sitting on the edge of the conference table, she grabbed Houston's hand, rubbed the back of it on her cheek, and kissed it. He squeezed her hand and smiled.

Matt was on his way into the conference room when he saw the exchange. *That's the kind of relationship I want,* he thought. When he entered, she asked for more whiteboards.

CHAPTER FIVE

"**H**ouston, I need to get into the accounting offices of Vladimir Ivanov," Sophie said out of the blue.

"How do you intend to do that?" Houston moved to a chair in front of her desk and sat down.

I need to find a way to meet one of Ivanov's inner circle.

"What's your plan?"

She called Rodriguez in and told him what she needed. He stepped out and spoke to Agent Smith.

"Smith can you track down the Ivanov's CFO's information. We need to know where he goes, when, with whom, anyplace we can run into him?"

"Can do." Smith got to work on it immediately.

Sissy called out, "Sophie, I have something." Sophie stepped out of her office and sat beside her. "I have intercepted a phone call from Yon; he contacted a fishing vessel. He's asking how much to transport a trunk to Japan." She pulled it up so the others could hear the translation.

"They must be finalizing the transactions. We have to find out what those emails say. Have you figured a way to capture the transactions?" Sophie asked, picking up a pen from Sissy's desk and clicking the pens tip in and out. A nervous habit she recently developed and was trying to break. Houston laid his hand over hers discreetly. She smiled at him and put the pen down. "Did he reference a date?"

"He's making arrangements for Friday. We're 13 hours behind, so still Friday or late Thursday."

"So, just under three days." Sophie moved to where Agent Timms was working with the decoder, "gentlemen, do we have anything we can use yet? We have three days to intercept." Agent Timms looked up at her.

"We're making progress, I could use Mathews if you can give him up," he requested. "This code is multilayered and sophisticated."

Sophie asked Matt if he could leave what he was doing and help Timms. Agent Mathews spoke with Sissy then headed where Timms and the NSA decoder were working.

Sophie was heading back to the conference room when Sissy stopped her. "Matt got permission to tell me your story, Sophie. I want you to know what you all did was amazing. I'm proud to be a part of this team."

"I appreciate you saying that Sissy, but you deserve to be here." She nodded in response to the compliment.

Smith came back with Vladimir's CFO's picture they had captured during surveillance.

"His name is Demitri Stepanov; he's related to Vladimir through his mother. Vladimir sponsored his entry into the US once he became a citizen, so he had someone he trusted to do his books. The one thing that may work for us is that he is a degenerate gambler and he also drinks too much. On the other hand, he always pays his debts. Vladimir shares his wealth by giving exorbitant wages to his family. Demitri would never turn on Vladimir." Smith informed them.

"That will make things difficult; Dimitri will fight for Vladimir on any arrest we try to make. Does he go out regularly to any specific location?"

"I have some pictures of Dimitri and Vladimir going into a Russian hot spot. A restaurant and lounge called Mari Vanna. They go at least three times a week. It belongs to another relative of Vladimir. He sponsored several family members; he appears to be very loyal to his roots. Dimitri goes to Starbucks every morning, the one on Pennsylvania Ave. He arrives at 8:30 am."

"If I ran into him there, do you think he would talk to me?" Sophie asked the team.

The men all laughed. "You don't think he'll talk to me?" She asked, embarrassed that they laughed.

"He'll talk to you," both Rodriguez and Houston said at the same time with a smile.

"Ok, then I'll meet him in the morning."

The team made a plan for this casual meeting, which will be anything but casual.

We don't have Detective Cartwright here to spread my name out to his CI's, how do we let them know I'm in town?"

"We'll have to go to Cosby for that; he can make the inquires to the other agencies and get us to the right people."

Agent Rodriguez assumed that task. They needed to get into the offices.

"We got it," Timms shouted, rushing into Sophie's office.

"We have it decoded. We had to tweak the decoding software that the NSA had, but we did it!" He handed her the decoded emails as several of the others came in to see what was going on.

As they all moved into the conference room, they congratulated the men on their success.

"From these, it appears he still thinks he's going to outwit his father and gain some funds of his own. His problem is he's trying to convince these buyers to pay 10 million each to cover his betrayal. I'm not sure any one of them will do it." Sophie said, then asked Timms if he could put the decoded emails up on the screen so everyone could read them.

"It looks like the last email says the Triads will go 9 million tops for twenty million in counterfeit. But the Akuza will do 10 million. It's their first stab at counterfeit and they want the best-made bills." Timms was reading out loud. It looks like the Winter Hill gang has lost out altogether.

"My guess is he will pressure Alexander for a down payment to make up the difference," Houston added.

They continued to read over the emails and talked over the best way to intervene.

"How can we get both transactions to happen at once, letting us capture them before Yon catches on?" Rodriquez was thinking out loud.

"Can we intercept and then resend emails back and forth to them, without them knowing?" Sophie asked.

"Yes," Sissy responded, moving her fingers quickly over the keyboard.

"Please send Yon the following message with the proper encoding, from the Akuza. We will pay what you want but must send a man to inspect the merchandise before shipping. We will deposit money after his inspection. Give address and time." She thought for a moment, "Agent Mathews, we need to capture everything coming in and going out from these guys. If we miss something, we will blow the whole deal."

"Do you want his text also?" Matt questioned.

Sophie moved over to his station, "Yes, everything."

"Yon hasn't sent an account number yet, so when he does, we can capture it and change it to one we choose," Matt informed her.

"Are we one hundred percent sure we can recapture the money we send to Yon?" Houston asked. He knew it would be Cosby's biggest concern.

Sissy replied, "I've been able to make it work when I was doing a job for the Secret Service. I'll set up an account."

"Agent Mathews, is there anything we're missing?" Houston rubbed the five o'clock shadow on his face.

"I can redirect the text, but the phone calls would mean one of us would have to play a role," Matt responded.

"Yon has never spoken to anyone except Alexander; it may not matter. Let's get someone in here who can speak Korean, to be safe," she turned to Rodriguez for a reply.

"I'll get on that."

"It's time to sell this to Cosby." Sophie prodded.

"You want to do it?" Rodriguez asked.

"No, you have a handle on what we're doing," Sophie said as she returned to the conference room.

Cosby immediately contacted the Seal Team working on this operation. He arranged for them to meet with the Task Force. With only three days to make this work, he didn't want any miscommunication.

Sophie finally got a plan on paper and wanted to run it through the team for comments. She had ordered dinner from Carol. Rodriguez volunteered again to pick it up. She got the feeling he was using this as an excuse to see her. After the group ate and cleaned up, Sophie stood.

"Ok, here's the plan. Acting as the Triad contact we tell Yon if he will accept the 9 million, they will pick up the trunk in Japan and he won't have to take the risk of further transport. Then we let the Triad's know they will have to transport the money themselves from Japan if they don't go above 9 million. Then Yon will have to reply with the destination in Japan and the time of arrival."

Sophie looked around to see if anyone saw a flaw in her thinking so far. "It's the best way to get the drop location. We sent a message to Yon that the Akuza wants to inspect the trunk before it sails. That allows us to get trackers on the trunks. Then our seal team can board the ship undetected. Replacing the money for something of the same weight and reseal it."

"There are so many moving parts, Sophie. Let's think of what could go wrong so we can have solutions in place," Rodriguez said.

"That gets us the counterfeit, but what about the payments to Yon?" Smith questioned.

Sophie made eye contact with Sissy. "Ms. Corban, can you address that?"

"The money is being redirected to a government holding account. Once we are in control of it, we can send the funds to Yon."

"But how do we get it back?" Smith was still confused.

"Since we control the account, I can recall the money within twelve hours."

"How sure are you of the timeline to recall it?" Houston asked.

"I've done it before. I'm pretty confident I can do it again." Sissy responded.

"I think it's worth the risk," Sophie said. The others agreed.

The Seal Team joined them. They went over the plan several times, allowing for the possibility of one or two trunks.

"Do you have someone that can speak North Korean for the meet with Yon on the dock, or do we need to request one? Rodriguez asked Sergeant Abbott, the team leader.

"We have a man on our team that speaks Korean. Plus, he knows what we need to get things ready for the onboard exchange. We would like to use our own tracking devices."

Rodriguez looked at Sophie, who had asked him to take the lead in this meeting. She nodded. Rodrigues continued, "we have no problem with that, but we would like to have a live feed of the operation."

"We can arrange that," the Sergeant paused, "you say we have three days to prepare?"

"We don't have that confirmed yet, but we'll let you know as soon as we do," Rodriguez got up to get some coffee.

After the Seal Team left, Sophie and Sissy sent the communications between Yon and the Triads. After Sissy got the bank account ready, all they could do was wait to see if both sides bought into it. It was 1 in the morning and there was no need for everyone to stay and monitor the computers. Matt and Sissy agreed to split the night and let everyone else go home.

"Make sure you call me if there's any movement, no matter what time it is." Sophie said.

It was 2 am when Houston and Sophie pulled up to their home. On the drive, Sophie asked the question that bothered her earlier.

"Why did everyone laugh when I asked if Demitri would talk to me? Was it that strange that he might?"

"Sweetheart, you don't realize how attracted men are to you. Any man in their right mind would jump at the chance to talk to you, that's all." Houston grabbed her hand and kissed her palm.

She smiled at his response. "Houston, just because you find me attractive doesn't mean everyone does."

He looked at her, shook his head and smiled. She had no idea how beautiful she was.

"Poor Bully has been on his own these last few days. Can he sleep on the bed tonight?" She asked, knowing how Houston felt about that.

"Absolutely not, that is a bad habit we don't need to start. We can move Bully's bed next to ours, so he's close." She wasn't happy, but she knew he was right. Sophie fed Bully and went outside and threw the ball for him a few times. Houston had put in a security doggie door for him, so he had been able to go in and out all day. But she still wanted to play with him for a few minutes. They set the alarm for seven and got in bed. Houston checked all the locks and set the security alarm before he laid down. At 5 am, the phone rang.

"Houston, tell Sophie it looks like they both bought it. We will continue to monitor the communications, to be safe." Matt relayed the message with excitement.

Houston decided to tell her in the morning since the phone didn't rouse her. He turned to kiss her cheek and saw Bully had squeezed himself onto the bed next to her. His legs were dangling over the edge, her arms around him. It was such an endearing spectacle he decided not to make him get off. He chuckled, kissed her cheek, and went back to sleep.

Houston and Rodriguez were in the SUV about a half block away from Starbucks. The plan was for Houston to call Sophie on cue and ask her to find a good Russian restaurant. If all goes well, she will be in front of Demitri, and hopefully, he will take the bait. She had an earpiece, and a mic on her watch. The trick was timing. She was waiting to hear from Smith.

Agent Smith was the lookout at the corner. She finally got the message he was on his way. Sophie straightened her skirt, licked her lips, and started moving to the door. Demitri got there first and held it for her. She said thank you and got in line. He stepped in line right behind her. Sophie's phone rang on queue.

"Hello." She waited for the question.

"I just moved here too. I would have no idea where a good Russian restaurant is. Who would I even ask?" She listened some more while turning slightly to the side.

"I'll try, I'm at Starbucks, when I get to my computer I'll look it up." She listened again.

"Alright, goodbye."

"Excuse me; I didn't mean to eavesdrop. But are you looking for a Russian restaurant in town?" Demitri asked.

Houston and Rodriguez high fived each other listening in on the contact.

"No, it's my fault. I was speaking too loudly. Yes, my husband insists we eat at a Russian restaurant at least once a week, he loves the food," she responded.

"I take it you just moved here."

"Yes, we moved from New York."

"May I introduce myself, I'm Demitri Stepanov," he said.

She stretched her hand out to him, "I'm Sophie Star."

They finally got to the head of the line. Sophie ordered a caramel macchiato. Demitri ordered a cappuccino and insisted on paying for hers.

"Shall we sit while we wait for our drinks?" He asked, directing her to a table for two by the window.

"Certainly."

"Why have you moved from New York, Ms. Star...I must say your name sounds very familiar." He queried as they were being seated.

"We needed to get a fresh start. I'm a CPA and a consultant, I plan on opening a firm."

"I work for Vladimir Ivanov I'm his CFO."

"I'm sorry that name isn't familiar to me." She furrowed her brow as if trying to recall his name.

"You're new in town. You'll hear Vladimir's name mentioned more as you do business here."

They heard their names called. Dimitri went to pick up the coffee.

Sophie stood when he did and waited for him to bring her drink. "Would you happen to know of a good Russian restaurant?"

"Yes, the best in town is Mara Zanna, here let me write down the address." He wrote it on a pad he took out of his coat.

"Maybe I'll run into you there sometime." He nodded his head to her and then held the door for her as they left the building. Houston saw that he turned and looked back at her as she walked away.

She got back in the SUV and they went over how they felt the introduction went.

"Your name rang a bell with him. That could be a good thing." Rodriguez said enthusiastically.

"Yeah, or a bad thing." Houston added.

The team discussed the possibilities of another contact with Dimitri. This time at the Russian restaurant. It would solve a lot of tactical issues if he would just offer her a job.

Sophie turned their attention back to Yon and the counterfeit transactions.

"Now we concentrate on money transfers. We need to confiscate the counterfeit money in mid-transport."

Houston laughed, "oh, is that all."

Sissy got her attention. "The last communications between Yon and the Triad's finalized at 9 million. The drop point now being at the Japanese docks. The Akuza finalized with the 10 million with drop off at the same destination."

They listened in on a call from Yon to Alex. Yon said he needed a one million dollar down payment for him to hold the other 10 million for him.

"Ms. Corban, do we have a place and time for the inspection of the merchandise?"

"I'm waiting on that info. Here it is — Friday 7 pm at the Port of Odaejin.

"I'll call Cosby so they can let the Seal Team know," Houston said.

The introduction to Sophie Star stayed on Demitri's mind as he walked into his office. He set down his briefcase and hung up his coat on the brass coatrack by the door. Then he did a search of her name on the computer and looked up all he could find on her. "That's it," he shouted out. Then mumbled to himself. "She was the woman who kept the Morano's on top for so many years. She created the App that Vladimir's organization used to check questionable new contacts. It checked VINs against confiscated cars, boats, and markings on confiscated drugs. It was a way to detect if the new contact was a cop using confiscated items in his cover or used confiscated drugs on a deal. Ms. Star kept Joe's criminal activity hidden from the DEA; they were untouchable. Until Nikko got careless," he remembered hearing that from Joe Morano himself when he came to dine with Vladimir. The two immigrants had met when Joe and Vladimir had first started business and had formed a friendship over the years. He headed over to Vladimir's office to let him know who he met. He planned on suggesting they try to hire her before she starts her own business.

Things were on hold until Thursday. It was a prime time to make another contact with Demitri. The only counterfeit money left in play was the money Alex was going to buy. If they can get into Ivanov's operation, they may be able to capture that too.

Houston and Sophie walked into the Mara Zanna at 8 pm without a reservation. The aromas of the Russian food waft in front of them.

"I'm sorry sir, without a reservation I can't seat you tonight." The Maître 'd said.

Sophie and Houston stepped out of line and were looking over the patrons to see if Dimitri was there. Houston suggested they get a reservation for the next day and try again. Houston went to make the reservation while Sophie kept eyeing the room. She heard the door open and saw Vladimir and Demitri walk in.

Houston notices and walked back over to Sophie. "Honey, do you have another restaurant you'd like to go try?" He asked, stalling.

"I wanted you to try the food here Demitri said it was the best." She said his name a little louder than necessary.

Dimitri heard his name and turned to see who was talking. When he saw it was Sophie, he walked over to her.

"Ms. Star, what a delight to see you again," he said. "Let me introduce you to Vladimir Ivanov, my cousin, and employer.

"Mr. Ivanov, a pleasure to meet you, and this is my husband, Houston Townsend."

"Are you eating here tonight?" Dimitri asked.

"We had planned to but we didn't make a reservation, so we'll have to come back," Houston replied.

"Don't be ridiculous; come eat with us at our table." Vladimir insisted.

"We couldn't possibly put you out like that," Sophie responded.

"Nonsense, it's a fortuitous meeting. Demitri said he ran into you but didn't know how to make contact. I have an offer I'd like you to consider," Vladimir said.

"Honey, I would like to try the food."

"If you're sure it won't impose," Sophie responded as she turned back to Vladimir.

Dimitri led them to Vladimir's reserved table. Houston held Sophie's chair for her, then the men sat down. The waiter brought over water, menus and a bottle of Vodka. Vladimir recommended the best dishes and they ordered their food. They passed the time with small talk about Washington DC and his move from Russia to the United States. He was proud to be a citizen.

They were finishing their meal when Vladimir said, "Ms. Star, you may not know that I was a close friend to Joe Morano."

Sophie got a knot in her stomach; she wasn't sure if he had any idea of her part in their takedown.

"I wasn't aware. Joe gave me my first accounting job. I liked Joe." She was sincere, twisting her glass of tea in tiny circles.

"He told me a lot about the way you shored up his business and protected them. He gave you credit for increasing their territory and adding the coca farm," he paused. "I would like you to do the same for my business."

"I had planned on opening up a firm with my husband. He's my partner." She took Houston's hand.

"Ms. Star, I can offer you a great deal of money. When you're done, you could always decide to go out on your own. Although you will find working for me is very lucrative. Demitri will want to retire someday and you could take over his position. He will tell you I am a generous employer." Demitri nodded his agreement.

"My husband and I are a team, Mr. Ivanov. I won't work anywhere without him."

"Of course, I understand completely. That is not an issue with me."

"What do you think, darling? It is an attractive offer." Sophie turned to Houston.

"I'm not opposed to it; we can start our own business anytime. We don't have the name recognition in DC as we did in New York. Vladimir's recommendation could be the vehicle needed to get our name out there."

"I assure you, Mr. Townsend, if you do for me what you did for Joe, we will recommend you to others." Vladimir assured them.

"I liked working for Joe. We could try it and see how you feel about our work and go from there." Sophie smiled.

"Excellent, Houston can meet with Demitri tomorrow to work out a contract and you can start right away."

Houston got the waiter's attention to get his bill.

"Absolutely not, your meal is on me. Just one of the small perks." Vladimir took the check and had Demitri take care of it. They said their goodbyes and headed out the door.

Houston called Fons on the way home and asked him to come down when they got there. They sat at the kitchen table and Sophie took out leftovers for Fons and heated them. Houston took a plate for himself. How he could eat again after stuffing himself at the Russian restaurant; she had no idea. They discussed how well it all fell into place.

Houston and Fons stayed up to go over strategies. Sophie said good night; she wanted to spend some time in prayer.

CHAPTER SIX

Matt and Sissy had replaced the texts back and forth from Yon, the Akuza and the Triad. Everything was ready; they were all waiting for the Seal Team to do their part. It was almost 4 pm on Thursday.

Sissy redirected the money sent from the Triad and Akuza to a government holding account.

Houston was in Sophie's office, waiting. He was lying on the couch; she came over and sat on the edge.

"Do you think you could get Bully designated a service dog? I would like him to come to work with me sometimes."

"Let me see what I can do. Are you alright?"

"My ideas seem so simple and workable in my head, but there are real people involved. What happens if I'm wrong or I miscalculated something? How do I live with that?"

"Any type of military or police action has its risk. Sophie, you spend an enormous amount of time trying to take all the risk out. These men need stopped. Sometimes it takes a toll we'd rather not pay."

"I don't think I can do this job, Houston. I'm not like you. You're brave; you look at risk as a part of life. I don't want anyone getting hurt because of some plan I came up with that goes awry."

He sat up and held her, "you are the bravest woman I know. But you don't have to do this. After this assignment, we'll sit down and discuss what you want. Ok?" He held her for a while.

"Our man is meeting Yon. He's wearing a camera and a wire." Smith hollered so everyone could hear.

They all gathered around the plasmas. The men spoke Korean, captioned in real-time for the Seals and Command. Deputy Director Cosby was in the room with them.

"I take it you are Nori's man coming to inspect the merchandise?" The sun was going down on the horizon.

"Yes, my name is..."

"No need for names." Yon interrupted.

The Seal member went to the trunk, careful to be out of the direct site of Yon. He scanned his surroundings to see if Yon had guards posted. He saw only Yon's bodyguard. The Seal opened the trunk and inspected the money. He locked it and placed the seal Yon gave him on the trunk, making sure to let the seal linger on the camera for 10 seconds. The Seal team only had a short time to reproduce it, and they couldn't get it wrong.

"It's all there. I will call my boss and have him transfer the money to the account you gave him. It will take less than 30 minutes."

"That's acceptable, but this trunk does not get on that ship until the money gets in my account."

"Understood."

"He made the call alerting the Seal team that the commercial fishing vessel would be leaving soon. The Seal Team's window of opportunity was short. They'd been waiting in international waters on a Mark V Special Operation Craft. The Seals needed to transfer to the CB-OTH. (Cutter Boat-Over The Horizon) To shadow the commercial vessel.

Yon also texted his contact at the Triad and insisted he send the money before the boat left the dock.

Command captured the text. Sophie was sitting next to Sissy, "it's time to send the money." She hit the send button and it was off. About ten minutes later, Yon got the notification of receipt and gave the all-clear. He watched the trunks loaded onto the ship.

The boat launched and headed for its destination to Hirado Harbor in Japan.

A clandestine boarding at high seas was a dangerous and treacherous undertaking. The Seals shadowed the vessel until it was evident that most of the crew were asleep. Multiple attempts were necessary to attach the rope ladder to the cleat because of the rough water.

Getting off the moving, bobbing craft and grabbing the ladder took its toll. The team nearly lost a man overboard. After boarding, they hauled up the duffle bags that contained the replacement paper. Then silently moved to the cargo hold.

They each had three large duffel bags. The 10-man CB-OTH attached itself to the hull and turned off the motor. Now they waited.

Yon rechecked the deposited funds and called Alex.

"Alex, do you have the million-dollar deposit I need?"

"I can have it in 24 hours," Alex replied.

"That's the most time I can give you. I have to have it transferred to my Appa's account by then," Yon was worried Alex wouldn't come through.

The team had monitored the call and knew Alex was under pressure to get that money.

Command waited for the Seal team to trade out the money.

"Command this is Stacker, we are in the cargo hold, we see the trunks and are getting ready to transfer funds now."

Then there was a sudden command change. "Hold!" Stacker whispered. "I hear someone coming." Tank acknowledged with a click. They hid and watched while a young Korean man was searching the cargo hold. He stopped at the trunks and was getting ready to open one when another man came in.

"What are you doing here?" The older one said.

"Nam-Gi, why did you follow me." They were speaking Korean. The Seals and command were being given the translation through their earpieces.

"Answer me, Dae-won."

"I'm jumping ship in Japan; I can't live under oppression anymore. Come with me, Nam-gi," he pleaded.

"And what of our parents? You want to leave them there to starve without us."

"I can't stay; I will die if I can't get away."

"What will you do, how will you live?"

"When the trunk was open, I saw what was in it. It's US Dollars, Nam-gi!"

"Yes, and do you see the destination is the Akuza's, and there's a seal on it. You touch one dollar, and they will track you down and kill you, our parents, and me."

"I won't put you at risk, but I also won't stay. I'm jumping ship in Japan either way."

"Alright, brother, I will help you. You can take all the money I have and start a new life. One of us should be free."

"I don't want to leave you Nam-gi, please come with me."

"Someday, after our parents are gone. I will come. You'll have to get word to me where you end up." They hugged, cried, and left the cargo hold.

"We're clear." Stacker relayed, and they went about the transfer. Once the money was in the duffle bags, Stacker put a tracker in the trunks and resealed them.

After lowering the duffels down to the CB-OTH, two of the Seals made the hazardous trek down the rope ladder. Tank and Stacker climbed over the rail and were climbing down when they heard, "HOLD." At the command. the men flattened themselves against the ship, doing their best to keep from swinging, their bodies in pain from hitting the hull of the boat repeatedly. Their hands were cramping, trying to keep from slipping down the wet rope ladder. One of the deckhands was walking the deck, smoking a cigarette. It was too dark for him to see the black rubber covered grappling hook attached to the railing.

Everyone in command was holding their breath. Sissy kept repeating, "don't stop, don't stop," to herself, speaking to the smoker. Houston and Sophie were praying God would send His Angels to hide the men.

The crew member stopped past the ropes and looked out onto the ocean. He finished his cigarette, tossed it overboard, and moved along.

"Go, go, go." The men finished propelling down and got in the waiting boat. They released the hook, and it dropped at their feet. They rowed until they were far enough away to keep from being detected, then turned on the motor. They went back to the Mark V Special Operations Craft waiting for them. It was over, and everyone was safe. Sophie took her first deep breath all day.

"Sophie, when do you want me to recapture the money," Sissy asked.

"I'll let you know." She replied.

Deputy Director Cosby called everyone together. "Excellent job in confiscating that counterfeit money. Now we have to make sure we get the real thing back from Yon."

"Yes sir, we're going to hold off as long as we can so the trunks can make it to Japan and on the way to the US. The other agencies want to find the route their using. The information will help them with other smuggling cases," Rodriguez reported.

"That's fine, but you get me that money back!"

"Yes sir."

"What about the last 10 million?" Cosby asked.

"Sir, you have to decide if you want to capture the counterfeit 10 million. If you do, we have to be willing to give up the million Yon wants as a deposit." Sophie explained to Cosby.

He thought about it for a minute. "Do you think we have a chance of getting our hands on it?" Cosby asked.

"Sophie received an offer to work for Vladimir last night. We have a way in. It may lead us to the money when he gets it."

"How did you do that?" He turned to Sophie.

"God has given us favor and a very proficient team." She laughed.

"Well, however you pulled it off, great work. Now get me that money back."

"It was 8 pm they only had eight more hours to recapture the money.

At 1 am Sophie asked, "does anyone know if the ship has made it to the dock in Japan yet?"

"I just got word it docked, and they are taking the cargo off the ship now."

"Ok, Ms. Corban, redirect the funds. There's going to be fireworks when he can't give his dad 20 million dollars, and the bills are out of reach." Sophie wondered what his father would do.

Alex had insisted Kim go to dinner with him. She tried to refuse, but he got agitated and asked if she wanted to keep her job, so she relented. After supper, he walked her to her door. She tried to say goodnight at the door, but he came in behind her. She had a small apartment, sparsely decorated. Everything she owned looked like it came from Goodwill.

"Kim, I need you to do something for me at work tomorrow," he said.

"Of course, what is it."

"I need you to take one million dollars out of the Capital account and transfer it to this account overseas." He handed her a paper.

"I can't do that without authorization from Demitri," she said, puzzled.

"I'm authorizing it." His voice was harsh.

"I can't; it will look like I embezzled it. I'll go to jail."

He slapped her, "you will do it. I have to have that money tomorrow."

"No, I can't." She pleaded, her hand holding her face where it stung.

"You will do it; do you hear me." She had stepped away from him.

"Don't make me hurt your family, Kim. I have their address; it's on your emergency contact form. I have friends in South Korea who would gladly do me a favor." He stepped close to her, "I need that money. Do you understand me?" He grabbed her wrist and wrenched it back.

"Please, leave my parents alone. Why do you want me to do this? Ask your father for the money; he will give it to you." She said, sobbing and gasping for air.

"He can't know about it. You do this tomorrow, Kim or I will have your work Visa pulled for stealing. They'll send you back to South Korea. Who do you think the immigration office is going to believe; you or me?" He didn't wait for a response. He left and slammed the door.

She fell to the couch, crying. Kim had no choice; she needed this job. It supported her family back home, and she loved living here.

Kim walked into her office with her head down. She tried to hide the big black and blue mark, and the swelling on her face, with makeup, to little effect. Kim let her long black hair hang over her face to help hide it.

"What on earth happened to you?" Her coworker Tom asked.

"I'm ok Tom, please don't ask me anything." She headed for her desk and put down her purse.

"It's Alex, isn't it? I see him bother you almost every day to go out with him. Did he do this?"

"I can't talk about it! Please, just let it be, " Kim whispered the last part.

She sat down and started working. Tom went back to his desk on the other side of the room. Kim brought up the Capital account and made ready the transfer. She pulled the offshore account number Alex gave her last night, out of her purse. Kim couldn't bring herself to push the enter button. She was getting ready to delete it when Alex came in.

"Have you done what I asked, Kim?" He came within a few feet of her and whispered.

"Please don't make me do this."

"Tom, you need to take a break, I need to talk to Kim," Alex said in a demanding tone.

"Demitri needs me to finish this right away, Mr. Ivanov. I'll take a break shortly."

Alex stepped closer to Tom, "when I tell you to do something you do it, I'm the boss here, Demitri works for me." Alex raised his voice.

"He actually works for your father," Tom retorted under his breath.

"Get out of here now or your fired and you can take the chance my father won't back me up."

Tom left, worried about Kim, but he knew he couldn't do anything to help her.

Alex came back to Kim's desk; he grabbed ahold of her hair and yanked her head back. "You have two minutes to get that transfer done, or I will keep the promise I made last night." She gave up, what good was her integrity, it wouldn't feed her family. She hit the enter button, and the money was gone. He let go of her hair, kissed her cheek, and said, "now that wasn't so hard, was it?" He headed out the door.

"Be ready by 7 pm I'm picking you up for dinner. And cover the bruise on your face. It's not attractive." After a few more steps, he turned to her again, "wear something flattering. I want to show you off." Now he was acting as if he owned her. That was the reason she refused to go out with him in the first place. The thought of it made her sick.

Kim went to the bathroom, locked the door. She couldn't go to the authorities no one would believe her; HR would never confront him. She would just get fired. Her situation was hopeless. Kim leaned against the sink, covered her face with her hands, and sobbed.

Sophie was at the command center while Houston went over to Mr. Ivanov's offices to talk to Demitri.

"Sophie, the money from Alex got deposited into Yon's account. Do I let it stand?" Sissy asked.

"We don't have a choice if we want the counterfeit, let it go," Sophie responded.

Houston walked up the stairs into the Ivanov accounting offices. A young man was sitting at one of the desks. According to a cup on his desk, his name was Tom. Houston stopped in front of him and asked for Demitri. He stood to greet Houston and let him know Dimitri hadn't come in yet, directing him where he could sit and wait. He saw two desks in the open foyer. Beyond that were two closed offices. A pretty, young Korean woman walked past him with her head down and sat at the other desk. He could see she'd been crying and she had a big bruise on her face. He wondered what on earth went on here.

Demitri came in a few seconds later. "Mr. Townsend, welcome, come into my office. But first, let me introduce my staff." Turning, he said, "this is Tom Dempsey; he's been here six months." Then he turned to Kim, "this is Kim Lee; she has been with us for two years now and does great work." They both nodded their hello's. If Dimitri noticed her bruised face, he didn't say anything.

They walked into Demitri's lavishly decorated office. Houston sat in one of the Valeria Luxury chairs. Dimitri took off his jacket and moved to his large oak desk, sitting behind it. Behind him was a credenza with pictures of what appeared to be his family and friends. The paintings on the wall were originals; he had no doubt. There was a bookshelf that covered a small portion of the wall to his left.

"Mr. Townsend, I feel the offer in this contract is very generous. Mr. Ivanov feels you and your wife would be a valuable resource to the company." He handed Houston the contract and waited while he read it.

The contract offer was indeed very generous. Houston added one stipulation. They wanted to be on the books as independent consultants. Dimitri got on his computer, made the correction, then printed it out. Houston signed it.

"Mr. Stepanov..." Demitri interrupted, "please call me Demitri."

"Dimitri, I do have one personal request. My wife would like to bring her dog to the office on occasion. Would that be acceptable to you?"

"Women and their pets." He laughed as he got up from his chair. "I see no reason why that would be a problem." He walked to the door, "let me show you where your office will be." Houston followed his lead.

Demitri took him to the office next door, being used as storage. The space was large and had a private bathroom included.

"I'll have this storage removed and have a nice desk, a small conference table, and a couch brought in by tomorrow. You will have a decorating allowance and can fix it up however you choose, but for now, you'll be able to function." He said, looking pleased.

"Your very generous, Demitri. Sophie and I will be here in the morning. What time do the doors open?" Houston was hoping they would get a key of their own.

"As soon as security can get all your information entered, they will give you a code. It will allow access to the building whenever you need it. But someone is usually here by 7 am. I come at 9 am after I get my Starbucks down the street." He smiled. "If you want to take the time now, I can have Kim take you to their office, and you can take care of it."

"That would be fine. I might as well get as much done as I can."

They stepped out and Dimitri asked Kim to take Houston to the security office. She didn't say anything and kept her head down the whole time. Houston knew a battered woman when he saw one, and this woman was one. Unfortunately, they were here undercover. Getting involved in her issues could blow their cover. God would have to make way for them to help her.

Houston got everything done and left with a code for them both. Security in this place was extreme. Sissy will have her hands full hacking into it. He headed back to command.

Alex gave Yon a call to verify he received the money.

"Yon, it should be in your account as we speak," Alex informed him. Alex was at his desk, tapping his pen, excited they had gotten this far.

"Good, I'll put the 20 million in my Appa's account tomorrow. I'll need to get the rest of this out of here as soon as possible."

"I'll get the money for you."

When Yon hung up, he went online to check his account; the balance was $1,000,000. $19,000,000 was gone! He jetted up from his desk, picked up his phone, and called in his computer tech.

"Kam, nineteen million dollars is missing from this account, I need you to locate it for me. NOW!"

Kam got into the account. He saw that at 2 pm Friday, the money moved from the Capital account into an account in Switzerland. From there, it went to the Caribbean, from there to Puerto Rico, then to Hawaii and on and on. It was still moving. He went to Yon's office to inform him of what he found.

"Can't you transfer it back to my account?" He stood up, pacing.

"No, sir, it's out of our control. It's gone."

"NO!" He banged his fist on the desk, "It is not gone, you get it back, or I'll kill you, do you hear me!"

"Sir, there is nothing I can do. It's gone." Yon walked over to him, pushing him against the wall. He wrapped his hands around Kam's throat and started choking him. Kam was clawing at his hands and gasping for air. His feet were off the ground. Finally, Yon released him. Kam dropped to the floor and scrambled out of there.

Yon was desperate. He only had 24 hours to get that money back. His father would have no qualms about killing him. His mother was the only one who treated him like a beloved son.

Panicking, he called his bodyguard, "take the rest of the day off," he told him. He didn't want his bodyguard shadowing him. Yon had to make plans to get out of North Korea with the 10 million in counterfeit bills. He transferred Alex's million to his account in Hong Kong.

Yon would have to go home to get to the hiding place under his floorboards. He would grab the counterfeit money along with his forged passport and documents. Yon had been planning to escape for years.

The computer on his desk notified him there were new emails. He opened the email from the Triad. When he read it, his body started shaking. The money was not in the trunk; it was gone. How did this happen? He would kill whoever did this to him.

Yon emailed the Triad back and told them the money was in the trunk when it left port. If it's gone, it happened on their end. He knew that wouldn't fly. If he didn't refund their money, the Triad would contact his father. He would find out what Yon had done. His Appa would have to reimburse them, or their reputation would be ruined, if not worse. Then his Appa would come for him.

Yon opened the email from the Akuza. It too stated paper, not money filled the trunk. They wanted an explanation now or their money back. Yon sent him the following email properly encoded:

Before I sealed it, your man inspected it.
If the money was not in the trunk when
you received it. I would ask your man what he did with it.

Yon was heading back out the door when he got notification of a reply:

'WHAT MAN!'

Yon responded:

The man you insisted inspect the money at the dock.

Akuza's reply was:

I made no such arrangements
with you. You have 2 hours to return
our money.

At that moment, it all made sense to him. Someone hijacked communications between them and broke the code. Whoever did this stole the money and the counterfeit bills. It was either some government or some uber techy criminal network. Either way, he was going to have to take the money from his Appa's company to pay them back. He sent a text to both the Triad and Akuza to explain what he thought happened.

Yon called in another accountant and explained what he needed. What he needed was nineteen million dollars. He needed it redirected from the firm's Capital account to refund his clients. The accountant would not do that kind of transaction without authorization. Yon screamed at him to get out. Giving the Triad and Akuza back their money wasn't going to happen. He needed to get the money promised from Alex and run. Right now, his own life wasn't worth a counterfeit dollar.

Yon would be dead if he stayed and dead if he left. What did it matter? Better the Akuza kill him then his own family. He decided it was time to leave the country.

Yon knew he couldn't miss his Appa's weekly business meeting. His Appa would send someone to look for him if he didn't show up. Yon needed more time than that to get away. He looked at his watch; it was 5:30 pm. It would take a half-hour each way to his house and another fifteen minutes to pack a few of his things. He would be late for the 7 pm meeting, but he'd been late before. His Appa and his uncles would be at the office until about 10 pm. They played mahjong and drank Yakju while discussing business. That would distract them for a while.

CHAPTER SEVEN

When Houston got back to command, the place was buzzing. Word came in that the trunk destined for the Triad in San Francisco arrived. The Akuza trunk also arrived in New York. The CI in San Francisco has already reported the Triad is in an uproar over their stolen money. Matt caught transmissions from the Triad's to Yon, demanding their money back.

"Sophie, should I let these emails through to Yon?"

She turned to Rodriguez and Houston, "what do you think, should we let Yon know his business is toppling?"

"Let it go, this is on a trajectory of its own now," Rodriguez commented. Houston agreed.

"Let it through, Agent Mathews." She passed on the direction.

"Akuza got their trunk. They are up in arms with the betrayal. They contacted Yon too." Sissy reported to the group.

"This will force Yon out of North Korea. He will put pressure on Alex to get him the rest of the money so that he can run from his father." Agent Smith conjectured.

Sissy put up on the big screen all the messages going back and forth. Even the final one from Yon when he realized what happened so everyone could see.

Izumi's two-hour deadline came and went with no response from Yon. The next thing he did was contact his colleague in Japan and order a hit. He wanted the heads of Yon Se-bin, his brothers, who are his partners, and Yon Min-ji, the son.

At approximately 7 pm, three men in a Zodiac Milpro, motored onto the shore of Wonsan, North Korea. They came ashore about three miles from the Yon headquarters. The men dressed in shozoku, katanas strapped to their back, pulled the craft to shore and tied it to a tree. The leader grabbed the rope from the craft and placed it over his head and around his shoulder. Without a word, they jogged to the offices of Yon Brothers Enterprises in the industrial area.

The notoriously unreliable electrical grid of North Korea caused a blackout. The intruders traversed the rugged terrain by using night vision goggles, virtually invisible. The men paused at the edge of a copse of trees next to the industrial area. They spotted Yon Enterprises.

To the east was a manufacturing plant and to the west a warehouse. Sixteen wheelers sitting dark, abandoned, waiting to be loaded in the morning. All was dark except Yon Brothers. The men could hear the generator from where they stood. A reward for funneling millions of dollars into the Supreme Leaders obsession. The missile program. Their support afforded the Yon's many luxuries.

They Crossed the road at the darkest point. Seeing the two guards, they avoided approaching the front entrance. The men moved to the back of the building, looking for another entry point. A window on the second floor was slightly ajar. Using themselves as a ladder, they stood on each other's shoulders, allowing the last man to open the window. He then dropped a rope down to the others after tying the end around his waist.

The three men moved ninjutsu, looking for the room where the partners held their weekly meeting. They stopped on the third floor when they heard men's voices. Accomplishing their mission in less than three minutes, they sent proof in picture form to Izumi, who ordered the hit. Then they were out in the cover of darkness again, heading back to their vessel. All of it done without a word said between them.

Yon had packed his bag and headed back to the office. He didn't dare miss the mandatory appearance at Appa's weekly business meeting. It would draw too much attention to not show up. He had snuck into the house, not wanting the servants or his mother to see him. Yon felt terrible about leaving his mother here to face the aftermath of his betrayal. He looked at his watch; it was taking him longer than he anticipated.

Yon got to the headquarters about 7:50 pm making his way to the third floor and headed to the conference room. When he opened the door, the smell hit him. He saw the scene before him and threw up. The heads of his Appa and uncles were lined up against the wall away from their bodies. His legs collapsed under him. He crab-walked backward until his back hit the wall. He couldn't suck in air. "APPA!" He cried. "Oh, Appa, I never intended for this to happen."

He closed his eyes and tried to get his strength back. This sight would forever stay burned into his mind. He sat for a long time before he realized he needed to get out of there. If he had been there on time, his head would have been lined up there by his Appa's. He stood and made it to the door. He made only one stop before he was out the back door of Yon Enterprises forever.

Yon didn't remember how he got to the private airfield. The fresh air brought his mind out of the fog as he walked to the plane. He had texted the pilot and told him to be there ready to go in 30 minutes. Disappearing was the only answer. Most citizens of North Korea were not allowed to leave the country. Yon Se-Bin and his son were an exception because of the amount of money he gave to the Supreme Leader. He was even allowed a private jet as long as the Supreme Leader had access to it.

He needed to get to Alex and make him come up with the rest of the money. He could start over with four million dollars.

"Nai, can we make it to Hong Kong without stopping to refuel?"

"Yes sir."

"Then do it."

Yon sat in the most beautiful leather seat money could buy and closed his eyes on the worst day of his life.

All sorts of intel from CI's and government agencies were flowing in. Dubbed Operation hijack, its actions were causing panic in some illegitimate circles.

Organizations around the world had gotten their counterfeit bills from North Korea. The big question was whether the Yon organization was trustworthy anymore. The team hadn't anticipated this benefit. They may have put North Korea out of the fake money business for a while. At least for the short term.

Out of nowhere, Matt shut down all communications coming in on the plasmas.

"What's going on, Matt," Rodriguez questioned.

"I need to talk to you and Houston in the conference room. Leave the computers alone, Ms. Corban," He demanded. Sophie and Sissy both looked at him, puzzled.

When he shut the door behind them, Matt said, "you need to warn Sophie before I put up this next communication."

"What is it Matt," Shaken up, Matt walked over to him.

"It's from North Korea to Izumi. It's a picture of the assassination of the Yon family."

He took a deep breath. "Their heads are severed."

Houston leaned his hands down on the table and let out a long breath. He had to prepare his wife for what was coming.

Houston walked into Sophie's office, knowing she was going to blame herself for the death of these men. He was praying God would give him wisdom on how to break it to her.

Sophie looked up from the computer when he walked in, "What's going on, the plasmas are all dark. Do we have a glitch in the communication system?" But then she noticed the look on his face. "What is it, Houston? What's going on?"

Houston went to the couch and asked her to join him. When she sat down, he turned to face her.

"When Deputy Director Cosby formed this task force, he had one thing in mind. And that was to take down the most dangerous criminal organizations. Sophie, we do what we do to protect other Americans from an evil they don't even know exists half the time. Criminals don't value human life; that's why we have to intervene and do what's right. What they do to each other is often brutal." He stopped talking and took her hands then looked straight into her eyes.

"What is it, Houston? Just tell me."

"We received pictures of an assassination in North Korea at Yon's headquarters. Yon Min-ji was not there, he's still alive as far as we know, but his father and uncles are all dead. Their heads severed."

Sophie's eyes went wide, she gasped. "What!" She got up and looked down at him. "Did you know this could happen?" She stepped to the office window to look at the plasmas, which were still black.

"We didn't anticipate this, no. But looking back, retaliation was not out of the realm of possibility. It was more likely that Yon would tell his father what happened. Get the money from him to pay back the Triad and Akuza. Thus, keeping their international reputation intact. Then move on. Chalk it up to the risk of doing business."

"Houston, those deaths are on me, it's my fault. It was my plan." She had her hands on her face crying. She moved back to the couch and sat down.

He wrapped his arms around her. Houston knew he was going to have to give Sophie a dose of reality. If she was to stay on the team, she can't blame herself for the unintended consequences of an operation. "Sophie," he said in that authoritative voice, "this is the job. We do what's right to save others." He moved away from her so she could see his face. "If you want off the team, I will back you up. But you must understand what we do is critical to the survival of this country and its citizens. By stopping North Korea from selling counterfeit funds, we hinder their missile program. Even if it's only for a few months, we did a service for this country."

She laid her head on his shoulder, crying. Not saying anything, Houston sat with her.

"What do you want to do, sweetheart?" His voice was soft.

She took her time to answer, "I'm not sure, I'll pray about it and let you know. I want to go home, Houston."

"Do you see my point of view on this?" He needed some indication of what she was thinking.

"I do, Houston. You're a lawman through and through. You see the lives saved and protected and can accept that sometimes evil men have to die to save good men. The Bible has story after story about evil being judged and punished. Evil deeds have consequences, and sometimes, evil men die without repenting. But I'm not built like you, I can't do that, yet. Maybe I won't ever be able to. So, I'm going to have to learn to accept it if I stay on the team. But I'm not sure I want to be a part of it." Sophie looked at him, "from the womb, you were called for this work. I'm not sure I can do it."

"Whatever you decide, I am behind you. You have God-given abilities and talents that can be used in many areas to benefit people." He hesitated before he asked if she wanted to see the pictures.

"No," she said. "I'll never be able to get it out of my head." Houston called for an escort to take her home.

"I'll come home as soon as I can, sweetheart. I love you."

Sophie nodded and laid her head on his shoulder. When the escort came for her, he kissed her and walked her out.

Matt had talked to Sissy to see how she felt about seeing the communication. She said she had no issues with it.

Rodriguez had requested Cosby meet them in the command center. He got there just as Houston was coming back in.

"Sir, we have some intercepted pictures of an assassination. It happened earlier in North Korea," Rodriguez explained.

"Put them up, Agent Mathew's," Cosby ordered.

The images on the screen were horrifying. Some of the men turned their heads away, gagging, trying to keep from throwing up what was in their stomachs. Lined up against the wall were three heads, identified as Yon Se-bin and his two brothers. Yon Min-ji wasn't there. There was total silence in the room.

Finally, Deputy Director Cosby said, "we should have expected this. I have no doubt it was the Akuza. They are brutal." He turned to the team, who were very sober.

"This is the job, gentlemen. We had to stop the transfers; it would have harmed our economy. The people we have sworn to protect. A portion of the profits made by Yon Enterprises funds the North Korean missile program. The United States is the target of those missiles." He made sure everyone was looking at him, "this is what we signed up to do. We are not responsible for what they do to each other."

He finished his statement and left the room; there was nothing else to say.

No one spoke. Matt removed the images and put up the new intel that was cycling.

Finally, Rodriguez spoke, "Houston, how did Sophie take it?"

"She believes it's her fault. I can't guarantee she'll finish this operation. We may be on our own."

"It would be a shame not to get the final ten million off the streets. Considering the price that was just paid for it," Rodriguez replied. "Maybe we can salvage the plan somehow."

"Maybe. Let's give Sophie some time to make a decision."

The men curbed the discussion for the night and went home. They needed to know if Sophie was out.

Houston sat in his car in the driveway of his house for a long time. *Lord, should I encourage her to stay on the team or persuade her to resign.* Rodriguez pulled in and went around back to the stairs up to his apartment. Houston had to go inside. Sophie would hear Fons upstairs and start worrying about why he wasn't home. Houston walked in and looked for her. Sophie was sitting in the kitchen; Bully had his head on her lap and she was petting him. A cup of hot tea was sitting on the table in front of her.

Houston walked to the table and pulled out a chair; he was stalling, not sure of what to do. He moved the chair next to hers and sat down while taking her hand in his. Neither spoke for a long time. Finally, Houston lifted her chin, looked into her red and puffy eyes and asked, "what do you want to do, sweetheart?"

"Those men would still be alive if I hadn't put this plan in motion," she sighed. "I can't be responsible for people's lives! If these men weren't right with God, they're facing eternity in Hell. Maybe if they had had more time, they would have chosen to turn their lives around. Now they have no more chances, and it's my doing." Tears were running down her face; she turned her head away from him.

"Sophie, God is no respecter of persons. He wants everybody to come to the knowledge of salvation. But you also know that he created people with free will." His voice was getting harsher. He couldn't understand why she took their deaths so personally. "You have no idea how many chances God gave those men to accept the truth. He loved them as much as he loves us." He kept pushing, not wanting her to fall into the same depression she had when Nikko died. He couldn't face that again.

Sophie stood up so abruptly that her chair wobbled behind her, startling Bully, who got up and backed away.

"STOP! Houston stop! You're not helping. You want me to be like you. I'm not you." She headed to the bedroom, with Bully following behind. "You don't understand me."

Those were the last words he heard as she slammed her door. Houston was on his feet, "Sophie, don't walk away. Let's talk this out." But he was talking to a closed door. He fell back into his chair, upset that she stormed off. He hated that! He hated that she wouldn't stay and work through it. He was angry she didn't see it the way he did. Upset, she didn't feel the same way he did about law enforcement, until the Lord started dealing with him. Then he recognized his failure and regretted it.

Houston put his head down on his folded arms and asked God to forgive him. He knew he went about this all wrong. *Lord, she's right, I don't understand her. I was scolding her like she was a child. But she is a grown woman and fashioned by you with the sensitivity you gave her. I'm sorry for stepping out of line, Lord.*

In the morning, Houston woke to the smell of coffee and toast. He took a shower and brushed his teeth, slipped on a pair of sweats, and headed to the smell of food. He went in and wrapped her in his arms. She was scrambling eggs on the stove.

"I'm sorry, Sophie, you were right. I don't understand you, the way I should. I scolded you like you were my child, not my wife, and equal. Please forgive me."

She turned the burner off and moved the pan aside, then turned and wrapped her arms around his neck.

"You're a good man and a good husband, Houston. You want to fix everything and that's a great quality. But you can't fix me or try to change me. That's God's job." She snuggled into his chest, "He's the only one who can change the way I view things and He's done it many times." She reached up and kissed him. "Of course, I forgive you."

He sat down and she brought over two plates of eggs and toast and then went to the refrigerator for orange juice. They ate in silence for a while.

"Houston, I've decided I will finish this assignment. It wouldn't be right to the others to leave in the middle like this. But then I'm done. I'm resigning."

Houston put his hand over hers on the table. "I'm OK with whatever you decide, sweetheart."

"I don't want it to affect you or Fons. My job allows me to work from anywhere. I like it here."

Houston just nodded his head. He wasn't sure what he would do if she weren't on board with the task force.

"I got Bully designated a service dog." He changed the subject. "We'll have to get him in training soon, but until then, he can go with you whenever you want. He has a vest. Fons and I will run to Walmart and get him a second bed, water bowl, and some toys, so he has what he needs wherever he is." Sophie reached over and ran her fingers through his hair, "you are the best husband."

They cleaned up the breakfast dishes and headed to command with Bully.

They met in the conference room. "Sophie, are you ok? I'm sorry we didn't anticipate this," Rodriguez had walked in behind them.

"I'm fine, Fons, it was a shock, but I want to see this operation through."

She turned to Sissy, "are you alright. I should have called you last night to check on you, I'm sorry."

Sissy looked at her a little perplexed, "Sophie, I'm fine. It was a shock, none of us saw this coming, but these are criminals, it's what they do."

They discussed their next steps toward retrieving the missing ten million. Then Houston and Sophie headed to Ivanov's headquarters.

Houston had the box of Bully's things and Sophie's briefcase. She had Bully on a leash as they headed into the accounting offices at Ivanov's. Kim and Tom were both at their desks. They stood up to greet them when they came in.

"Hello, Ms. Star, my name is Kim Lee, I'm your lead accounting assistant, and this is Tom Dempsy. Let me show you to your office." She led them into the office Demitri had cleaned out for her.

"Thank you, Kim. I'll need your help getting settled." She noticed the bruise and swelling on her face.

They got the office arranged the way she wanted and plugged in the company desktop computer. She needed passwords to get into the accounts. She called Kim in to help her navigate. Houston was getting Bully settled into his corner on his new bed and set his toys down. He got water for his bowl from the private bathroom in the office.

"Kim, when will Demitri be here? I want to let him know I would like to do an audit of the accounts as my first task."

Kim's eyes got large, she gulped and answered, "he'll be here shortly, he had a meeting with Mr. Ivanov."

"Thank you." Sophie settled in to start familiarizing herself with their accounting system. She was using the audit as a pretext to find out where Alex got the money to send Yon. Houston had his computer out at the conference table in the office. He moved the table, so he was able to see out the door when it was open.

Less than an hour later, Demitri came into her office and welcomed her. Sophie discussed what she wanted to do. He gave her the codes to all the accounts and authorization to go through the files. She started working on it as soon as he left. She needed one question answered. Were funds from the money laundering co-mingled with Ivanov's legitimate businesses? If he ran them through an offshore account, it would be harder for her to track.

At noon Houston suggested they take Bully for a walk and get some lunch. Sophie didn't want to stop what she was doing, but he told her he wanted to do a reconnaissance of the property. He wanted to see how many security guards, and how many cameras were set up. When she stepped out to let Kim know they were going to lunch, she saw Alex talking to her. He had his hand wrapped tightly around her upper arm. It looked like he was ordering her to do something. As she got closer, she heard the last part of the conversation.

"..be ready by seven; don't make me wait." Alex was saying.

Houston knew she was going to get involved, so he moved up beside her.

"Alex Ivanov, I presume?" she held out her hand, "I'm Sophie Star, and this is my husband, Houston Townsend."

"I know who you are. My father told me you are going to improve our computer security and help us to expand our business. I don't know you, but I doubt you can do either." He ignored her extended hand.

"Well, let's hope you're wrong." Sophie responded. Houston was incensed by his rudeness.

She turned her attention to Kim. "I wanted to let you know I will need you to stay late with me tonight. I want to finish my task, and I'll need you to clarify some things for me."

"She can't, she's going out with me," Alex answered for Kim.

"I'm afraid not Mr. Ivanov, she's my assistant, and I need her."

Alex started to get in her face but saw that her husband was watching him closely. Then he heard the dog growl and decided he better watch himself. Besides, his father for some reason, wanted this woman working for him.

He put on a fake smile. "Ok, Ms. Star, I can give up one evening with Kim to make your transition easier." With that statement, he left without saying goodbye.

Sophie went to Kim, "are you alright?"

"He forces me to go out with him," she realized what she had said, "oh, I'm sorry that is not your problem. I'll be happy to stay as late as you need me, Ms. Star."

"Thank you. It won't be too late. I didn't like the way he was treating you. Is he the one who gave you that bruise?"

"I can't talk about it," Kim replied.

"Alright, Kim, Houston and I are going to lunch. We'll be back shortly."

Alex got a text from Yon to give him a call on a secure line. He went to his father's conference room and called from there.

"Alex?"

"Yes, Yon, is everything alright?"

"No." Yon went on to explain all that had happened in the last 24 hours. "I'm staying in Hong Kong for a few days. Then I'm going to New York. I need the rest of the money; I need to hide, Alex. They killed my family and will not stop until I'm dead too."

"I'll do everything I can to get that money for you, Yon. Stay in my condo here in DC while you're in town. No one will look for you there. Do you have the bills with you?"

"Yes, I will transport them myself. After what happened, I can't trust anyone."

"I'm sorry about your family Yon." Alex was sympathetic to his loss. "Who could have done this?"

"Some governments have the capabilities, yours, for instance. Other than that, only a few organizations are that sophisticated. I have no idea, but they have put a target on my back. If they wanted to shut my Appa's organization down, they did a masterful job of it."

They said their goodbyes. Alex decided he was going to make Kim do another transfer. If Ms. Star found the embezzlement, it would only implicate Kim. She could swear he told her to do it, but all he had to do was deny it. He would hate to see her go to prison; he did like her. But better she goes to jail than his father finds out he stole from him.

Sophie was through most of the accounts. There was nothing that indicated the money from Ivanov's illegal businesses funneled into his legal accounts. Houston finished setting up the mics and cameras. He checked with Command to verify the connection.

Sophie opened the Capital account. There was a transfer to an offshore account number that looked familiar.

"Houston, look at this." He moved over to her desk. "Isn't this Yon's account?"

"It looks like it. Let me check with Ms. Corban." He called and got confirmation.

"We knew he sent it, but it came out of the Capital account without any authorization. That's a violation of their policies." She searched some more to see who transferred it. It was Kim.

"Houston, he's setting Kim up."

"What do you want to do about it?" He walked back to his computer.

Sophie knew he was going to need three more million dollars, and they needed that money to transfer to Yon. They decided to wait for that before they confronted her.

Sophie made a list of reports for Kim to do. She wanted Kim's staying late to look legitimate.

Kim had just made it home and locked the door behind her when someone knocked on it. She looked through the peephole and saw it was Alex. *Maybe he'll think I'm not home, the lights aren't on,* she hoped rather than believed. He knocked again louder. She continued to ignore him.

"Kim, I know you're in there. I saw you walk in. Don't make this hard on yourself. Open up." At first, he spoke quietly, then the pounding got harder, and his voice got louder and angry. He tried the doorknob; it wouldn't turn, so he shook it and pounded on the door again.

Fear started to grip her. She slid down the door and sat on the floor, pulling her knees up to her chest, wrapping her arms around them. She rested her head on her knees.

Alex was angry. Kim wouldn't answer the door. He would knock it down, but that would bring out neighbors. Alex needed that money transferred in the morning. He was about to leave when he heard something on the other side of the door. He squatted down and whispered through the door.

"Kim, I know you can hear me. I need you to transfer three million dollars to this account in the morning." He slipped the account number under the door. "If you don't do it, your work visa will be pulled by noon, and I will have you arrested for embezzlement." He knew it wasn't the way immigration worked, but she didn't. "You better understand me, girl. Do it by 10 am or suffer the consequences."

Kim picked up the paper he slid under the door and held it in her hands, listening to him threatening her. Knowing she would have to do it, there was no choice. He would tell the police about the million dollars she already transferred without authorization. No one was going to believe her. She heard him walk away. She still sat frozen to that spot, tears running down her cheeks. All the light from outside had dissolved. She was sitting in the dark, listening to a light rain hitting her window. Who could she trust?

CHAPTER EIGHT

The next morning at Ivanov's offices, Houston got word that the other three million dollars were sent to Yon. They decided to confront Kim with the information.

"Kim, could you come into my office please," Sophie called out to her. She came in.

"Please sit down." She did.

"Kim, can you explain a transfer you made for a million dollars to this off-shore account a few days ago? And another one this morning? I don't see authorization for it."

Kim's eyes got big; Sophie could see the fear. Kim put her hands to her face and started crying; her words came out muffled. "You won't believe me. No one will."

Sophie moved over to a chair next to Kim and gently brought her hands down from her face. "How do you know unless you tell me." Houston hadn't moved from his spot at the conference table.

Kim told her of being forced to do the first transfer. She brought her left hand up to her cheek, where there were still remnants of the bruising. "Alex hit me. Hard," she said. "Then he came to my house again last night. I pretended I wasn't there, but he saw me come in. He shoved the account number under my door. Alex said if I didn't transfer three million dollars by 10 am today, he would make me regret it."

She turned her face away from Sophie. "I can't lose this job. My father was badly injured at work in South Korea. He can no longer work. They live on what I send them." When Sophie didn't reply, she took a deep breath and continued. "But if I stay, he will make me do more things I don't want to do. Not just at the office," she paused and looked down, ashamed. "He wants me to do other things with him. I don't want to be in a relationship with him, Ms. Star. He is a bad man."

Sophie finally spoke. "I believe you. Alex is setting you up. In case the embezzlement is discovered before he can pay it back. And there is a good chance he can get away with it."

"If he finds out I told you. He will hurt me or have someone else do it. Not all of Ivanov's businesses are legal. They associate with some pretty dangerous people."

"I'm aware of that, Kim." Sophie got up and went back to her chair behind her desk. "It might be wise for you to leave here."

"Are you firing me!? No, please! They'll send me back to South Korea. Alex told me that."

"Not necessarily, Kim."

"If I can find someone else to sponsor your work visa, you can stay."

"I don't have another job. Even if I did, Alex would come after me." Kim lamented.

"Are you willing to leave DC?"

Kim just looked at her, confused. "Leave?"

"Yes, I know where you could get a job, but it's in another state. To do this, you will have to work with authorities to get an immunity deal on the embezzlement. You would have to help them prosecute Alex. Can you do that?"

"No, no! He has already threatened my parents in South Korea."

Sophie pointed to Houston, "do you see that man over there." She looked to Houston, "as we speak, he is making arrangements for you to travel to another state safely."

"How would I live? It took me a long time to get this job."

"I have a friend who has an accounting firm in Washington state. He will hire you. It won't pay as well as here, but I can pay your rent for six months. I'd be glad to send you to school to get your CPA license if that's what you want. But I need you to help me with Alex."

"Why would you and your husband do that, Ms. Star? You don't even know me."

Houston moved from his place at the conference table and leaned against the desk, looking her in the eyes. "The Bible says, 'If anyone has the world's goods and sees his brother in need yet closes his heart against him. How does God's love abide in him? Little children let us not love in word or talk but in deed and in truth.' (1 John 3:17-18) We're doing what our Father tells us to do."

"I was you, once, and someone helped me. Has anyone ever told you about Jesus?" Sophie added.

"Yes, there are many Christians in my country. But we are Buddhist."

She told Kim how Suzie invited her to church and how Jesus changed her life. She let her know that Suzie would help her once she reached Lake View. Kim hung on to her and cried.

"I do want to go, Ms. Star. But I don't understand how you can help me get immunity and a new work visa."

"I just can. Trust me."

"What about my parents?" Kim asked.

Sophie turned to Houston.

"I will see if I can get them a temporary emergency visa to come to visit you for a few months. Hopefully, this will be over by then," Houston told her.

Houston instructed Kim to go home and pack only the things she would need for a week. He would send someone to pick her up and take her to the airport. Houston handed her everything in his wallet, about one hundred fifty dollars. He added that they would have an account set up for her at the local credit union. When she got there, there would be money in it to hold her until she got her first paycheck.

Sophie spoke up, "a friend of mine will pick you up and take you home with her until I'm able to get housing for you." She hadn't spoken to Suzie yet, but she knew her well enough to know she would help any way she could.

"What about the rest of my things. I don't own much; the apartment was furnished?"

"Don't worry. We will have a moving company send the rest of your things to you. Just leave the key with the person who takes you to the airport." Houston replied.

After they said their goodbyes to Kim, she left, and they shut down the computers and left the office.

Houston and Sophie headed to the command center to set in order the promises they made Kim. Sophie got ahold of Special Prosecutor Trindi Martin from DOJ. She told her what she had promised Kim. A new work visa and immunity if Kim cooperated. Sophie asked if she could take care of it. Ms. Martin said she would get approval and get back with her.

Houston got ahold of the Korean embassy, asking if the forms could be filed online for an emergency visa for Kim's parents. He had the authority of the DOJ behind the request to ensure it would happen.

After leaving command, Sophie called Suzie to tell her a little about Kim. She wanted to know if the other half of the duplex was empty. Suzie told her it had been on a short-term lease. A businessman, who had a job to oversee in Lake View would be leaving in a week. Sophie asked her to get permission to rent it to Kim. She let her know she would send six months' rent in advance and told her Kim's parents might join her for a few months. Suzie offered Kim a place to stay until the apartment was vacant.

"Suzie, please do for her what you did for me. Introduce her to Jesus."

"Sophie, you know I will." Sophie did know, Suzie's life was about telling others the way to salvation.

Houston stopped at the Chinese Restaurant by their house, for a takeout order.

Sophie got the call late that night that Suzie settled Kim in her spare bedroom. They would hold Kim's things in storage until the apartment was ready.

Alex hadn't talked to Kim since she transferred the money to Yon. He tried calling her several times and even went by her office. When she wasn't at her desk, Alex assumed she was in with Ms. Star. He decided to wait and go by her house later that evening and take her out to dinner. Alex owned her now. She would have to do whatever he wanted or go to jail.

It was dinner time when he went to pick Kim up. He knocked. When Kim didn't answer the door, Alex put his shoulder to it and broke in. The house was dark. He walked to her bedroom and saw that her clothes were gone.

"You think you can hide from me, Kim. You'll regret this little game," he yelled out to the empty room.

"Houston, Mr. Ivanov, wants to talk to us, but I need to get this done. Will you go and see what he wants?"

"Sophie, I'm not leaving you without protection in this place. It's not protocol, and even if it were, I wouldn't do it." He responded. She moved to his side.

"I'm fine. We have no reason to believe any of us are in any danger right now. Please go. We need to keep a good rapport with Mr. Ivanov to make this work."

He wasn't happy about it; his gut told him not to go. "Sophie, I'll go, but only to tell him we'll get back to him as soon as possible."

"Thanks, Houston."

Houston left to go to the office building right behind the accounting offices. The grounds were green and lush. There was a fountain surrounded by colorful Iris, Bergenia, and other flowers he didn't recognize. The building itself was much newer than the one he just left. The inside decor was ostentatious, very Russian, lots of gold overlay. Houston headed to Vladimir's office, intending to make it short.

By the time Alex made it to the office, he was fuming; he had been stewing about it all night. He walked up to Kim's office, thinking she may have moved to another apartment. Alex couldn't believe she would leave her job. She wasn't at her desk; he turned to Tom.

"Where's Kim?" He asked.

"She hasn't come in yet," Tom replied.

Alex went over to Sophie's office and walked in the door without knocking. She looked up and noticed his belligerent demeanor.

"Can I help you, Alex," she asked as he stepped closer to her desk.

"I'm looking for Kim." Alex barked.

"She's not here." She stayed seated, trying to keep some distance from him.

"I can see that. I want to know where Kim is. She has been spending a lot of time with you lately." His irritation evident when he spoke.

"I'm her supervisor; of course, we spend time together."

"I have the feeling it's more than that," Alex moved closer.

"I have no idea what you're talking about; your personal life is not my concern. However, I noticed you tend to be abrasive with her; you need to give her more respect."

Agent Rodriguez was at command watching, and he could tell this wasn't going to end well. He decided to text Houston and let him know he needed to get back to her office.

"Mr. Ivanov, Sophie and I are in the middle of working on a secure link for your organization. She didn't want to be rude and not show up; I thought I would come to let you know she isn't available right now."

"That's fine, Mr. Townsend. I pay her to work not to chat with me. I had some questions; maybe you could answer them for me?"

"Of course, Mr. Ivanov," a text pinged. Houston looked at it.

Rodriguez text. **Get back to Sophie.**

"Mr. Ivanov, I have an emergency, I'll get back to you."

Houston ran across the common grounds and headed to her office.

"Ms. Star, I've been watching you, and you're poisoning Kim's mind against me. I want to know where she is. What have you done with her?"

She got up, "I would like you to leave, Alex."

"I'm not going anywhere until you tell me where Kim is." He was right in her face. She backed up but got pinned against the wall.

"Where is she!? You need to stay out of my business. Do not interfere with my relationship."

"What if she doesn't want a relationship with you?"

"You do know where she is, tell me!" He was inches from her yelling.

"Get away from me!" She tried pushing him away. She barely moved him an inch; the attempt just made him angrier.

"Not until you tell me, and I'm not afraid to encourage you." He raised his fist as a gesture.

That's when Houston came into the room. He saw Alex's fist in the air, leaped over the chair and grabbed his arm. Houston spun Alex around and punched him in the face. Alex straightened up from the punch and swung at Houston's jaw, but Houston moved out of the way. Houston came back at Alex and slugged him in the stomach, doubling him over. He grabbed his arm and bent it behind his back just as security came into the room.

"Take this joker out of here before I kill him." He pushed him toward security.

Alex was gasping for air but managed to say, "you just made an enemy. You and Ms. Star need to stay out of my business!"

Security followed Alex out of the office.

Houston went to Sophie and accompanied her to the couch.

"Are you alright, sweetheart, your trembling. Get your purse; we're out of here." He started to stand.

"Houston, please give me a minute, I need to calm down."
He got up and started pacing, he was angry, what if he had
come in a minute later. That man would have hit his wife. He
was boiling mad.

"I shouldn't have let you talk me into leaving you," he said
heated.

"But you came in time and protected me. I'm alright," she
said, but there was a small tremor in her voice.

"He could have hurt you, Sophie!" He grabbed her purse
and helped her up, putting his arm around her for support as
they left the office.

Vladimir caught up to them, calling Sophie's name before
they got in the car.

"Ms. Star, are you alright? I heard what happened."

"I am now, thank you. I just need to go home," she replied.

"Of course, I'll see you tomorrow." He looked at Houston.
"can I speak to you for a minute."

Houston helped Sophie into the passenger seat and then
moved to where Mr. Ivanov waited.

"Mr. Townsend, I must tell you; I would normally retaliate
against you for *touching* my son. But I understand you felt you
had to protect your wife." He looked Houston right in his eyes.
"I won't forgive it again."

"Mr. Ivanov, I have no intention of *touching* your son again
unless he threatens my wife or me. And trust me, then I will do
more than give him a few taps."

"Keep in mind what I said. I will take care of Alex."

By the time they got home, she had calmed down, but Houston hadn't. He was getting more troubled. Houston had been fighting the fear of losing her. It started after Nikko paralyzed him with the snake venom and kidnapped Sophie right in front of him. He couldn't do anything then, but he was never going to let that happen again.

Houston talked to Rodriguez on the way home and told him they were at the house for the night. He also mentioned he planned on taking Sophie off the task force. They went into the house, and she sat on the couch. Bully instinctively came and jumped on the couch next to her and put his head in her lap. She was stroking his fur.

"Please sit, Houston, you need to calm down."

"I can't. If I had been ten seconds later, Alex would have hit you. You're off this case. We can get that money some other way."

"Please sit down; let's talk about it." He relented. She cupped his face in her hands and kissed his lips.

"There is no one who will look out for my safety and protection the way you do, and you did protect me, Houston. You're right; I should have honored your instinct not to go. That's my fault, but can we talk about it?"

"Sophie, the thought that you could be hurt again is more than I can take."

"But I didn't get hurt. You were there when I needed you. But this mission's best chance is the one we agreed on."

"I don't care. You're not putting yourself in harm's way again."

She knew he needed time to calm down. She got up and put one of Carol's premade dinners in the oven. Then she went back and snuggled with Houston on the couch and watched TV until the dinner was ready. He had his arms wrapped around her, still protecting her; it helped him. They ate dinner but didn't talk much, then went to bed.

In the morning, she got up early and made breakfast. When Houston came out ready to go to the command center without her, she stopped him.

"Houston sit down and eat breakfast; we need to talk."

"Sophie, please don't ask me to put you in that situation again."

"Can we at least talk about it. You know I respect your opinion. And I appreciate your commitment to my safety. But your fear of me being in danger is unreasonable considering our choice of careers. I know you'll make sure I won't ever be alone at the office again." He got up and squatted down in front of her chair.

"Sophie, how would I go on if I lost you. I can't even imagine it without losing my composure." He laid his head on her lap.

She combed her fingers through his hair, "do you think for one minute, it would be easier for me if I lost you." She said more sharply than she intended.

He looked up, "no, of course not."

"I would never ask you to quit your job because I'm afraid of losing you. Being able to work with you takes the edge off of my fear. If something happens, I would at least be there with you to help in some way. The main reason I joined the task force was to be with you."

He took her hand and kissed her palm, "what am I supposed to do Sophie, it scares me."

"We trust God with our lives and protect each other. I'll do whatever you want me to do because you ask out of pure love. But I would like to stay on the task force."

"If I agree, will you listen to me when it comes to your protection?"

"Absolutely." She responded. He stood up and paced a few minutes.

Houston decided that if Max and his police dog Bully Sr., the father to their dog, were on the premises, she would be safe. He knew Sophie would be comfortable with that. They were part of her protection team during the Morano task force.

"I want Max and Bully Sr. with you every minute you're on Ivanov's property. If Cosby doesn't go for it, we'll both quit the task force."

"Sweetheart, I wouldn't ask you to do that."

"I know, but if I ask you to, then I need to make the same sacrifice."

"I can accept that." She kissed him and went to get dressed.

Once at headquarters, Houston went to Cosby's office. His secretary ushered him right in.

"Sir, did you hear what happened yesterday?"

"Yes, Agent Rodriguez came in and informed me. I'm sorry, Houston, is Sophie alright?"

"She is, but I'm not. I need her to have Max and Bully with her when she's on Ivanov's property."

Cosby didn't say anything for a minute, "Houston sit down." He took a seat across from Cosby. "Generally, I would have never allowed a married couple to work together for this very reason. But this team works together better and more successfully than any other team I have ever seen. It's an anomaly. I believe a good part of the reason is because of the stable dynamic your and Sophie's love bring to it. So, I can't ignore your request. If my wife worked this job, I would feel the same way. Make it happen."

Houston felt much better when he left Cosby's office.

Houston and Sophie were at the conference table in her office at Ivanov's.

"We need to get Sissy in here. If we can hack into the security and find out where Vladimir keeps his real books, we'll be able to do more. So far, we know Yon is on his way here with the counterfeit millions. We might need men on the ground for this one, can we do it with just our team?"

"It depends on what your plan is, Sophie. What do you have in mind? Do you want to conference in the team?"

"Yes, lets video conference with them from here." She decided.

Houston texted Fons,

Rodriguez, can you get everyone together to brainstorm via video conference.

In a few minutes, they were all connected. They discussed getting Sissy in Ivanov's headquarters with them. Then they considered the best way to get their hands on the money.

"We know Yon will be at Alex's condo, and I seriously doubt he will let the money out of his sight with what just happened to him. Do we want to steal it?" Smith asked.

They discussed that for a while and then Timms came up with an idea.

"If we let the transaction happen and let Yon leave with his money. I have no doubt he will never go back to North Korea. So the money won't go to the missile program and that worry will be off the table. We don't know how Alex plans on dispersing it to get his profit. Now he thinks he doesn't have to pay back his father because he framed Kim. The fact that she has disappeared helps his case. Now he has 10 million dollars to spend free and clear."

"What are you saying, let him get it into circulation?" Sophie questioned.

"No, of course not, not all of it, maybe 1 million. There are very few maps on where and how these counterfeit bills circulate. If we have a chance at mapping it, isn't it worth finding out? I'm sure the US Treasury would want that information. Worst case scenario, 1 million hits the street, but that's manageable. Then we can confiscate the rest."

"Wow, that's quite a departure from normal protocol Agent Timms," Rodriguez stated.

"Isn't that what Sophie's modeled for us. Think out of the box." He replied, throwing her under the bus with a smile.

"Even if we do let a million slide through to track it's trajectory; we need to tag it to do that. And the rest of it in case we lose track of it somehow," Rodriguez remarked.

"Check with the Secret Service, Fons. They work with counterfeit money. They may have a way of doing that. Ten million is a lot of money. It could take hours to do it," Houston said. Yon would be coming soon and they needed to solidify a plan.

Sophie headed to Demitri's office to try to get Sissy hired.

She knocked on his door. "Sir, do you have a moment for me," she said as she poked her head in the door.

"Come in, Sophie, what can I do for you?"

"You know we lost Kim. Alex got physical with her, and she left the city to get away from him." Sophie spoke as she sat in the chair across from Dimitri.

"I didn't know the whole story, but that doesn't surprise me. Alex is not like his father. He is an entitled punk that doesn't have a tenth of his father's street smarts or business sense. Do you want me to replace her?"

"I was hoping I could hire an assistant; one I have worked with before. I received a call yesterday saying she moved into town. If that's alright with you, it will help me stay on track rather than taking the time to train someone."

"As long as security can vet her, I don't see why not," he smiled at her. "How are you coming with your assessment of our structure?"

"I have found a few troubling things, but I don't want to say anything prematurely. I would rather finish first."

He nodded, "I understand, Ms. Star. Let me know when you are ready to give me your report."

"I will. Having this new assistant will help me finish up."

She stood and thanked him as she went out the door.

Sophie headed back to her office and told Houston he went for it. Houston called to let Sissy know. Max and Bully showed up an hour later, setting up just in front of the door to the office.

Sissy was in security at Ivanov's in an hour, and Houston had a contract ready for her to sign.

"Ms. Corban, can you get into the security cameras?" Sophie asked when she finally stepped into her office.

"I'll work on that. Can I use the conference table for a desk for a while? I don't want to do this at Kim's desk; it's to open." Houston moved over to make room for her.

"Remind me to negotiate a bigger office for you next time." Houston laughed.

They spent the rest of the day working on their projects. Houston was on with command to set up a schedule for tailing Yon and Alex. They brought in a few undercovers from the FBI they had worked with before. Cosby had reluctantly approved their plan. He knew it was risky, but the benefit would be noteworthy if it worked. They had to get into Alex's condo when neither Yon or Alex were there and mark the counterfeit money. It was the only way to surveil every bill electronically. To be on the safe side, they decided to tag all the money. It would take two men an hour to do it, but it was necessary. The whole team was out getting HUMINT.

Houston decided he wanted to give Sophie relief from the stress of the last few days. He let Rodriguez know they would be taking Saturday off.

Houston wouldn't tell Sophie what he had in mind for their day off. She thought maybe a spa, or a day on the lake. As they drove deeper into the Virginia countryside, those ideas disintegrated. She was watching the scenery when she noticed a sign that said, 'SKY DIVING.'

"Tell me you are not taking me skydiving, *PLEASE!*" She said in a panic.

"Princess, you'll love it. When you jump out of that plane, there is no adrenalin rush like it. Besides, it's my turn. I went horseback riding with you on your turn."

"Yes, but you love horseback riding." Pointing to the plane, she added, "this is jumping out of a plane!" She gave him her best suspicious look, and playfully said, "have you taken out a large Life Insurance policy on me recently?" Houston burst out laughing. Sophie couldn't hold a straight face any longer and started laughing too.

"You'll love it, I promise." He took her hand and kissed her palm.

When they got to the hanger, they joined others in a crash course on how to jump safely and when to pull the cord. Sophie listened intently, hoping to come out of this without being splattered on the ground.

Her instructor told her that she would be jumping in tandem with him today. He gave her a wingsuit, a helmet, goggles, and added gloves for warmth. Houston, Sophie, and her instructor got on the plane and waited for the altitude to reach 12,500 feet. Sophie and her instructor jumped first, then Houston jumped. It was scary and exhilarating at the same time. She was screaming and laughing, Houston linked up with them for the ride down.

She didn't know if he could hear her, but she hollered, "I'm going to kill you when we get down." He was laughing at her; he knew she was enjoying it even though she wouldn't admit it. *He knows me too well*, Sophie thought as she watched the ground coming up on her fast.

Houston let go and dove ahead about fifty feet before pulling his cord. He wanted to get on the ground and secure his gear. He was right there when Sophie came down on a soft landing. He unhooked her from her 'buddy' and helped her take her helmet off. She slugged his arm a few times. He just laughed at her, "you know you loved it." She finally relented and gave him a big hug.

"I must say it was exhilarating." He kissed her and grabbed the gear to put in the waiting truck to take them back to the hanger.

They chatted on the drive home and had fun reliving the experience. Houston pulled in at a casual Italian restaurant someone recommended. It ended up being a very romantic dinner. They both enjoyed the quiet ride home. Sophie watched the Loblolly Pine go by. The farmers use them as windbreakers along the highway.

Houston reached over and took her hand in his. "What are you thinking, princess?"

"I was just thanking God for you. I love you so much, Houston." He glanced over to her and kissed the hand he held.

"I love you too, sweetheart."

They got back at dusk. Rodriguez was upstairs, and Bully was outside playing with his toys. After calling Bully inside, she turned to Houston, who was cleaning the dog dishes to refill them.

"Thanks for a great day, honey. You always manage to take me out of my comfort zone. But don't think for a minute I won't get even." He swallowed her up in his arms and kissed her.

"You make my life exhilarating enough, princess."

"And you make my life a roller coaster." She laughed.

"Does that make me 'Apollo's Chariot'?"

"No, you'll always be my soft landing.'" He kissed her again.

CHAPTER NINE

Sunday, they attended a Church they located close to their home, with Rodriguez. After they ate lunch out, they headed to the command center. The others had gotten there earlier.

Sophie sorted through all the HUMINT they had gathered in the last couple of days, putting it up on the whiteboard in a logical order. They had all gathered around, looking at the arrangement on the boards.

"What do you see, Sophie?" Rodriguez asked.

"Yon arrived last night, but he hasn't left Alex's condo. The Secret Service told me about their newest top-secret spyware. It's an odorless spray that can be tracked by satellite." Sophie relayed.

"That's amazing. Does the Secret Service think it can be sprayed on money and track it effectively?" Timms asked.

"Yes, they've used it before, although on smaller amounts and it worked."

"That solves that problem. Now we just have to get Yon out of the condo." Matt added.

Rodriguez stepped up, "I think I have an idea. I hadn't told any of you yet, but Cosby came by earlier and told me the President wants us at his Donor Dinner Monday night. He wants to meet us, and he thought it would be a nice treat for us to meet at the White House. Oh, and he said this wasn't an option. When the President invites you to dinner, you show up in monkey suits."

"What are you saying Fons, how does that get us in the condo?" Smith asked.

"I get it," Houston stood, "we get Cosby to find someone to invite Alex as a guest and tell him he can bring a friend. If it works, we get Alex and Yon out of the house for several hours. But how in the world does an invitation filter down to Alex Ivanov?"

"That problem is above our pay grade. We let Cosby work that out," Rodriguez said.

"I like it," Sophie agreed.

Since it was Sunday, they called it a day and headed out, leaving Rodriguez to present the idea to Cosby.

Houston had been dressed in his tux for an hour; it was almost 6 pm. He was sitting on the couch watching sports with Bully lying at his feet. Sophie came out in a navy Oscar de la Renta fit and flare silk leaf strapless gown. It had white applique leaves and stopped above the ankles. She had Jimmy Choo black patent leather mules with a crystal strap. On her ears, she wore her two-carat diamond earrings. Her left hand had her wedding ring and a four-carat tennis bracelet. Houston stood up when he saw her, smelling her perfume. He took her hand and gave her a twirl, "how can you be this beautiful and be with me?"

She laughed, "you had me under your spell, prince charming." They both laughed and went on their way.

The Task Force walked into a beautifully decorated White House Banquet Hall. Round tables seated ten, dressed in white tablecloths and matching white seat covers with the president's seal embroidered on the back. On the tables, short square mirrored vases with white geraniums and roses set atop a round mirror piece. The table setting included three glasses, a coffee cup, and silverware. Cloth napkins folded like a butterfly added to the beautiful setting. More significant free-standing floral arrangements were scattered around the room. The head table was longer, several rectangular rather than round put together. The centerpieces ran along the surface of the tables every eighteen inches. One larger arrangement sat in the middle made up of red, white, and blue roses.

The organizers had seated the team at different tables to have them mingle. Houston had eased Sophie's hand onto the crook of his elbow. He placed his hand on top of hers. Houston couldn't help noticing men's heads turning; he knew she looked stunning.

Houston whispered in her ear. "I don't know how Cosby did it, but there they are, Yon and Alex sitting at a table with some wealthy donors."

"Who's at the condo looking for and marking the counterfeit bills?"

"Secret service guys. I hope they brought a safecracker with them; I doubt it's just laying around the house."

Sophie and Houston were seated with some wealthy guests that were in the oil business; that was fortunate. Houston could easily keep a conversation going. A couple of women at their table were not invited but were the guest of others. They were young and pretty, dressed a little more daring than Sophie's taste. The meal took an hour and a half to serve. When done eating, Sissy came to Sophie's table and whispered in her ear. She excused herself and went with her to the lady's room.

"You look beautiful, Sissy. Who are you sitting with?" Sophie couldn't see her from their table.

"Thanks, Sophie, you too. They set me up with Matt as my date, and we're sitting with four Republican Senators and their wives. Matt is up on his politics, so it makes for interesting conversation." Then she lowered her voice, "Matt looks very handsome tonight in his tux." She chuckled, "I can't believe the money in this room, Sophie. My mom won't believe I'm hob-nobbing with the President. I was always the anti-establishment rebel of the family. I guess we all grow up."

"My parents would have loved this for me. God works in mysterious ways." Sophie headed for a stall. They finished freshening up. As they walked back into the dining room, Sissy stopped her and gasped. "Sophie, look at that woman, she is blatantly flirting with your husband." Sophie looked and shook her head with a little smile.

"Doesn't that bother you, Sophie? I'm going to tell her a thing or two." Sissy headed for their table.

Sophie took her arm. "Sissy, you don't know my husband that well. Houston will in no way entertain another woman's flirtations. I feel bad for her, he responds rather rudely. My heart is safe with him."

Sure enough in a few seconds as they were walking over, he removed her hand from his arm. He made it known he was a married man and not interested. The young woman stood up with a shocked look on her face and left the table. Sophie went behind her husband and kissed his cheek, not saying a word about the incident.

An hour later, Deputy Director Cosby came over and collected the team to lead them into the Oval Office. Houston asked Cosby if the Secret Service had located the money. Cosby said no, but they were narrowing it down. The President and First Lady came in. Deputy Director Cosby started introductions. When he came to Sophie and Houston, the President stopped.

"Ms. Star or rather Mrs. Townsend, you're the one who took down the Morano network. Nice work, we are lucky to have you on our side." He shook her hand.

"Mr. President and First Lady, it is my honor to meet you. I wasn't alone, everyone here was an integral part of that takedown, and they also saved my life in the process."

"I'd love to hear the whole story." The President responded.

He moved to shake Houston's hand. "Agent Townsend, your name has come up several times. Your colleagues and superiors respect you. I'd like to have you come and play golf with me some time."

"Thank you for that, sir, it would be my honor," Houston answered as he then took the First Lady's hand. The president went on to the rest of the team and acknowledged them.

Once they were escorted from the room, Houston asked Deputy Director Cosby if the team could be excused for the evening.

"Not yet, I'd like someone to keep an eye on Yon and Alex. The team at Alex's needs to know when they leave here." Houston had moved a few steps when Cosby stopped him. "You may not realize it, but this meeting was an important introduction. The President is critical to sustaining our Task Force funds." He turned and left, as did the rest of the team.

They went back to their tables, each one trying to keep Yon in their sites.

"Houston, look who's coming our way." He looked and saw Yon and Alex coming directly to them.

"Mr. Townsend, Ms. Star, I had no idea you had these kinds of connections," Alex said with his normal arrogant tone. "Let me introduce you to a friend of mine. Yon Min-ji, this is Mr. Townsend and Ms. Star, they work for me." Sophie was taken back by his comment; she knew he meant to give the illusion he was superior to them. Houston stood when they came over.

"Mr. Townsend," Yon reached out his hand to him, "and Ms. Star, I must say you look quite stunning tonight." He took her hand and bowed over it.

"Thank you, Mr. Yon, how kind of you to say. But I prefer Mrs. Townsend when I'm not at work. Are you here long?"

"A few more days, I'm finishing some business then leaving town. It was quite a privilege to come to the White House. Some of Alex's friends were invited but couldn't make it, so they offered him the invitations."

"I see, well I hope we run into each other again before you leave. Maybe we could have dinner," Sophie said.

"It would be a great honor, Mrs. Townsend."

Alex said goodbye, and they went off to mingle with the wealthy. Houston and Sophie went to find Cosby to see if they had found the money yet. They found him with his wife talking with the Senate majority leader. They waited until noticed, then went over to talk to him.

"Let me introduce you to my wife," Cosby said.

"Trish, this is Mr. Houston Townsend and his wife, Sophie Star-Townsend."

"It's a pleasure to meet you both. You look lovely, my dear," She said.

"Thank you, Mrs. Cosby and you look stunning in your gown."

"Thank you dear but call me Trish." She got called away by some friends, and they were able to ask Cosby about the mission.

"Last I heard they were using some electronic gadget to get into the safe and looking for any kind of hidden room. There wasn't one on the blueprints, but that doesn't mean anything."

UNINTENDED CONSEQUENCES

"Is it alright if we leave, Rodriguez will stay and keep an eye on Yon and Alex."

"As long as someone keeps an eye on them, then that's fine." Cosby moved over to be with his wife.

Sophie slugged his arm, "you can't just volunteer Fons like that."

"You want to go home, don't you?"

"Well, yeah, but..."

"Then don't complain."

Houston tracked down Fons to tell him he wanted to take Sophie home. "Fons, Cosby said someone had to stay to make sure the men at Alex's condo knew when Yon and Alex left.

"So you volunteered me, right?"

"Well, Yeah." He smiled at Fons.

"Go ahead, I'll stay, but you owe me."

Sophie touched his arm. "Thank you, Fons."

Sophie went into her room and changed. When she came out, she saw Houston sprawled out on the couch; he had taken off his jacket and tie. His head was on the armrest. His left arm outstretched, pointing the remote at the TV, turning to the sports channel. His right leg was touching the ground. She came in and jumped on him and kissed him all over his face.

Houston laughed, "I'm not complaining, but what's this for?"

She kept kissing him, "I saw that woman trying to seduce you tonight, it looked to me like you brought her down a peg. I wanted you to know I appreciate your faithfulness." He captured her lips and held them.

"What would I do with another woman, I've already got my hands full with you." He laughed. Sophie was the first to

105

hear the apartment door open at the top of the stairs. She jumped up.

"Hey, Sophie, you got some food; Oops, sorry, did I interrupt something?" He said with a laugh.

Houston got up and lunged at him. Wrestling with him as he did with his brothers. Laughing, he got out the words, "I'll make you sorry." Fons was grappling, trying to get a hold on Houston. Sophie went to the kitchen and grabbed the other dinner she had Carol make. She brought it back with her and watched them, enjoying the laughter of the two wrestlers trying to get a hold on one another.

"Fons, would you like to watch television with us," Sophie asked, seeing Bully had gotten in the mix.

"Tell her no thank you," Houston had his arms wrapped around Fons's chest on the ground.

"No, thank you, Sophie." He finally got lose and stood up. She handed him the cooking pan, ready to go in the oven.

"How did you know?" he asked with a grin on his face.

"I must have ESP or something," she smiled. Houston had come around her and wrapped his arms around her from behind.

"How did you get home so soon?"

"I asked Matt to stay and watch Yon. I told him to call us if he hears anything about the money."

Fons said thank you and went back upstairs. "And lock the door, from both sides." Houston hollered after him. He heard it lock and laughed.

"I noticed you had an extra dinner in the fridge, that was nice."

"He's the man my husband chose to watch his back. I'm going to do everything I can to keep him healthy," she turned and kissed him.

"You know he has a crush on Carol?" Houston said.

"I know," her only response. Houston followed her back into the living room.

He left it at that—a conversation for another day.

"Now, where were we?" Houston asked.

They were asleep when the phone rang. Houston answered.

"Hello?"

"Houston, I thought you'd want to know. They found the money in a safe room. They sprayed it with the tagging solution. We're all set."

"Thanks for calling Matt, I'll let Sophie know."

"Sissy, we are going to have to give Vladimir and Dimitri something. They won't keep me here if I don't have anything to offer. What if I let Vladimir know about Alex stealing the money? I can tell him that the laundering business is in jeopardy because of the way it's set up?" Sophie said.

"I understand why we need to give them something, but what do you think he'll do when he finds out his son's a thief?" Sissy was sitting at the conference table in Sophie's office.

"Initially, he will be furious and want to punish him, but in the end, he will take up for his son and try to keep him out of jail," Houston said.

"I'm thinking, the DEA and FBI had years to try to get something on Vladimir. He's too smart now and has distanced himself on paper from any of the illegal businesses ever to get a conviction. If I can convince him to get out altogether, we get the same result. He ends his illegal enterprises.

"Vladimir needs to see Alex as a detriment to his freedom and livelihood. If I can convince him that the government could confiscate his legal businesses if they can connect them in any way to Alex's illegal ones, then we can go after Alex without his father running interference. We could shut down Alex's entire network." Sophie said, leaning back in her office chair.

Houston thought for a moment, "I don't like the idea of Vladimir getting off without any jail time. The rest I like."

"Honey, that's the purist in you, you see everything in black and white, it's why you're in law enforcement. But reality points to the fact there is little chance of ever getting a conviction on him. But if we can shut down his illegal enterprises, we will have accomplished our mission."

"There is one more thing," Houston said. "No matter how mad Vladimir might be with his son. Even to the point of letting go of his son's little empire. He will fight to keep him out of prison. I'm sure of that."

"Well, then we will have to make sure we have an iron-clad case," Sophie replied.

Houston left to talk to the team about their new approach. He let Max and Bully know he was going.

"I'm going to use Kim's computer, see if I can find any direct routes to the information we need." Sissy got up and headed for Kim's desk.

An hour later, Alex came up to the offices and noticed Sissy at Kim's desk.

"Who are you?" He asked.

"I'm Kim's replacement, Sophie hired me."

He sat on the edge of her desk. "My name is Alex Ivanov; you work for me. Let me take you out to dinner; I like to get to know my employees."

Sissy gave him a look, "Sophie warned me about you, she said you abused Kim. I'm not interested."

Alex got up in a huff, "I suggest if you want to keep your job, you treat me with a little more respect."

She laughed, "you might scare the women you're usually around, but you don't scare me."

Max was watching this play out, laughing to himself, but ready to intervene if necessary. Alex came stomping over to Sophie's office, intending to storm right in.

Max got up and stood in front of the door, "can I help you, sir."

"Get out of my way; I need to talk to Ms. Star." Alex tried to push by him but stepped back when Bully Sr., growled.

"I'll let her know you're here. Please wait." He left Bully at the door to watch him.

Max went in and told Sophie the whole story. She laughed, "I love that girl." Let him in Max, thank you." Max let him in, closing the door and standing with Bully on the inside of the office.

"Excuse your man, Ms. Star," he said indignantly. "I want to talk to you alone." He moved to one of the chairs and sat down.

"I'm afraid that's not possible, my husband hired him, and he was told not to leave me alone with you. What is it I can do for you, Mr. Ivanov?"

"I want to know why you replaced Kim and what right you had telling that woman I abused her predecessor."

"I replaced her because it's obvious Kim's not coming back. And I told her the truth about you so she could make an informed decision if you asked her out. Is there anything else I can help you with?"

Alex jetted up and slammed his fist on the desk. Bully started growling and yanking on his leash, trying to get to him. It startled Alex, he turned to the dog who was on his hind legs trying to get to him.

109

"I suggest you calm down, or Max may not be able to control Bully," Sophie instructed.

"I came here to pass on an invitation from Yon for you to have dinner with him. He would prefer you to come without your husband, but if you insist, he is also welcome."

"There is no way I would have dinner with Yon without my husband. I will ask him and see if he is interested. I will let you know." Alex headed to the door.

"Get him out of my way." He waved his hand toward Bully.

After he left, Max asked Sophie if she was alright. After being assured she was, he went back to his post.

When Houston got back, she told him the whole episode with Alex.

"You were right to bring on Max and Bully. Thank you, sweetheart." She hugged him.

"That's why I do it; you give such good rewards." He smiled and reciprocated the hug.

"She let him know about the backhanded invitation to dine with Yon."

"Who knows what information we might glean; it could be worth the time."

"I agree, I'll send a message to Alex." They went over to the conference table to discuss the team's input. They decided to go ahead with the new plan.

"The US Treasury was interested in mapping how the bills circulate. An opportunity like this doesn't come by very often. They want us to let at least half a million pass through so they can see how it flows into the economy. A lot of benefits can come from your plan, Sophie." Houston said.

"It was Agent Timms idea. He deserves the credit."

They decided to wait until morning to talk to Vladimir, so they locked the office, and they all went home.

Thursday morning, Houston and Sophie headed to Vladimir's office. They had decided on the best way to present the information. Houston felt Vladimir would respond best to Sophie; she agreed. They asked his secretary if he had a minute for them. She came back and escorted them in.

Vladimir stood and shook Houston's hand, "What brings you to my office today?"

"Mr. Ivanov, in doing my audit I have found some disturbing information. Since it involves your son, I felt bypassing Demitri would be the delicate thing to do."

"What is it, Ms. Star?"

"I have found that money is missing out of your Capital account..."

"How much?" Vladimir interrupted, leaning forward on his desk.

"Four million. I traced the first million to an account of a man named Yon Min-ji, a North Korean. He is the son of the head of Yon Enterprises. This organization is known for its high-quality counterfeit bills. Another three million followed that into Yon's private offshore account. The transfers were made without proper authorization."

"Who made the transfers," Vladimir asked, tapping his finger on the pad in front of him.

"Kim Lee, Sir."

"So, that is why she disappeared."

"No, she was being set up by your son, he used force and intimidation until she finally gave in and agreed to do it. She left because she knew he was setting her up."

"And, of course, you only have her word for that."

"No, Mr. Ivanov. I understand this will be difficult for you to believe about your son, but my information is irrefutable. You don't have to accept it, but it's all true. There is no connection between Kim Lee and Yon Min-ji. But there is proof of multiple communications with Alex and Yon."

They could tell he was having a hard time believing his son would do this. "Is that all you have for me?"

"No, but you may not be ready to hear it," she said patiently. Looking down at her hands then back up to Vladimir, giving him a moment to absorb what he'd already heard.

"Keep going."

"I'm afraid your son's activities have opened you up to government confiscation. In addition to prosecution by the US Treasury and the IRS."

His face got animated, "what do you mean by that?"

"For me to be confident, I need your other set of books."

She explained Alex's laundering businesses are not audit-proof. Although the money filtered through the right kind of companies, the corroborating paperwork is shoddy at best. Any sort of IRS audit would bring up huge red flags.

"I will do my best to insulate you. However, I do not doubt that within a year or two Alex's businesses will be raided by some government agency.

"What are you suggesting I do?" He asked a little surprised.

"My suggestion is you separate yourself from your son's illegal businesses. Get out of it altogether if you choose to go that way. You've transformed your criminal enterprise into some very lucrative legal businesses. Is there any reason to stay on the wrong side of the law?"

"Ms. Star, I have been considering this myself. Before Joe died, he had decided it was time to get his family out. Was that your influence?"

"His son Thomas was trying very hard to get his father to see the wisdom of that decision. His son Nikko was the only holdout. Unfortunately, his choices cost him his life."

"Yes, it was merciful that Joe didn't live to see it. It's not easy, Ms. Star, to separate from family, be it by death or by family trouble."

Sophie told him that Alex's check-cashing businesses were in the most jeopardy.

"It might be too late to get him out of it before an audit catches up with him. He should have opened them with shell corporations. He could have created computer-generated foreign investor profiles, to explain the income."

"Is there any way to unravel it, Ms. Star?" Vladimir had grabbed the pen on his desk and was turning it end over end on the desk pad.

"I won't promise anything. But removing any trace of you shouldn't be too complicated. What do you think, Houston?" She asked, turning to him.

"I think it's the safest thing for you, Mr. Ivanov."

"I feel I have given you the best advice I can. If you want us to be done, I'm alright with that. Demitri may have advice that you feel more comfortable with." She had said everything she could to plant the seeds.

Vladimir reached into his desk and pulled out a hard drive. "This is the other set of books. Do what you can for my son, and I will do whatever you suggest. I don't want my son to go to jail, Ms. Star, can you see to that?"

"I'm sorry, Mr. Ivanov, I won't even pretend to make that kind of promise. Time is our real enemy here."

They took the hard drive and went back to her office. Sophie was working with Sissy, going over the books. Matt joined them by secure video and downloaded everything on the hard drive. Houston ran the original back to Mr. Ivanov's office.

When he got there the secretary was gone, he heard loud voices coming from Vladimir's office. It sounded like Alex was in with his father.

"Papa, it's a lie, are you going to believe that woman over your own son?"

"How could she have known about Yon if it wasn't true?"

He couldn't come up with an answer. "I'm your son, that money belongs to me just as much as you. Why shouldn't I be able to make my own decisions?" Alex turned defensive.

Houston heard what had to be a punch to the face, Vladimir must have hit his son. "I told you we do not do business with the North Korean's, that should have been enough for you."

Houston moved closer to the door at an angle that made sure he wouldn't be seen and watched. Alex raised his hand to his face and turned away. "Papa, you don't have the stomach for this business anymore. Retire and let me show you how it should be done." Vladimir turned him around and punched his son in the stomach. Then he grabbed his collar to raise him back up from his bent-over position. His face was inches away from his son's.

"You little punk, you think you can take me out? I'll chew you up and spit you out. Now get out of here so I can decide what to do with you."

Houston hid in the coat closet so Alex wouldn't see him. He left it open a crack so he could see when Alex walked by. Alex's face was bloody and he was still slightly stooped over from the gut punch. He came out of the closet when he was sure Alex was gone. Houston waited outside Vladimir's office for five minutes before he knocked.

"Mr. Ivanov?"

"Yes, come in." The confrontation with his son visibly shook him.

"I wanted to get this back to you before you left, sir."

Ivanov was sitting behind his desk, staring blankly out the window. "Thank you, Houston. Your wife was right, you know, about Alex."

"She generally is, sir," Vladimir responded with a forced smile.

Houston handed him the hard drive and went back to the office. He told them what he had heard and seen. They locked the office and headed home for the day.

Houston and Sophie decided to eat at Olive Garden on their way home. As they were leaving the restaurant, she got a text from Yon with a time and place to meet for dinner the next evening.

Alex got home and went to his room, he cleaned up his face, and took off the shirt that had blood on it. He was so sure no one could track the money to him. Kim was the one that was supposed to get blamed. It was 'that' woman's fault. Now he would have to pay it back. He only needed it long enough to pay Yon. He would have to find a fast way to dispose of the counterfeit bills now. It would minimize his profit, but even if he came out of this with a few million, it would be his to do with as he pleased. He went to the living room where Yon was waiting for him. He was going to take him to some clubs since he would be leaving in a few days. Alex had no intention of telling him what happened.

The team met at command the next morning. Sissy and Matt were going through every item of Vladimir's second set of books. The rest of the group were in the conference room.

"Do we want to wait to see what Alex does with the counterfeit money? Or do we take him down now?" Rodriguez was voicing the dilemma.

"His dad gave him a pretty bad beatdown last night. It wouldn't surprise me if he panics and tries to sell it so he can pay his father back. What do you want to do Sophie, it's your plan?" Houston turned to her.

"Let's give it a little time. The laundering operations aren't going anywhere in the next few days. I'd like to get the whole network and the counterfeit bills for the Secret Service and US Treasury. Like Timms said, this opportunity may not come up again," she explained.

They all discussed it and agreed to give it a couple of days. Then Houston, Sophie, and Sissy headed to Ivanov's headquarters. They gave Max the heads up; they were on their way.

When Houston and Sophie got in, Demitri asked them to come into his office.

"Ms. Star, I understand you found someone embezzled money during your audit."

"Yes, sir."

"I would have appreciated you telling me before you went to Mr. Ivanov."

"It was a difficult call for us, but because it was his son, I felt I should keep it quiet. I hope you understand."

"I do. Vladimir has never seen his son's flaws. You opened his eyes; I don't think he would have taken that from me. Vladimir listened to you about changing his direction too. He wants you to do your best to insulate him from possible prosecution." Dimitri turned his chair to look out the window. "Vladimir wants me to talk Alex into closing all the laundering businesses. He'll back him in the Casino as long as it stays legit. If Alex refuses, I'm to cut Alex off and sever business ties." He turned back to Houston and Sophie. "I already know how that will turn out."

"It must be difficult for Mr. Ivanov. He loves his son," Sophie sympathized.

"Alex wants to make easy money. He launders for cartels as well as gun traffickers, the money's easy and abundant, just his style. He'll probably end up like Joe's son."

"Is he going to make Alex pay back the money?" Sophie was curious.

"I'm sure he will, to teach him a lesson. Can you do anything to reorganize those businesses for Alex?"

"I told Vladimir I would try, but I think it's too late. Any audit would go back far enough to question where the influx of money came from. Going back to doctor the books without the necessary documents to back it up would be seen through by an experienced auditor.

"I might be able to save some of the newer ones." She had no intention of doing it, but it would give them a reason to stay if they need it.

Dimitri thanked them and they went into her office where Sissy had been working. She was able to isolate the businesses used for laundering. She also found the names of the criminals with whom Alex did business. If we capture the grunt that brings in the drug money, the DEA may be able to go up the chain, making deals to get bigger fish.

"Let's get that information to command when we're ready we can let SRT in on it. They will have to plan the takedown." They spent the rest of the day duplicating documents needed to prosecute the case.

"Sophie if you want to get changed before we go to eat with Yon, we're going to have to leave."

She acknowledged him, and they locked the office and headed out.

CHAPTER TEN

It didn't take her long to change while Houston fed and played with Bully until she was ready to go. He hadn't heard of the restaurant before, so he put the address in his MapQuest for directions.

They walked in, and Houston gave the Maître 'd Yon's name. He directed them to his table. Yon stood up as they approached and acknowledged them.

"I'm so happy you were available for dinner."

"It's our pleasure, Mr. Yon," Houston responded.

They ordered from the menu, and in a few minutes their beverages arrived. They made small talk until their dinner came.

"I'm afraid I have an ulterior motive for asking you to dinner, other than the pleasure of your company."

"And what would that be, Mr. Yon?" Houston asked while acknowledging the waiter.

He turned his eyes toward Sophie. "I know a great deal about you, Ms. Star. When introduced at the White House dinner your name rang a bell with me. I Googled you and refreshed my memory. I knew there was more to the story, so I asked a few of my contacts here in the US for the unpublished version. You are quite famous in some of the more infamous elite circles, Ms. Star. I'm aware of your part in making Joe

Morano an inordinately wealthy man. While keeping him insulated from potential prosecution; word gets around."

"I'm afraid my part in the wealth of Joe Morano became exaggerated as it spread, Mr. Yon."

"You're too modest. Please call me by my given name Min-ji." She acknowledged his request. "But even if only a portion of it is true, I need your services."

"What do you have in mind." Houston voiced his reluctance.

Yon went on to tell them what happened to his family. It was hard for him to relate without choking up. After composing himself, he went on.

"I ran for my life. My Appa never treated me like a son; I was more of a servant to him. Anyway, I don't have access to his equipment now. What I do have are the plates my father used to make his counterfeit bills; they are the best in the world. Almost impossible to detect. And I have access to the distributor who supplied my father the paper and security strips for the bills. I need to start over. I need to change my name and get set up properly.

"My Appa thought I was incapable of learning the business; he was wrong. I'd like to hire you; and your husband, of course." He nodded to Houston.

Houston was concerned the noise in the restaurant would hinder his mic from picking all this up. Yon went on to explain his plans, and that he had no intention of going back to North Korea, he would set up in a new city.

"I would love to stay in the United States, but law enforcement here is too tight."

"Where then, China?" She asked.

"That's what I was thinking, but not the mainland. The government there is almost as corrupt as North Korea, and they would want huge payoffs. I love Hong Kong. As a Special

Administrative Region, it retains some of its independence from China. I would have a better chance there."

"I don't know Min-ji, we have a job here, and I'd like to finish it. I wouldn't want to live in Hong Kong. What do you think, honey?" Sophie didn't want to show how much they wanted to get their hands on those plates.

"I think I would be interested in being a partner rather than a consultant." Houston answered.

Yon turned to him, "I would be open to that, with your wife's talent, we would be set for life." Yon was getting excited about the idea. They finished dinner, and Yon asked them to give him an answer before he left town.

The weather was perfect for driving; the sky was clear, blue. It was warm but not hot. Not that it mattered. The car regulated the temperature automatically. Dark eyes was following the GPS to the address the PI gave him last night.

After two weeks of searching, Dark Eyes hired a man he had worked with before to find Sophie. What she was doing in DC, he had no idea, but now he was only a few hours away. There wasn't much to see once he got out of New York City and hit I-95. A few trees or old telephone poles lined the freeway for a while, then metal towers carrying electrical lines took their place as he got closer to DC.

Traffic was getting heavy; concrete overpasses started flying by. Dark Eyes was getting closer; he looked at the clock. Three hours had passed already. Sophie's address in DC was only 30 minutes further. He moved over to the fast lane so he wouldn't get slowed down. He could feel his pulse rate go up with anticipation of seeing her again; he'd missed her.

Dark eyes wasn't ready to end this little infatuation, or whatever it was. He needed Sophie to be conscious of his existence. But how would he do that? He would think of something.

He pulled onto her street. The sun was going down, but he wanted to see where she lived, maybe even get a glimpse of her. Pulling over two houses down, facing hers, he grabbed for his binoculars in the glovebox. The house was a two-story Colonial. *Nice. You're doing well for yourself, Ms. Star.*

He grabbed the door handle intending to look in the windows; until the garage door opened. Dark Eyes slid down in the seat, not knowing which direction they were going and watched. The vehicle's rear turned toward him, and they drove off in the other direction.

He sat up in the seat and decided to follow them. He couldn't tell for sure who was in the SUV because the windows, like his own, were highly tinted. He could only make out two figures.

They stopped about fifteen minutes away, at a Thai restaurant called Little Serow. Dark eyes pulled into the parking lot well behind the SUV, as Houston came around to open the door for Sophie. "You look very nice tonight, Ms. Star," he said out loud to himself.

Sitting there, watching them enter the restaurant, he was tempted to go inside. There was no risk to it, and he was hungry. He pulled down the mirror on the visor and ran his fingers through his hair. Grabbing the sports coat in the back seat, he got out of the car and headed for the front door.

The seating area was full; he searched to see if he could find where they were. The hostess approached him, explaining the wait would be an hour. Pulling out a hundred-dollar bill, he again asked to be seated. She pocketed it and asked him to wait a moment while she found a place for him.

She came back a few minutes later, grabbed a menu, and led him to a small table for two in the very back of the dining area. He didn't mind because it allowed him to see the entire room.

Finally, he saw her profile across the room. Smiling, he gave his order to the waiter and watched.

Several times her eyes scanned the dining room, and he thought he caught her eyes once. Dark eyes wondered who the Korean man was, that sat with them. He couldn't tell if it was business or pleasure. Their movements and facial expressions gave no indication.

He observed them through dinner and watched as they said their goodbyes at the front door. He finished his meal and left to find a hotel close to the Townsend home.

After leaving the restaurant, Sophie called headquarters while Houston drove. She put her phone on speaker.

"We heard, Sophie," Rodriguez said without a hello.

"Can you get ahold of the team that marked the money and see if they saw any kind of box that those plates could be in," she requested.

"Sure, I'll get right back to you."

He went to Cosby's office and let him know what was happening and what he needed.

"If Yon is telling the truth, he must have taken the plates after he found his family dead. I wouldn't have thought his father would have trusted him with the location, based on what Yon has said of him." Cosby weighed the truth of Yon's story.

"My guess is Yon found out that information through the years and kept it to himself. Knowing someday he planned on going out on his own and would steal them," Fons suggested.

The call back to Cosby came in from the Secret Service. The men said they saw nothing in the safe room that could have held the plates.

"Our funding would be guaranteed for years if Sophie can figure a way to get her hands on those plates," Cosby remarked.

Rodriguez headed back to command. Cosby needed to make some calls to get approval for the expanded operation. By the time Houston and Sophie came in, the place was buzzing. The team was fielding calls from a dozen agencies wanting to help.

"What is all this, Fons?" Sophie asked.

"Everybody and their dog want to know if they can be involved."

They shut down the phones for a moment and went into the conference room to discuss it.

"How do we get our hands on these plates?" Timms asked.

"We're trying to insinuate ourselves into his plans. He wants Sophie to get him organized, but that won't get us to the plates, we need to be part of the production." Houston spelled out his rationale.

"That was quick thinking on your part, Houston," Sophie replied.

They went on to discuss the problems. The first being, Yon was leaving in a couple of days and they had no idea where the plates were. Next, they had to finish the operation they were on. Ten million counterfeit dollars were still in play. They hadn't come up with an answer by the time they called it a night. They would work on a plan over the weekend and meet again on Sunday night. Yon was leaving on Tuesday.

Sophie cleaned up breakfast dishes while Houston turned on a Saturday football pregame. Fons and Matt were coming in ten minutes to watch the main event. Carol made up all sorts of finger food, and Sophie made sure there were soda and coffee enough to float them all away.

"Honey, I plan on going shopping this afternoon while you are in a football fog. But first, I'm going to take Bully for a walk at that park a few blocks over."

"Alright, princess," he got up and went to her, "are you sure you don't mind me inviting the guys over for football?" He had his arms around her.

"Of course not, it sounds like great fun. I'm meeting Sissy at the mall. We want to go to Nordstrom's grand opening."

"Use the household card," he said.

"No, I'm planning on buying some Christmas gifts, I'll use my card," she replied.

"Ok," he kissed her and went back to the game.

She put the leash on Bully, put on her coat, and headed to the park.

Sophie checked out the quaint businesses as she jogged. She stopped to let Bully dig at a root that fascinated him for some reason. "Houston has to come here with us Bully. It's almost like the park by our condo in New York." Bully barked as if responding. Then the feeling she had of being watched returned. Sophie hadn't felt it since leaving New York; until now. She looked around but saw no indication someone was watching her.

Dark eyes got up early and dressed in dark blue jeans and a hooded sweatshirt to fit into the Saturday crowd. Today he was going to find a way to let her know he was there. In his vehicle was an M-24 sniper rifle with a Leupold Mark 4 scope, the rifle broke down into two pieces. He added some clothes to hide the outline of the rifle and placed it in a small duffle. He found it to be the most innocuous way to carry it.

Waiting for a glimpse of Sophie, the radio played Andrea Bocelli; he liked the romantic lyrics. He hadn't been there long when he saw Sophie walk out the door with her dog on a leash. She had on tan ankle boots, dark blue jeans, and a tannish fitted aviator leather jacket. *Classy,* he thought admiring her style. He had seen a park on his way over. It seemed like the logical place to take her dog. He would have to get there fast and find a spot to wait for her.

Dark Eyes drove past the park and noticed fashionable little shops in older buildings fixed up for small businesses, lined the street across from it. The shops all butted up to one another with flat roofs. He parked around the corner. *There has to be access to the rooftops for heating and cooling,* he thought.

Dark Eyes headed to the alley carrying his duffle. Sure enough, there were access ladders to the roofs. Placing his duffle on his shoulder, he made it to the roof of the building directly across from the park. He walked to the front where there was a three-foot wall surrounding the perimeter, part of the façade. He knelt behind it and took his rifle with its suppressor and scope out, putting it together in seconds. The binoculars were the next item he took out, looking through them to find her.

Sophie was coming around the corner, stopped at the light waiting for it to change. He exchanged the binoculars for his rifle scope and followed her. "Now, how am I going to let you know I'm here?" He whispered out loud to himself. "I could give you a little love tap, that would get your attention."

Sophie was jogging the path about five yards in from the street. He tracked her through the sparse trees, separating them. She stopped to let her dog take the time to smell his surroundings. Then he saw her turn her head and look straight at him. Startled, he ducked down behind the wall. *No, there's no way she can see me.* He brought his head above the wall again and caught her in the scope. She was walking with her pet down the path. *"You feel my presence, don't you, Sophie? We have a connection."* The idea swelled inside him, making his pulse race.

Sophie stopped again, this time facing him, watching her dog dig at a root that had grown above the ground. She smiled as she watched him. He aimed at her; she looked up again. "Yes, Sophie, I'm here," Dark eyes whispered out loud. He took a deep breath, calmed himself, and squeezed the trigger.

Before the quiet whoosh could reach her ears, something hit her arm. The force thrust her backward into the big oak behind her, knocking her unconscious. Bully instinctively looked up to where the sound came. He went to Sophie, whining and barking, nudging her to get up. When she didn't respond, Bully started running to his house, the leash dragging behind him. He came in the doggy door and directly to Houston, barking; no one paid attention. The guys were yelling for their team that got a touchdown. But Bully started biting at his pant leg and pulling at him.

"What is it, boy, we're watching a game. Sophie, come get Bully." When she didn't answer, he began to get concerned.

"Sophie," he hollered. He got up and started looking for her. Realizing he didn't hear her come in.

"Where is she Bully?" Houston said. By then Matt and Fons were paying attention.

Bully went back out of the doggie door and started running. Houston grabbed his gun out of the drawer, where he kept it and followed.

Dark eyes watched through the scope for a moment; he had to get out of there. The park wasn't busy, but someone was going to see her on the ground. He only wounded her, but the velocity of the bullet had thrown her backward, and she hit her head. She was unconscious, but he knew she would be alright. He took his rifle apart and headed down the ladder. Pulling the hoody up on his sweatshirt, he calmly started walking to his car.

Houston was the first out the door trying to keep an eye on where Bully headed. Fons and Matt followed a few feet behind. A block from the park, Matt noticed a man wearing a hoody carrying a duffle bag. It looked out of place to him; he stopped just past the man and turned around. The man was turning the corner; his back was to him. Matt didn't get a look at his face. He thought about following him, but finding Sophie was a more urgent task.

Houston saw Bully cross the road heading into the park and followed. Soon he saw a body on the ground.

"Call 911," Houston said, running to Sophie, kneeling on the ground beside her. Fons called it in and gave them their location.

Houston checked her for injuries. There was a knot on her head, bleeding, and a rip in her leather jacket and blood running down the sleeve. He took her jacket off and could see a bullet had grazed her.

"Sophie," he patted her face, "wake up, sweetheart." She was still out, but she had a steady pulse. Relieved, he sat on the ground, laying her head on her folded jacket in his lap, waiting for the ambulance.

128

Matt and Fons were checking out the area, searching for a bullet, or anything that might explain what happened.

"Fons, look at this," Matt said. Fons moved over to the tree. "That looks like a bullet hole." He was ready to take the bullet out, but this wasn't their jurisdiction, so he left it. They had to be careful not to give away their law enforcement connections. Being part of the Task Force was a Top Secret assignment. But they could certainly point out what they saw.

Matt estimated the trajectory of the bullet. It had to come from the roof across the street. They headed over there to check it out. Climbing the ladder, they went to the front of the building and had a perfect line of sight to where she had fallen. Fons noticed some scratches on the cement wall but no casing.

"Matt, the shooter must have used the cement wall for his stand. Look at the scratches." He touched them, some loose cement dust from the scratched surface coated his fingers. Matt agreed. They heard sirens moving closer.

They hurried back to the park and waved down the police car.

At the hospital, Sophie woke in the emergency room. The doctor stitched the gaping wound in her arm with twenty stitches. He was more concerned about her head injury. He sent her off to get an MRI.

The Doctor determined she had a concussion. It would leave her with some dizziness and nausea for five or six days.

"Sophie." Houston whispered to her, "how are you feeling?" He was sitting by her side, kissing the palm of her hand. Matt had taken Bully home for him, and Fons was in the hallway making calls letting the team know what had happened.

She opened her eyes, "my head hurts. What happened?" Her voice barely audible.

"It looks like someone took a shot at you, throwing you back into a tree. You have a concussion. Do you remember anything? Did you hear a shot?" He had so many questions.

"No, I didn't hear anything, and I didn't see anything suspicious. But..."

"But what?"

"Houston, I've had a feeling someone's been watching me since we were in Paris." She spoke softly, her head throbbing.

"What!" His voice was loud and accusatory, "why didn't you say something?" He was on his feet.

"Please don't yell at me, Houston." She moved her hands to cover her ears.

"I thought it was paranoia, because of Nikko, Houston. I was afraid if I told you, you would insist on getting me twenty-four-hour protection. I wasn't going to go through that again."

"And how did that work out for you? You're in the hospital, Sophie!" He was so angry with her for keeping this from him.

"Tell me when it started." He sat back down to listen.

Sophie told him everything she could remember. She told him the feelings started with the Champagne at the condo. When she finished, she said, "please don't be angry with me, Houston."

Houston *was* angry. Sophie knew exactly what she was doing by keeping this from him. The sight of her on the ground had caused a flashback to when he was helpless. The day Nikko kidnapped her; Houston had failed her then. Today he failed her again. It was crushing him.

Nikko had injected him with a snake venom that left him paralyzed but completely aware. He watched while Nikko knocked Sophie out and kidnapped her, not able to do anything about it. At that moment, powerless, he felt his death would have been a blessing. He made promises to her that he would never let anyone hurt her again. *How can I keep my vow if she doesn't tell me what's going on?*

Houston stood up and told her he was going to send in the policemen who were waiting to get her statement. He stepped out of her room and saw Fons speaking to the two officers who had been at the scene. He stepped up to them and introduced himself.

"She's awake now if you want to take her statement, Officer Brown." He read the officer's name on his uniform. They nodded and went into the room.

"Houston, do you think Alex could have done this, or rather hired someone to do this?" Fons asked.

"I don't think so, Fons. Sophie just told me she felt someone has been watching her since Paris." His tone was agitated. He told Fons everything Sophie had just relayed to him.

Fons looked away toward her room then back to Houston. "We could be looking at this all wrong. Maybe we have two separate incidents on our hands."

Houston put his hand up and rubbed his five o'clock shadow. "You think she could have a stalker and someone who wants her dead?"

"I don't know, but we can't just assume it's one person."

He grabbed Houston's arm and moved him out of the flow of the people in the hallway. "Who does Sophie think it is?"

"We haven't discussed that yet. I was too upset; I left the room after she told me about the stalker."

"If it's not Alex, then who else? Thomas?"

"I really can't see Thomas putting a hit out on her. Yes, he said horrible things to her when Nikko died. But he was grieving. Deep down, I think he still loves her."

"What about someone in Nikko's organization. Someone carrying a grudge, who blames her for the organization going down?"

"It's possible, Fons. But most of them are either in prison or have moved on. I don't think any of them liked Nikko enough to avenge him."

Houston noticed a man walk in. He was stocky, not more than 5' 7", wearing a navy suit off the rack with a wrinkled light blue dress shirt. He walked to the nurse's station and asked for Sophie Townsend's room while showing his badge.

She was getting ready to answer when Houston stepped up and addressed him.

"Are you looking for my wife, Sophie Townsend?"

The detective turned to him and replied. "Yes, I'm Detective Valdez. I'm assigned this case. You're Mr. Townsend?" He extended his hand, Houston shook it.

"Yes and this is Alfonso Rodriguez." Turning to Fons. "Sophie's in room six. The police are in there with her now taking her statement."

Detective Valdez took out his notebook and pen and said. "Then why don't we take this time for you to give me your statement."

Houston told him everything that happened. Fons added where he found the bullet and that the sniper's nest was on the roof across from the park.

"Is there anyone you can think of that may want to hurt your wife?"

Houston gave Fons a look and saw him nod his head in agreement. "Yes, my wife and I are working for Vladimir Ivanov. She had a run-in with the owner's son Alex.

The detective looked at him for a moment. "How long have you worked for them?"

"A few weeks. My wife is a consultant and CPA."

"Are you aware of their illegal activities?"

"We wouldn't know anything about that. We work on Ivanov's legitimate businesses." Houston stated flatly.

The detective's face showed he wasn't inclined to believe it. "Is there anyone else?"

"I can only think of one other person." He hesitated, "Thomas Morano."

The detective looked confused. "Are you talking about the New York Morano's?"

"Yes, my wife handled their books for years. She was dating Nikko, Thomas' brother, at the time. He died in a police shootout; Thomas blamed Sophie for his death."

"Your wife has some infamous clients, Mr. Townsend." He closed his notebook, not expecting a response, and headed toward Sophie's room.

Houston stopped him and requested that he and Fons be able to watch when they interrogate Alex.

"Mr. Townsend, my Captain is not likely to approve that. He has a stringent policy about who can be in the viewing room. But I'll ask"

"Thank you."

They all headed to room six.

CHAPTER ELEVEN

The Doctor kept Sophie overnight for observation. Houston stayed in the recliner next to her bed. The Doctor released her the following day, with instructions to stay in bed for a couple of days and not to drive.

Once Houston got her home, and in bed, he sat with her. "Houston, I'm sorry I didn't tell you."

"Sophie, I vowed to take care of you. I take that very seriously. But I can't do it if you don't trust me."

"Sweetheart, I do trust you." She took his hand to her cheek and leaned into it. "I know my protection is one of your deepest concerns." She sat up straight, the sudden motion gave her a wave of nausea, "but if you can try to see it from my side for a moment. I thought I imagined it. And on top of that, I knew you would throw up a twenty-four-hour protective detail around me." Looking him in the eye, she continued, "Houston, I can't go through that again. I don't want my life restricted, none of this is your fault. I decided to take on the Morano's, not you. It's over now; I want to have my freedoms back. Can you understand that?"

Houston sat still, moving his eyes away from her. "I know that you want that, Sophie, but there will be times you will have to acknowledge my expertise. Can you do that? Trust me to do what's best for you."

Sophie took her hand and rubbed it down his face feeling the unshaven whiskers and seeing the hurt on his face. "Sweetheart, I will always trust my life in your hands, but can you keep in mind how I feel, too?"

Houston laid his hand on top of hers on his cheek and nodded. "I will, but unfortunately, it's out of my hands now. Cosby has ordered security for you, whenever Fons or I are not with you." He looked at her, "I'll make sure it's just until we find out who's after you."

"Thank you, Houston." She laid back down.

"Can you think of anyone other than Alex, who might want to hurt you?"

"No. But there's something else that's bothering me."

"What is it?"

"Houston, hitmen are expert marksmen. Nothing was obstructing his view of me; I think he hit me exactly where he intended."

"That's been bothering me too. Why didn't the shooter take the kill shot?"

"Do you think he just wanted me to know he was out there?"

Houston didn't have a good answer for that. "Maybe it is just a stalker who's escalating and not a hitman." He could see she was having trouble keeping her eyes open; he ended the conversation. "You rest, I'll keep you up to date with everything we find. Right now, I'm going to watch the interrogation of Alex at the police station." Fons had called him earlier and told him Cosby cleared the way for them to view the interrogation. "Is there anything you need before I go?"

"No, I'm good. Who did Cosby send to watch over me?" She asked with her eyelids sliding closed.

"It's Deputy Marshal Samuels."

"Wake me when you get back, ok?"

Houston kissed her cheek and left the room, closing the door.

Houston and Fons were in the viewing room watching from behind the one-way mirror. Alex was sitting facing them with his attorney by his side. Detective Valdez and Officer Brown walked into the interrogation room and sat down.

"Mr. Ivanov, my mane is Detective Valdez, and this is Officer Brown, we have a few questions for you."

Alex ignored them; his attorney spoke up. "I'm Frank Geraud, Mr. Ivanov's attorney, why have you drug my client down here."

"Mr. Ivanov, are you familiar with a woman named Sophie Star-Townsend?" He asked.

"Ms. Star, yes, she works for my father and me as an accountant," Alex answered.

"Where were you yesterday afternoon?"

"I was playing golf at Kenwood in Bethesda."

"Can anyone verify that?" Valdez asked, pushing a notepad and a pen in front of him.

"Yes. I was with friends." He grabbed the pen and wrote down their names. He finished writing and pushed the pad back to the detective.

"Were you aware someone tried to kill Mrs. Townsend yesterday?"

Alex looked genuinely shocked. "No, why on earth would someone want to kill her?"

"That's what we'd like to know. I understand you had a run-in with Sophie and her husband." He added.

Alex looked at his attorney, who nodded his head. "It was a misunderstanding. I was looking for another employee who disappeared. I thought Ms. Star knew where she was. I got a little animated with her; her husband came in and thought I was going to hurt her. He slugged me a couple of times. That was the end of it. I wouldn't kill anyone over that, and if I did, it'd be him, not her." His attorney was not pleased with that last comment.

"I understand you told him he had made an enemy." The detective pushed on.

"I was humiliated," he said.

"What about the information they took to your father, were you upset about that."

He saw Alex's face turn indignant.

"It was all a lie; my father knew it. He plans on firing her for lying to him. I certainly wouldn't kill anyone over it. Firing her will be my revenge."

Houston looked at Fons, "that guy lies better than I tell the truth."

But they agreed his surprise at the attempted murder appeared to be genuine. It's not likely Alex had anything to do with it.

They watched as the detective finished the interview and let them go. The detective and officer came in to talk to Houston.

"Mr. Townsend, I have to say he doesn't look good for this. He has an alibi, not that he couldn't hire someone, but his answers seemed to be legitimate." The detective said.

"I agree; it does seem like he isn't our man. But the only other person is Thomas Morano, and he isn't a likely suspect either."

"Thomas Morano brother to Nikko Morano, the boss of the crime family who died last year?" Officer Brown asked, surprised. "How was your wife mixed up with him?"

"Nikko was obsessed with my wife before we married, he kidnapped her, then died in a police standoff. His brother

138

blames her for his death. But I find it hard to believe he would take a hit out on her." Houston responded.

"Well, we'll get in contact with Mr. Morano and see if he looks like a person of interest."

"Thank you, Detective Valdez, please let me know if you bring him in. I have no problem going down to New York if you have to interview him there." Houston requested.

Houston called to tell Dimitri; Sophie wouldn't be in for a few days. He explained what happened, then headed home to check on her. Bully was on the bed lying next to her. She was fast asleep. He went over and shooed Bully off the bed, then went out to the kitchen and looked for something to make her for lunch.

Bully followed, going to his bowl, looking for food. Houston obliged, then went to the fridge. It was full. Matt must have wrapped all the food Carol made for the football game and put it away when he brought Bully back after the shooting.

Hearing Fons coming down the stairs, he took out some of the leftovers to make lunch for them. He pointed to the rest of it in the fridge.

"Fons, take as much as you like up to your apartment with you. Sophie would insist."

"Thanks, I'm not going to look a gift horse in the mouth. When are you guys going to let me ask Carol out, I need a girlfriend like her?" He'd been trying to get an answer for weeks.

Houston laughed, "Sophie's afraid if you guys start dating and then break up, she would lose her chef."

"Who'd be foolish enough to break up with someone who can cook like this. Besides, Carol's gorgeous." Houston shook his head at his response.

"You'll have to take it up with Sophie; I'm staying out of it." Houston laughed.

They ate lunch and talked about security.

"It's going to be challenging until we figure out who's after her," Fons stated.

"Sophie brought up a good point. She doesn't think a hired hitman could have missed his target like that. She was in direct line of fire."

"That's been nagging at me too. There's something else going on here, Houston."

Houston was cleaning up the kitchen, he stopped, turned, and leaned up against the counter. "She thinks the shooter wanted her to know he was watching her. That's as good a theory as any we have so far."

After more speculation, Fons went to his apartment with his arms full of leftovers. Houston went in to see if Sophie was awake; she wasn't. He had sent Agent Samuels home when he got back from the police station. He'd work from home.

He took Bully outside and sat on the steps, watching him run after shadows. Houston's mind was navigating all the different scenarios possible to explain what happened. Bully came and sat next to him, putting his snout under his hand to get his attention. "You did a good job Bully, taking us to Sophie. We have a big job keeping her safe." He stayed for a while, petting Bully.

Fons had gotten a call from Detective Valdez. He had contacted Thomas Morano, he and his attorney would be at the NYPD tomorrow at 10 am. Houston asked Rodriguez what the plan was to meet with Detective Valdez. He said he's taking the 6 am shuttle. Houston and Fons bought tickets for the same shuttle.

They made it to the NYPD by 9 am. Houston decided to see if he could find Captain Cartwright.

"I'm glad I caught you," Houston said, seeing him standing outside his office. "Captain, congratulations on your promotion." The Captain turned to see who was calling his name. Smiling and reaching out his hand when he saw it was Houston and Fons.

"Houston, what a surprise. Is Sophie with you?" Shaking his hand while looking around for her. Houston told him what had happened and why he was there. He asked if any of his CI's had any indication that news of Sophie's involvement with the takedown had gotten out.

"I don't think so, if it had it would be big news," Cartwright replied. "Can I come and watch the interview with you? I'd be interested to see his reactions."

They headed to where Detective Valdez was waiting for Thomas Morano. At precisely 10 am Thomas Morano came in with his high-powered attorney, Mr. Fitz.

"Thank you for coming in, Mr. Morano. My name is Detective Valdez from DCPD. I have a few questions for you?"

"What's this about, the officer that called wouldn't tell us anything?" Mr. Fitz said a little annoyed.

"All in due time, Mr. Fitz." He directed them to the chairs in the room on the opposite side of the table. "Where were you on Saturday afternoon, Mr. Morano?"

"On a yacht fishing with a few friends."

Detective Valdez pushed a pad and pen in front of him, "Can you write down their names, please?"

"Not until you tell us what this is all about, Detective." Fitz chimed in annoyed.

Thomas agreed and added. "Why am I here, Detective?"

"When was the last time you saw Ms. Star, Mr. Morano?"

Thomas looked shocked at the question, "Ms. Star, this is about Sophie?"

"Yes, someone tried to kill her on Saturday."

"Is she alright?!"

Houston was in the viewing room with Captain Cartwright and Fons. He watched Thomas intently looking for any indication he could have done this. All he saw was the man who hid Sophie from his brother to save her life. A man who deep inside loved her. In that split second, he knew it wasn't him. Thomas still cared for her. Then he saw his countenance harden again.

"Yes, it only grazed her arm; she has a concussion."

Thomas' voice became cold and distant, "so why are you bothering me, I haven't seen her since she got my brother killed."

"Is that how you see it? Ms. Star got your brother killed."

Mr. Fitz warned him not to answer that.

"Mr. Morano, do you have reason to want Ms. Star dead?" He asked directly.

Mr. Fitz tried to tell him not to answer, but he waved him off. "I have every reason, but I did not try to kill her."

"Maybe not directly, but with your finances and connections, you could hire someone."

"That's enough, Detective," Mr. Fitz stood up. "This interview is over."

They left, and Detective Valdez came into the viewing room.

"I don't see it, Mr. Townsend."

"I have to agree." Captain Cartwright added.

"He did look concerned when you told him someone tried to kill her. His alibi means nothing because he would never do it himself. He still could have hired it done." Houston weighed up the interview.

"Is there anyone else that has come to mind in the last few days?" Cartwright asked.

"No. You know Sophie; she doesn't have enemies."

"Houston, I will keep an eye on him and get my people to check their contacts for any word someone was looking for a hitman."

"Thank you, Captain. Please come down and see us when you get a chance. Sophie would be thrilled."

They all discussed it a few minutes longer, and then they headed out to get their flight back to DC.

Sophie's two days of confinement to bed were over. Houston had left for New York with Rodriguez. She asked Agent Samuels to take her to command.

After each team member greeted her and asked how she was, Sophie thanked them for their calls of concern when she was out.

They were back on track to close in on Alex's laundering businesses. Sissy had made up a chart on what days money would come into each store. Agent Smith called in Lt. Denison to approve the plan. It was his SRT that would execute it.

"Lieutenant Denison, we have to initiate the raids at the same time. We also have to be sure no one gets away to warn the others until it's all over." She stepped over to where he stood at the whiteboard, looking over the charts. "Is it doable?"

Denison rubbed the back of his neck, taking time to think. "We'll have to have someone run the counters. We don't want the normal patrons to get suspicious. The prosecutor wants footage of the action live; that's a pain. But it's doable."

"We have that covered. Ms. Corban has hacked into their surveillance system, and we're going to record it."

"Do you have the warrants?" He asked.

Sophie turned to Agent Timms for the answer. He responded, "yes sir, Deputy Director Cosby has them all ready to go for Friday."

"That's only two days. We haven't even done our surveillance yet." The Lieutenant liked to do his own recognizance.

"Sir, we have hours of surveillance at each location. You are welcome to take copies to study their routine," Sissy said.

"OK, send that to my office. I'll let you know in the morning if I have any concerns." He went on to another subject. "I know we want to capture the businesses laundering money for the cartels. But why wait for the bagman? We can find a better time to raid them. The big bosses in these organizations aren't going to be the bag men. We'll only get a few mid-level criminals." Denison questioned her timing on the raids.

"You're right, of course, but my goal is to shut down Alex Ivanov and put a crimp in the cartels pocket. I'm hoping the DEA can flip these mid-level men to give up bigger fish for leniency. Maybe they can work their way up the chain," Sophie answered.

"That could work. Alright, Ms. Star, I'll get back to you." Denison nodded to the team and left.

Houston and Rodriguez made it back to command by 2 pm. He noticed Sophie was in the office with Bully. He went to her and kissed her cheek, "How are you feeling today?"

"Better, but I'm ready to go home." He could tell she had a headache. Houston told her about the interview.

"He still hates me." Houston saw the pain of that in her eyes. "I need to go see him and try to explain." She started gathering her files.

"No, he doesn't hate you, he still loves you that's the problem. He can't reconcile the two. Give him more time, Sophie. I know you can't stand for him to think ill of you, but he's not ready to see things the way they happened yet. You have to accept that for now."

"Houston, I can't let him think I killed Nikko, he saved my life, I owe him."

He squatted down in front of her, "darling, he has to work through this by himself. When he has, then we'll see him. Can you trust me on this?" Houston wasn't jealous; he understood other men's attraction to her. Thomas wasn't ready to let go of his anger at his brother's death.

Houston put in one of Carol's premade dinners in the oven while Sophie went to change. When she came into the kitchen, he asked. "When are you going to relent and let Fons date Carol?" He laughed.

She turned to him, "that was random. I do think they'd be good together. What happens if it doesn't work, how do I take sides?"

"Why don't you let them work it out?"

"Yeah, right, what planet do you live on?" She scowled at him.

Houston walked over to where she was standing, wrapping his arms around her, he said, "give them a chance, princess. It could turn out great." She reciprocated, wrapping her arms around his neck.

"Alright, but if it doesn't turn out well, you are handling the repercussions."

"It's a deal." They sealed it with a kiss.

Houston pulled the dinner out of the oven and placed it on a hotplate on the table.

"We have to contact Yon before he leaves tomorrow. What have we decided to do?" Sophie asked.

"I think you should call him; he will respond to you better and let him know we want to partner with him. Tell him to go ahead of us and look at locations for the business. Warn him not to sign anything until you get him set up and protected. He needs convinced we want to help him. Let him know we will come as soon as we finish up our job with Ivanov," Houston said.

"That's a good plan. I'll call in the morning." Sophie said while setting the table.

Moving on to more pleasant phone calls, Sophie told Houston she called Suzie to see how Kim was doing. Kim's family arrived the same day the apartment was ready. They were so excited to be together again. Kim was doing very well and had spent a great deal of time with Suzie until her parents came.

"Suzie asked us to pray for them. She invited the whole family to Church Sunday. Kim seemed interested, but Suzie wasn't sure she would come without her family. Their family have been Buddhist for many generations."

"I know stepping away from what you believed was the truth for so many years is difficult. But we can pray that God will drop the scales from their eyes and they can see the truth."

After breakfast, Sophie made the call to Yon. He was pleased with the idea and said he would be leaving in the evening. He would send his address in Hong Kong when he finds a place to stay.

Houston and Sophie were heading to the office at Ivanov's headquarters. Max and Bully Sr. were already there. Tom stopped her before she got to her office door.

"Ms. Star," he whispered, "I know you're doing more here than an audit." He moved to the other side of the desk closer to her and Houston. "And I know you hid Kim from Alex. She didn't deserve what he was doing to her." Sophie waited for him to continue.

"I thought you should know. I saw Alex coming out of your office when I got here this morning." He headed back to his seat, "if there is anything I can do to help you, let me know."

"Do you have any idea what he wanted, Tom?" Sophie asked.

"No, but I don't trust him," he sat back down behind his desk.

Houston whispered to Sophie that he would do a sweep as subtly as possible. While Sophie sat at her desk working at her computer, Houston walked the room checking for cameras or listening devices. Command had included a bug detector in his gear bag. When he reached her desk, the light started blinking. He followed it to the air vent on the wall. Realizing they could use this to their advantage, he texted Sophie and asked her to follow his lead. She nodded her head. Then he texted Sissy to let her know Alex had put a camera in Sophie's office.

"Sophie, Mr. Ivanov was pretty angry at his son. Do you think he will give him an ultimatum to get the money back in 48 hours, or he'll disown him?"

"It does seem extreme but finding out your son stole money from you is tough to swallow."

"He had to be buying counterfeit. Why else would he send money to Yon Min-ji, a notorious counterfeiter?" Houston asked.

"Well, if that's what he did with the embezzled fund, he could either sell it or get rid of it through his check-cashing businesses. The problem is he would lose too much money in the exchange selling it outright. And it would take too long to filter it through his businesses. They don't keep that kind of money on hand," Sophie explained.

"Then there is really no way to get his father the money back in 48 hours." Houston summarized.

"There is only one way to get rid of it all, fast."

"What's that, Sophie?"

"If it were me I would take the bills and put them in the safe at the casino, switching dollar for dollar in the cash cage. They must keep at least that much money on hand for the floor. One clean sweep, and it's done. Not subject to audit detection. Vladimir wouldn't even know. He didn't want the Casino mixed up in anything illegal.

"To bad for him, he made an enemy of you. That's a pretty safe plan."

"Yes, changing money straight across leaves no trail."

They went back to work and continued communicating through text. Houston was also in communication with command. He asked Rodriguez to get a warrant for the casino, ASAP.

Alex was monitoring the camera from his office on the floor below his Papa's.

He laughed to himself that he had outwitted the so-called brilliant mind of Sophie Star. Yon was leaving in a few hours, and he promised to drive him to his private jet. He never confided in Alex what that dinner with Ms. Star was all about.

When Yon was gone, he was going to take Sophie's advice and move the money to the casino. Disseminating it through the cash cage's vault was a great idea. He'd laundered one million between his check-cashing companies. Now he would move the balance of counterfeit bills into the Casino safe and take out the real deal. They always had millions on hand.

Dark eyes had missed Sophie yesterday, because he followed her husband to the airport. So today, he came early to make sure to be there before she left.

He didn't know how long he could play cat and mouse with her, even though he enjoyed this distraction from his routine. Dark eyes poured himself another cup of hot coffee from his thermos, enjoying his playlist over the SUV's speakers. He was drinking the last gulp when he heard the garage door opening. Putting away his thermos, he turned on his engine and waited for them to pull out.

He stayed several cars behind switching back and forth in lanes to keep from detection. Houston and Sophie pulled into the Ivanov Enterprise facility. Dark Eyes followed the access road that paralleled the freeway. After driving a few yards, he pulled over, taking his binoculars to see where they were going.

Dark Eyes saw them pull into the parking area of the larger of the two structures on the property. He watched her husband open her door and walk with her into the two-story office building. He started searching the windows to see if she would enter one of the offices on this side. He could only see a few offices from where he was watching.

After ten minutes, he saw that Sophie was not in any of them. Turning the binoculars to the grounds surrounding the complex, he noticed a dirt road. The road seemed to horseshoe the property, most likely for their security vehicles. He drove about fifty feet and turned on the private road. The sign read 'Private Property Keep Out'. *Perfect,* he wanted everyone to keep out so he could use it.

Dark eyes drove to where he estimated the back of the buildings should be. He couldn't see it anymore because of the wooded incline that separated the road from the buildings. Pulling off the road as far as he could, he got out, taking his binoculars and headed up the incline. Leaning against a tree at the top, he started searching the offices.

Finally, he saw her husband in a second-floor office sitting at a table. If he was there, so was she. *This spot couldn't be more perfect,* he thought. The woods would conceal him. Soon he saw her come into view through the window. *Well good morning Sophie. Do you feel me watching you today?* At that moment, Sophie turned to look out the window. It was exhilarating, thinking she could feel his presence.

He watched her for nearly an hour, then decided someone might see his car. He hiked back to the car and went back to town. The thought of getting close to her was playing in his mind.

They all met at command in the conference room. Sophie requested Prosecutor Martin and Director Bean be there. The SRT team assigned to the Task Force was already there waiting for instructions. Their leader Lt. Troy Denison was well respected. He was talking to Houston about the operation.

When everyone was there, Sophie opened the meeting, bringing them up to date.

She asked Ms. Martin if she had obtained a warrant for Alex's casino. She answered in the affirmative.

Sophie turned the meeting over to Houston.

"Here's the plan. Friday between 8 and 9:15 pm, we're expecting cartel bag men to bring money into Alex's check-cashing businesses. Alex usually deposits it into an offshore account, layering it through several other banks around the world in different increments. Then he keeps his cut and gives the money back to the cartels as loans to some legitimate front. Loans that they never pay back. Your job is to interrupt that flow." Houston redirected his attention to Lt. Denison. "Here's where things get tricky. We are also expecting Alex to exchange the rest of his counterfeit money into the vault at the Casino. He can't know about the raids on his check cashing sites, or he'll bolt."

Sophie interrupted, asking Ms. Martin. "If we can capture the transfer at the Casino on camera, will that be evidence enough for prosecution?"

"I'll have to monitor it to be sure." Ms. Martin continued. "The US Treasury wants this to work. They will be able to confiscate the businesses involved and take millions of counterfeit bills out of circulation. It also shuts down a crucial source for laundering money for some of the major cartels."

Fons took over and explained to SRT what they needed.

"Lieutenant, we need your men to take them down stealthily and hold them inside the buildings. The aim is to take down as many cartel bag men as possible. To do that, we will have to synchronize the teams. The fact that there are so many and they come at different times makes it problematic. We'll also have to keep this quiet until we catch Alex switching money out of the Casino safe. We need to catch him in the act, and we don't have a time frame on that."

"We don't have much time to get this put together. Does anyone have concerns we haven't addressed?" Cosby asked.

"Will we be leaving any of the counterfeits in circulation per our mapping request?" Director Bean questioned.

"Sir, Ms. Corban has been videoing the check-cashing business on Westmont and other sites. She captured Alex trading a large amount of cash across the board. We're assuming it's counterfeit," Matt interjected.

"Do you want us to leave it in play?" Lt. Denison asked.

"Yes, we want that money in circulation," Bean said. We will keep a few of the check-cashing businesses open for use in other operations.

Sophie turned to Director Bean. "Do you want to take down the Casino since our SRT team will be busy with the other operation? This would normally fall in your jurisdiction."

"Yes, I'll get my men briefed after the meeting. Will you be directing that takedown, Ms. Star, or do you want my Tier One Response Team to do it?" Bean asked, respecting her propensity to run her live operations. He had no problem with women in leading positions.

"Yes sir, I would like to run if from here, will your men be OK with that?" Sophie replied.

The Director assured her that would not be a problem.

Cosby closed the meeting, "We'll meet here two hours before takedown. That's it for now."

Some of the team got together, tweaking their plan. Then left to get the gear ready.

CHAPTER TWELVE

It was Friday morning, and Sophie prayed no one would be killed or injured in the upcoming operation. After breakfast, they headed for Ivanov's headquarters. They left Alex's camera where it was and worked online and through text. Sophie had her computer on the accounting pages of the company for the benefit of the camera. Max and Bully were at their post outside the door, and Sissy was working from Kim's station.

It was evident that Tom was getting more curious every day about what they were doing. Their time here was running out. They needed to wrap this up fast before they blew their cover. Houston got a text from Detective Cartwright to give him a call.

Houston stepped out of the building and returned the call.

"Captain, do you have news for me?"

"I'm afraid so Houston, and it's not good. There is a hit on Sophie; it's Giovanni Brusco." Cartwright heard Houston take in a deep breath.

"I've seen his handiwork up close. The rumor is he created his version of the infamous, 'Murder Inc.'. Giovanni or one of his associates gets paid a couple hundred thousand dollars for a hit. If one of them gets caught, he will never give up a client's name. The hit cannot be canceled, with one exception; if the assassin dies, 'the contract' ends with his death."

"That's him Houston, whoever is after Sophie, it's serious. You need to get her protection until we can find him," Houston could hear the concern in Cartwright's voice.

"How do we find him? There isn't even a picture of him anywhere. If outsourced to one of his men, that's even worse." Houston said, getting distressed at the hopelessness of this situation.

"I know you and Sophie are Christians; if you ask me, prayer is the only answer. But I will do my best to work on it from this end. You need to get the FBI involved Houston. They want this guy as bad as we do." He took a breath, "are you going to tell Sophie?"

"I don't know yet. Thanks Captain, we're better off knowing what we're up against."

Houston called Rodriguez and told him what he found out and asked him to let Cosby know. He didn't want anyone else knowing since he hadn't told Sophie yet. He saw no reason to scare her. After tonight's raid, they would be going to Hong Kong. There would be little chance of anyone knowing where they were, giving the FBI time to try to catch this guy.

The weight of this new information was consuming his thoughts when he went back into the office. Sophie immediately noticed his demeanor had changed and went over to him.

"Sweetheart, are you alright?" She slid her hand down his cheek. He grabbed it and kissed her palm.

"Yeah, everything's fine, I have a lot on my mind." He smiled and went to his computer. As a US Marshal, he had an authorization code that allowed him to get into their files. He could have gone through the task force, but he didn't want anyone asking questions. Since the US Marshals hunt fugitives, they would have the thickest file on Giovanni. He turned his computer away from the camera and Sophie and started searching. What he found was even more troubling. Giovanni invited only the best and most experienced hitmen into his company. They pool their money to invest it.

The company has amassed almost a billion dollars between the investments and the contracts. When a member retires, he takes his portion and finds a replacement for himself. Once assigned a 'contract', it is active until it is complete or until the hitman is dead. The agreement does not pass on to another hitman. It is too big a risk that it would compromise the organization. In that case, they refund the money to the client, and they have no further contact. It's worked for them for 30 years, and most of the men have retired and replaced themselves. Giovanni is the only original member left. They believe he could be in his fifties: no fingerprints, no pictures, no idea where he lives.

It was five o'clock and they all needed to get to Command. Houston was hyper-vigilant while escorting Sophie to the car. She noticed but didn't say anything. She let him take control of her security since the park incident. The command center was buzzing when they walked in.

The heads of the agencies involved were here wanting to watch their teams in action. Houston, Fons, and Sophie were overseeing the mission. Ms. Martin was scanning the cameras making sure she would be able to get what she needed to prosecute. Sissy and Matt were running that part of the operation. They had recorded the normal functioning of the business for a couple of days. They planned to run it on a loop while the takedown was going on.

The SRT team's body cams footage was on the plasmas. They were in place and ready for the word to breach once DOJ had what they needed. Ms. Martin was watching the transfer of cartel money to the check cashing business at the Holgate site. She nodded when she had what she needed. Then Agent Rodriguez took over. Matt transferred the security camera footage to the loop.

"Alpha team breach now," Rodriguez ordered.

The Alpha team went in without incident. They detained the carrier and the man making the transfer to the cartel. Within a half-hour, the same go-ahead went out for the Westmont. All teams were to hold until everyone had breached. Everything was going well. The only issue was whether Alex took the bait by going to the Casino. They ran the risk of getting the small target and losing the big one. The teams sent a man to run the business upfront, while the rest hunkered down in the backroom waiting.

The team ready to breach the Corner café, called in.

It was the only business of Alex's they were raiding that wasn't a check-cashing front.

"Sir, this isn't going to work. There are too many civilians coming in and out. The restaurant workers are coming out back routinely to smoke. We have a currier in sight, but if we breach, there will be too many witnesses."

"Hold your position," came the command.

Houston and Rodriquez were discussing the situation with Sophie.

"Charlie Team, do not breach! Let this currier go through. If the next currier comes and you have an opportunity, then take it down. Otherwise, abort. We can't have an incident that will bring attention to our operation until it's complete."

"Understood," came the response from the team leader.

"We will still have the video feed Matthews and Ms. Corban hacked. Maybe Ms. Martin can use that as leverage somehow." Sophie theorized to the team.

Alex didn't want to draw any attention to himself, so he kept his Friday routine. He left the office about 6 pm and went to his standing reservation at Mari Vanna's. Then he planned to go to the Casino after picking up the nine million.

At his condo, Alex opened his safe room and took the two Samsonite Ripstop 30" duffle bags and headed to the Casino. He planned on being there by 9 pm.

The surveillance team on Alex called in that he was leaving his condo. The two rolling duffle bags could easily contain the nine million. The team stayed on him.

Sophie turned to Matt, "can one of you move from the SRT operation and move to the Casino surveillance?"

Matt responded, "yes, ma'am." Then he turned to Sissy, "I'll take over the casino." He then redirected his computer to that location.

Alex rolled the luggage into his office and sat at his computer. Not wanting the security at headquarters to see him switch the money, he called and told them he had a security expert coming in to upgrade the surveillance. They would be offline for fifteen minutes.

As soon as Alex shut down the cameras, he hurried to the room that held the massive safe for the Casino – using the keypad to access the room. The safe was sitting in the middle of a cell, not unlike a large prison cell. He accessed the door through another keypad and made his way to the safe. The safe was a Diebold Titan walk-in. Its thick outer door was left open during business hours. Only Alex and the head of Security had the safe combination. The inner door, a steel gate was locked and could be accessed by a key. Alex unlocked it and headed inside. The Cash Cage's head cashier was the only other person with the steel gate key.

Matt was recording Alex as he made his way to his office. He went to his computer and made a call. Out of nowhere, the plasma that was tracking Alex went dark. You could hear a universal gasp by the room.

"What's going on, Agent Mathews?!" Houston questioned.

Matt was frantically checking his connections and his access to the Casino cameras. "I don't know sir." Then he turned to Sissy. "What do you see?"

"The security at Ivanov headquarters got a phone call. Then the Casino cameras went black." She responded.

"Agent Mathews, we need that surveillance!" Houston repeated.

"It looks like Alex turned them off from his office," Matt said.

"Can you get us back in?" Came Houston's reply.

"Ms. Corban, can you segregate the Ivanov's security from the Casino? If I can get into Alex's computer, I can turn them back on; I don't want them calling Alex to let him know." Matt ordered.

"Can do," Sissy replied.

Matt and Sissy were working franticly, their fingers moving in light speed. The cameras were down for two minutes already.

Sophie recalled Charlie Team from the corner restaurant. There was no way to take the last courier down without being seen.

"Agent Mathews! We have lost three minutes." Houston's voice was getting urgent.

"I need another minute," Matt whispered.

"We don't have a minute Agent Mathews." Houston snapped.

"Ms. Corban, do you have Ivanov's security isolated?" Matt asked.

"Yes."

"Ok, I'm in Alex's computer. I've found the application for the surveillance." He was talking to himself, mainly.

"Agent Mathews! Can you do it?" Houston finally asked.

Matt didn't answer right away. Then finally, "got it!" he hollered as the camera came back up and recording.

The Special Prosecutor let out a breath she didn't even know she was holding. She turned to Sophie, "we need to get him while he's in the safe. That will be hard to explain."

Sophie turned to Director Bean, "Sir, can you have your men go in."

His team had been waiting for word. They had studied the blueprints already and were watching on the feed from Command.

"Breach!" The Deputy ordered.

Command watched as the Tier One Team breached the same door Alex had entered and hurried to the Safe. They used a handheld decipher to get the code to the outer door. Once they entered, Alex heard and stepped out of the safe; he had nowhere to go. There was only one way in, one way out, and the exit was blocked with uniformed armed men.

The team leader instructed Alex to get down on the ground with his hands on his head. He ordered his forensic specialist to photo the state in which they found the safe. Then he took out a small black box. He ran it over the money on the shelves, locating the tagged counterfeit.

The SRT teams and Tier One Teams took the money to Secret Service headquarters and Alex to FBI headquarters. The money will end up at the US Treasury, where it will be destroyed.

Director Bean called out over the comms, "well done. I'll meet you at headquarters."

"Understood," came the reply from the team leader.

The Special Prosecutor felt the case was strong and would hold up in court. DOJ secured all the videos needed to make the case and left copies there for backup. Lt. Denison released his teams to close down the businesses. All detainees were to go to the FBI headquarters for interrogation.

The DOJ would confiscate the businesses and decide what to do with them. Ms. Martin was sure Ivanov's attorney would fight for the release of the Casino. It was not actively involved with money laundering. Either way, Cosby would make sure the Task Force received a big chunk of all they commandeered.

Verbalizing his approval of their work, Deputy Director Cosby gave them a few days off. He wanted them back on Monday. They still had more to do. Namely, to get those counterfeit plates from Yon in Hong Kong.

Cosby asked Houston and Rodriguez to meet with him in the conference room.

"Rodriguez told me about Giovanni Brusco. I'm ready to bring in resources to protect her, Houston," Cosby said.

"You know protecting someone from a hit is nearly impossible. An expert assassin can shoot from anywhere. The sounds direction is distorted by the echo of the expended round," Houston said.

"Let's get the US Marshals and the Secret Service involved. They're trained for this." Cosby leaned against the conference table. "We'll find out who's behind it. Have you told the team yet?"

"Not yet, I haven't even told Sophie. I'll tell her this weekend. We'll be going to Hong Kong next week anyway; we'll be safer out of the country."

"Alright, Houston, we'll make some decisions on Monday. Good job on this, we did more than we set out to. If we can get our hands on those plates, it will be a windfall."

Cosby left, and Houston and Rodriguez went back out with the team to help shut things down.

It was one in the morning before Alex got his required phone call. He called his father, "Papa, they raided my Casino, I'm in jail. Please send one of the attorneys to get me out." He was having a hard time holding it together.

"I know, Alex. It's worse than you know. They have confiscated all the check-cashing businesses. They raided the companies while the cartel's carriers were there doing the exchange. It's bad. Ms. Star warned me you had put us in jeopardy, but I hesitated to believe her." He composed himself, "I'll send someone, I can't promise they can get you out." His father hung up and called his attorney.

Vladimir reluctantly called Ms. Star; he needed to ask some questions.

Houston and Sophie were getting ready to leave Command when her phone rang.

"Hello?"

"Ms. Star, I apologize for calling so late, do you have a minute?" Sophie moved to her office so she could close out the noise.

"Of course, Mr. Ivanov. What can I do for you?" She was waving her hand, trying to get Houston's attention. Matt noticed and let Houston know Sophie wanted him.

"You were right, the Secret Service and the FBI closed down Alex's businesses and hauled him off to jail." Houston came in and closed the door. Sophie put her phone on speaker. They listened to Ivanov explain what happened.

"Mr. Ivanov, I'm sorry, I know this must be hard on you. There was no way for me to fix it in time."

"I know, Ms. Star, I wanted to be sure my businesses won't get sucked into it.

"I went back and reorganized your company. Then I backed it up with documentation, covering Alex's deposits. So you're fine. I don't see how they could link them up with money laundering. I hadn't gotten to the Casino. Did you have any piece in that?"

"Yes, I'm the owner of record. I insisted it stay clean. I was hoping Alex would move away from the money laundering and run it legitimately."

"I'll come in tomorrow and make some determinations. Then I'll let you know. I'm sure a good attorney could argue the Casino had nothing to do with it. There was no connection other than Alex trying to swap funds." She took a moment before adding, "do you think you'll be able to get Alex out?"

Sophie could hear Vladimir take a deep breath. "Not until they allow bail. My attorneys are working on it, but he's still in holding and won't get before a judge until Monday."

"Tomorrow is Saturday. Will you be in the office?" Sophie asked.

"I'll be there at ten to meet you, Ms. Star."

"I'll talk to you tomorrow then, Mr. Ivanov. Goodnight."

He said goodbye, and Sophie called Ms. Martin. "Do you have any plans to prosecute Vladimir Ivanov?"

"I don't see enough evidence to make it stick. I'd rather put my energies toward his son. You did say he was not involved in any of the illegal businesses anymore, right.?"

"He did support his son's endeavors. But I agree our window of opportunity to prosecute Vladimir has passed. The goal of this operation was to shut down Alex and keep the counterfeit money from circulation." She looked around at the team through her office window. "And the Task Force accomplished that mission." Sophie added with a proud smile.

"I agree with that," Trindi said.

"Will Alex be able to get out on bail? He might run," Sophie increased the volume on her cell because of the ambient noise of the team shutting down.

"Our evidence is as good as it gets, but it isn't a violent crime, so it's up to the judge we get."

"Thanks, Ms. Martin, I needed to know where we were on this."

"I'll need to get more information from you, Ms. Star."

"Call me. I can meet you anytime," Sophie responded.

Houston listened to the conversation, "are you disappointed we can't get Vladimir too?"

"It's not that. We accomplished what we set out to do, shutting down the avenue for a drug dealer to launder their money. At least for now," Sophie said.

"What's the problem then."

I'm concerned Alex might get out on bail."

"Yeah, there is a good chance of that. But that's not our department. We kept the bills from circulating and closed down his laundering outlets. That's more than we were commissioned to do." Houston took her hand to help her up, and they headed for home.

They reached Ivanov's headquarters at ten the next morning. Sophie wondered why Houston had Max come today since Alex hadn't bailed out yet.

They headed to Vladimir's office. His office door was open, Vladimir's secretary wasn't in on Saturday's. They stepped to the door and knocked. Vladimir sat in his chair, looking out the window, watching the leaves blow in the wind. He stood up and waved them in.

"Thank you for coming in today, Mr. Townsend, Ms. Star. I wanted to hear what your opinion is about my exposure in all this." He put out his hand to Houston, who reciprocated. Vladimir stepped behind his desk again and sat down.

Sophie sat in the chair across from him, "Mr. Ivanov, I have searched everything. I am confident if you're on anyone's radar that you could pass muster. I would suggest that you don't handle the sale of any of Alex's businesses that weren't involved in the raid last night. If it's found you co-mingled funds, then you could get implicated. Let his attorneys do it and set it in a trust fund for his legal defense."

"I'll make sure to follow your advice." He turned his head for a moment, "his attorney says the evidence is very compelling against him, as it would be since it's all true. I never wanted my son to taste of prison. I was in prison in Russia, if I had the opportunity to kill myself I would have. Luckily, my wife's family had clout, and they managed to bribe my way out. That's when we came to the United States. Americans are the only ones who don't appreciate living here."

"Mr. Ivanov, I'm sorry your son chose the path that he did, but you have good attorneys I'm sure they can make a deal for him. I'd hate to see him run and be a fugitive the rest of his life," Houston added.

"I'm afraid your right. Alex would jump bail, but I won't help him unless the plea bargain isn't reasonable. I love my son, Mr. Townsend, very much."

"We have done all we can do for you now, Mr. Ivanov. Demitri is more than capable of handling all your companies, so this will be our last day." Sophie stood.

"I'm sorry to hear that, if you were inclined to stay, I would make it worth your while."

"I have another client who needs my attention, but thank you."

He came around the desk and hugged her and kissed her cheeks, Russian style. He then shook Houston's hand.

"Come back if you're ever in need of a job. Demitri will make sure you get your compensation." He smiled, but it didn't reach his eyes.

They headed toward her office to gather their things.

Sophie was looking out the window, thinking how sad it is that young men like Alex get drawn in by the lure of easy money and power.

Giovanni followed Sophie and her husband back to the Ivanov Headquarters complex. He passed by the entrance and went to the side road behind the compound. He turned the SUV around and pulled off the road, grabbing his duffle and walking up to the top of the incline, his feet scuffing the ground causing the earthy musky scent to reach his nose.

The ground was dry. He made himself a sniper's nest and put his rifle and scope together. Then he watched the office through the binoculars.

Twenty minutes later, he watched Sophie and her husband walk hand in hand across to the main building. Dark Eyes watched as Sophie whispered something in her husband's ear;

they laughed. Then she leaned into his arm and smiled up at him.

After watching them go inside, a tsunami of reality swept over him. Dark Eyes was alone, his life's accomplishment amounted to the company he built and his bank account. There was no wife, no kids, no one to whisper to, or fight with, no one to miss him when he died. Dark Eyes believed there was no God, so there was no life after death. He would be dust in the universe. Watching her with her husband and all that meant drove a dagger through him. Sophie had everything, he had nothing. Dark Eyes couldn't live with that reality. It was time to eliminate her and all she represented.

The windows of the newer building were tinted so he couldn't see inside. He sat up and shook the debris from his Carhartt long sleeve twill shirt and Khaki pants.

A familiar feeling coursed through him. One he readily acknowledged and embraced, hatred. He hated Sophie; her existence mocked him. He loved no one but himself, he was his own god. Dark Eyes didn't want or need anyone else. This little fantasy of a connection with her was a joke, a charade. It wasn't real. What was real was his contract on her, his business, and his ego.

Dark Eyes watched again as they came out of the building and back to her office. Fifteen minutes later, Sophie stepped over to the window. He put down the binoculars and picked up his sniper rifle. He eyed his target. Then her husband came to the window, wrapped his arms around her waist, and kissed her. They separated. *How poetic, she can die in his arms,* he thought with a sinister laugh.

Dark Eyes took a deep breath and placed his finger on the trigger. As he pulled, the office door opened, and Sophie moved. The shot broke the window but missed its mark. He got off another shot, but he lost sight of them. Her husband had thrown himself on top of her and knocked her to the ground. Dark Eyes thought he might have hit him.

He watched through the scope; saw the man who interrupted his shot rushing out of the office. He knew he was coming for him. Dark Eyes grabbed his rifle, duffle bag, binoculars, and took a quick sweep of his nest. Picking up his spent casings and ran down the hill to his car.

Huston slowly moved off of Sophie, careful to move the broken glass away from her. Without a word, Max and Bully headed to the only place the shots could have come.

Tom came running in. "What's happening?"

Houston moved Sophie to the corner of the room away from the glass and set her on the floor. "Tom, I need you to stay here with her." He took his back up piece from his ankle and handed it to him. "Shoot anyone who comes through this door that you don't recognize." He hadn't noticed his shoulder was grazed with the second bullet. He was running on adrenaline.

Houston kissed his wife's forehead, locked the door behind him, and ran to catch up with Max.

CHAPTER THIRTEEN

Bully was at least fifteen yards ahead of Max. On top of the incline Bully stopped to sniff the place where the shooter had been lying. Max caught up just as Bully took off again down the other side.

Max made it to the road and saw that Bully was chasing a vehicle. There was no way for them to stop it, so he whistled a command for Bully to end the chase and return.

Houston made it to the road as the SUV turned onto the access road. "Did you get the license plate?"

"No, it was too far by the time I got here." Max squatted down to pet Bully Sr. and told him 'good job'.

Max could see Houston's disappointment. They walked back to the sniper's nest to see if there was any trace of evidence left by the sniper; nothing. They hurried back to the office.

Sophie wasn't sure what was happening. Houston threw himself on top of her; glass was raining down on them. Rolling off of her, he grabbed her under her arms and dragged her to the corner. Then he checked to make sure she hadn't been hit by the bullet or cut by the glass.

Sophie heard Tom come in and ask Houston something; then he sat down beside her. He was asking her questions, but she couldn't understand him. It was all white noise.

Guilt consumed her thoughts. Old guilt over Nikko's death came flooding back. He'd still be alive if she hadn't interfered with his life. Now, here she was, ruining someone else's life. Vladimir was losing his son; Alex would spend years in jail. Yon's family was brutally murdered. All because of her actions. No wonder people wanted her dead. It was all her fault. *What am I doing? I have no right to judge these people, to ruin their lives.* Her body started to tremor.

Houston ignored the security guards that had been outside the office door. Tom wouldn't let them in.

"Tom, it's me, Houston. Open up." He could hear Tom come and unlock the door. Tom handed Houston back his weapon like it was a hot potato; he was not a gun enthusiast.

"Max call Timms, ask if any satellites were over this area and if so have him pull all the data." Houston said while walking over to Sophie. He could see she was going into shock. Her face was pale and she was staring at the wall.

Tom was explaining to security what he knew. Houston called Fons and said only, "I need help, now!" Houston made arrangements for Max to put their things from the office in his SUV and take the SUV home for him. Max offered to take Bully Jr.. Houston reached in his pocket and gave Max his keys.

"Don't worry about anything," Max said, "I'll take care of it. Where are you taking her?" Max asked.

"I'm not sure. Away from here, until we find who's after my wife." Houston sat by Sophie, putting her light jacket around her, and holding her close, while he waited for Fons.

Sophie's thoughts continued to torment her. Her mind managed to latch onto a familiar voice. Houston. He came and sat next to her, putting his arm around her. She was shaking. Sophie heard Houston speak to Tom; then something warm wrapped around her.

Fons had no idea what happened when Houston called him. The task force's cameras were already taken down. Sissy had disconnected from the Ivanov's security feed. But Fons didn't need to know why, when he heard Houston needed back up, he headed to the door. As he was leaving, he heard Timms holler that Max called in. Someone shot at Sophie, they want him to get all the satellite footage available. Fons told him to do it; he also instructed him to tell Cosby what was going on. He drove like a mad man, weaving in and out of traffic, trying to get to his partner.

Running up the stairs, he walked into the office. There were three security guards there talking with Tom. Houston wouldn't speak to them; he was sitting with Sophie. Max backed up Tom's story.

Fons went over to Houston, who stood. He helped Sophie up and grabbed her coat that fell off her shoulders. He tossed it to Fons and pointed to her purse. Fons grabbed it.

Sophie's knees buckled after a few steps. Houston scooped her up and headed down the stairs to Fons's SUV parked in front of the office building. Whispering to her on the way, "I've got you, princess, you're ok."

"Fons, I need a blanket. She's in shock." He said as he placed Sophie in the back seat. Houston scooted in beside her, taking the blanket and pillow Fons handed him and placed her back on his lap. He held her close and wrapped the blanket around her.

Fons got in the driver's seat and asked, "where are we going?"

"Trenton," Houston said, "to the ranch."

Sophie was still trembling, sobbing. Houston held her and prayed to let the words filter into her spirit; Fons joined him. Soon the trembling stopped, and he whispered again in her ear, "Sophie, you're safe, I've got you." Her body relaxed; she fell asleep.

When they were still several hours away from his home, he called his father. He told him about the hit out on Sophie, and he was heading there to get her away. Houston also told them he had nothing with them, they left without going home. His dad said they would take care of whatever they needed.

When Fons stopped for gas, Houston scooted out from under her. He laid her head on the small pillow and made sure she was covered. Houston grabbed the first aid kit to clean and wrap the wound on his arm. Then he went into the store, paid for the gas, and grabbed some Pepsi and deep-fried burritos for him and Fons. He got into the front passenger seat. He needed to talk to Fons about how they were going to keep his wife safe and alive.

The only other time Dark Eyes had been afraid of being caught was the first time he killed a man. He killed him in anger, not for pay. It was also when he first learned that killing came easy for him.

He hadn't planned on killing Sophie today. Hate overtook him; embodied him. Dark Eyes never did anything without being prepared in advance, except today. He had to go back to the hotel and pick up his things. If he didn't check out, it would bring lots of questions and possibly the police. It was risky, but he had no choice. He had done one thing right. When he followed Sophie's husband to the airport, he rented a second car under another alias. He parked it in the long-term parking.

Dark Eyes always had a backup escape plan. When coming to DC, he studied side roads and secluded areas to hide, if need be. Doing these things had kept him from getting caught more than once. His mistake was in getting caught up in some ridiculous fantasy that he had a connection with Sophie.

Dark Eyes pulled into the rental car return at the airport and parked in the 'Gold Club' return section. He didn't have to go inside or wait in line. He grabbed his suitcase and duffle bag. Then ran over to the long-term parking shuttle across the street. The shuttle was full, but he kept his hat pulled low on his head and didn't make eye contact with anyone.

After getting off the shuttle, he put his things in the car, a newer champagne-colored Toyota Camry. He wasted no time getting on the freeway back to New York. He still had to finish this hit, and he knew Sophie's husband would take her someplace he felt he could defend. It was likely to be either their penthouse condo in New York or the family ranch in Trenton, New Jersey.

It was almost dark when the SUV lights passed across the kitchen window of Houston's parent's home. His parents stepped out of the kitchen onto the porch.

Fons was first to get out of the SUV. He looked up at Houston's parents and acknowledged them with a nod. Houston stepped out of the passenger's door and went to the back door and woke Sophie up. Disoriented, she sat up. He helped her out of the car, and they walked up the stairs. Lily took her face in her hands and kissed her cheek. Sophie acknowledged Jack with a weak smile; he reciprocated. No words passed between them.

After going inside, Lily said, "There is a new nightgown, underclothes, and toiletries for her upstairs in your room, Houston." He started walking her upstairs.

"Spring brought some of her clothes for her to wear tomorrow," Lily added as she watched him go upstairs.

"Thanks, mom," he spoke with a weariness that was audible.

In the morning, Houston woke and headed to the bathroom to shower and change. He expected Sophie would be awake when he got out, but she was still asleep. He went to rouse her. Sophie told him she wanted to sleep.

An alert ran through Houston. The last time she couldn't be roused, she was in a deep depression. Nikko had just died, and Thomas blamed her. Houston never wanted to see her go into that dark pit again.

"Sophie, you need to get up, princess." He sat on the edge of the bed, brushed the hair away from her face, and kissed her forehead.

"I can't Houston. I'm too tired. Give me another hour or so."

Sophie turned away from him; her voice lost in the movement. He was going to push it until he heard a knock on the door.

"Houston, it's me. Breakfast is ready." Lily spoke through the closed door.

Houston opened it and stepped out. "Mom, I'm worried about Sophie, she won't get up."

"You go down and eat breakfast. I'll stay, it will give me a chance to pray for her." She reached up and patted her son on the cheek. "She's been through a lot, give her time to process it."

He bowed his head and thought for a moment, deciding if he should tell his mom about her bout with depression. "Mom, I was there when Sophie went into a deep depression. It started just like this."

"Go. I'll watch her." Houston leaned down and kissed her cheek and headed downstairs.

Jack and Fons were at the kitchen table eating. Houston grabbed food off the stove and sat with them.

Jack let him get most of his meal down, then asked. "Son, what are your plans from here?"

After swallowing what was in his mouth, he answered, "I plan on getting ahold of Cosby and get us out of the country. We're in the middle of an operation. The task force can investigate the hit while we're gone."

"That's not a bad idea. There's no way this hitman will be able to track you to Hong Kong." Fons added.

Houston was on the phone with Cosby making plans. Cosby insisted on sending Marshal's and FBI men to protect her until they were in the air.

They agreed that Rodriguez and Timms should be their backup in Hong Kong.

"I'll send a helicopter in the morning with the men. I need you and Fons to come in and pick up documents and write up a closing report on the Ivanov matter. Since you have to pack anyway, you may as well come in. So hop a ride back. We'll have to get an operative in Hong Kong to meet you with all the surveillance and tracking equipment you need. You'd never get it through the airport security here." Cosby was wrapping up the call.

"No problem, sir. I do have one request."

"What is it," Cosby replies.

"Could you have Timms get ahold of Max and have him send Bully Jr. with the men coming in the morning. It will make Sophie feel better."

"Not a problem. See you in the morning."

"Thank you, sir." Houston ended the call.

Lily played Christian music from her playlist on her iPhone. Then sat next to the bed, praying and reading her Bible out loud. Even asleep, the words would reach Sophie's spirit.

Sophie finally stirred, opening her eyes, lifting her head. "Lily?"

"Yes, dear." She responded by moving over to sit on the edge of the bed. "How are you?"

Sophie turned over to look at her. "I'm tired. Where's Houston?"

"He's downstairs eating breakfast. Are you ready to get up now?" Lily asked.

"No." Sophie laid her head back down on the pillow.

Lily considered her response. "Sophie, my children don't know this, but I have had two serious bouts with depression in my life. Through it, the Lord has taught me some precious lessons."

Sophie sat up with her back leaning on the headboard. Not answering but listening.

"Jack was often gone for months at a time when we first had children. Being a wildcatter, he went where they were drilling. I had two kids on my own and money was tight. Just trying to feed them was a trial. I let myself get discouraged; my mind kept looping the same hopeless thoughts over and over.

"The only relief I had from those thoughts was sleep. Pretty soon, I only got out of bed to feed the kids and send them to the neighbor. I got out of bed less and less. If it hadn't been for my loving neighbor, the children wouldn't have been taken care of at all. My neighbor finally called my husband, and he took an emergency leave to come back to find out what was going on."

Lily raised her eyes to meet Sophie's. "We were both Christians at the time. Jack's faith has never wavered; he didn't understand what was going on with me. He kept telling me to pray, but I couldn't pray for myself.

"My mind kept looping my failings. He stayed and took care of the children. Then he would sit by my side for hours and pray and read the Bible out loud, as I was doing for you. He was thinking about taking me to the doctor for medication, but he knew I didn't want that; he gave it some time. I'm not against doctors or medication, it just wasn't what I wanted.

"I could see how this was tearing him up inside. Blaming himself." She moved back to her chair and held her Bible to her chest. "Finally, I came out of it. But I had gone down to the darkest pit of depression and coming back was exhausting. Jack prayed for me when I couldn't pray for myself. He filled the room with the Word of God. That's what gave me the strength to claw my way back.

"It happened one more time but not as severe. The devil lies to us and tells us we are not in control of our minds. But the Bible says, 'For God has not given us the spirit of fear; but of power, and of love, and of a sound mind'. 2 Timothy 1:7. It's not easy. You have to force yourself to do things you don't want too. Like read the Word aloud. There is something powerful in the spoken Word, and praising God when you don't feel it. It takes time for your thoughts to catch up with your spirit.

"There's one thing I learned. There is a place where discouragement passes over into depression. You have to

177

recognize it and control it before it does. I learned to do it with God's help. Despair comes to all of us at one time or another. I had let it torment me. I couldn't stop the thoughts looping in my mind.

"After my last bout of depression, if I started to struggle, I would listen to uplifting Christian music and meditate on the Word. Jack bought me the Bible on CD. It's not easy, but with God's help, you can do it.

"Then you have to get out of your bubble. Find someone else who needs help or prayer and go pray for them. Helping someone else, helps you." Lily reached for her hand.

"Sophie, if you need help, let someone know. Houston, me, or anyone you trust. We will always pray with you and help you through it. We need each other." Lily stood in front of her, still holding her hand. "Would you like me to pray with you?"

Sophie nodded her head and closed her eyes.

A few hours later, Houston saw Sophie coming down the stairs. Her hair was damp from the shower, and she was wearing some of Spring's clothes. Dark wash slim-cut jeans with a button-up flowered top with a collar. Not Sophie's style, but she looked great to him. Spring's shoes didn't fit, so she was wearing the low heels she had on when she came. Fons and Houston were wearing blue jeans and T-shirts that his brother Teddy brought over for them.

He smiled at Sophie as he went to hug her. "Dad's making lunch. Are you hungry?"

Sophie shook her head. Houston was going to insist, but Lily caught his eye and mouthed to him not to push.

"I want to sit on the porch swing," Sophie spoke with a weary whisper and headed for the porch.

"I'll come to sit with you when I'm done, sweetheart."

After lunch, Fons asked Jack if he could use one of the horses to check out the perimeter of the property. He wanted to look for any sign of an intruder. Jack decided to ride with him.

Houston went outside and sat with Sophie. She wrapped her arms around his waist and laid her head on his chest. He put his arm around her shoulder. Houston sang church songs to her that she liked, and they sat there for a long time.

Sophie finally asked, "why is someone trying to kill me?"

"I don't know, sweetheart, but we're going to find out." He turned to look in her eyes. "Captain Cartwright called me. He said an informant had heard a notorious 'hitman' named Giovanni Brusco was in the country. He started a 'Murder for Hire' company."

Sophie furrowed her brow, "why does that name sound familiar to me?"

"I don't know, but we'll catch him. Cosby is sending men in the morning for backup until I can get you out of the country." Houston took his hand and raised her chin to kiss her. "I promise you, princess, I won't let anyone hurt you."

"I know, Houston."

He got up and held out his hand to help her up. "Let's go feed carrots to the horses." She placed her hand in his, and they walked to the corral.

Giovanni had spent the day sitting outside Sophie's condo building. With his binoculars, he could see into the French doors off the balcony. The place looked empty; the designated parking space for her penthouse was vacant. He needed to be sure before he moved on. Giovanni put on some gloves and loitered outside the side entrance. He waited for someone to exit so he could grab the door before it shut. Taking the stairs to avoid cameras, he made it to the top floor. After picking the lock, he quickly stepped inside and closed the door. The only light came through the French doors leading to the balcony.

He moved through the condo and checked each room. He entertained himself by going through Sophie's things. He stopped at the wedding picture on her dresser. "You are a beautiful woman, Sophie Star," he said out loud.

Giovanni locked the door behind him and made his way back to his vehicle. Before leaving, he made a call to accept the invitation to dinner the next evening from old friends. After that, he had decided to visit his favorite night club in New York. He knew once this contract was complete, he would have to go back to Italy immediately. He wouldn't be back any time soon.

The next morning after breakfast, Houston heard the chopper coming in. He and Fons went outside with Sophie to wait for it to land.

"Please don't leave, Houston," Sophie pleaded.

He turned to her, "I'll only be gone a few hours, sweetheart. I'm going to pack our clothes and pick up the documents we need for our trip to Hong Kong. You'll be safer here with all the protection Cosby's sending."

Sophie was watching Houston and Fons greet the men getting off the helicopter when she heard a bark. "Bully?" Then she saw him running for her. She ran and met him. "Oh Bully, I'm so sorry we left you behind. I love you boy." She lavished him with praise and affection.

Houston stepped up with a smile. "He can stay here on the farm while we're gone, he'll love it."

She stood up and hugged him. "Thank you, honey."

Sophie recognized most of the men that were there to protect her. She went over to thank them.

A few hours later, Houston and Fons walked into the Command Center. It was full, the whole team, along with men from other agencies they work with were there.

Agent Smith went to greet them. Houston asked, "what is going on here?"

They came to offer their help and services to protect Ms. Star. He noticed Cosby talking to Special prosecutor Trindi Martin.

Cosby noticed him and came over, patted him on the shoulder and said, "let's bring you up to date with what we've found so far." They walked over to Matt and Sissy's workstation.

Matt and Sissy had been going through the Satellite images from the day of the shooting, trying to find video of the incident while it happened. They had located two and queued them up to the plasma.

The feed started about an hour before the shooting. The group was looking at the security road behind the knoll. There was a black Ford F150 parked off the road. No one was in it or around it. The area was wooded, so they switched to infra-red. They saw a figure walking to the top of the knoll. He stopped and sat down. They fast forward to the time of the shooting. The man was lying on the ground. Then yellow flashes came from his rifle. In a few minutes, the man got up and started running; two other figures showed up on the screen.

"That has to be Max, and Bully," Matt informed them.

They were right on the tail of the shooter. Then they stopped at the nest, and that's when the shooter got too far ahead. They switched off the infra-red and saw a man get in the pickup; he had something in his hand.

"That looks like it could be a rifle with a silencer." Lt. Denison pointed out.

"Can we zoom in on the man or the vehicle?" Director Bean, from the Secret Service, asked.

Matt did the best he could, but the more they zoomed, the more pixilated the picture became. They saw the figure speed off and then saw Max come out of the trees. Bully was running down the road, but the shooter was already gone. Then they saw Houston catch up to them.

"We were so close, Fons, Max was right on his tail," Houston said, disheartened with the thought.

"Agent Mathews, could you track that pickup with one of those satellites?" Houston asked.

"We have about five minutes left of data from this satellite. Less than that on the other, but we tracked it as far as we could," he replied.

"The Lieutenant's men have tapped into traffic cams and some private surveillance. They were able to track the vehicle." Cosby added.

Then Lt. Denison explained, "we were able to track him back into town. Then he started using alleys, and we lost him."

"We'll keep looking at traffic cams, no doubt he will try to leave the area," Matt said. They all agreed.

Cosby, Fons, and Houston went into the conference room and discussed the trip to Hong Kong.

Lt. Denison interrupted them in the conference room. "Houston, you need to hear this. Go ahead, Cortez." He put it on speaker.

"Sir, Ms. Star is planning on leaving the ranch, and she won't let any of us escort her. She says she knows who's after her and is going to handle it herself."

"What!" Houston shouted, "get her on the phone." Cortez took the phone to Sophie.

Houston took the phone off speaker so he could talk to her privately, but everyone was watching him.

"Hello?"

"Sophie, what in the world are you thinking? You can't leave the ranch. I want you to stay there until I get back, then we can talk about it." He was trying to control his tone. Sophie didn't respond well to ultimatums.

"No, I know who is after me, and I know how to put an end to it," she said with conviction.

"How do you know who it is?"

"I'm not going to say anything until I confront the person myself, Houston, so don't ask me any more questions."

He knew ordering her to stay wouldn't work, so he sat down and calmed himself.

"Sweetheart please, you can't do this, wait for me. I'll go with you; promise me you won't go alone."

"No, I know what I'm doing."

"Please, please wait for me, do that for me."

"Houston, if I wait you have to give me your word you will come as my husband and not as an Agent. You *must* let me do what I plan on doing without stopping me and with no interference. And you must promise no one will track us. That's the only way I'll wait. Do I have your word? You'd never break your word to me."

He thought for a moment, "Yes, I give you my word. We go in the morning. Alone."

Everyone was waiting for an explanation. Houston told them she had figured out who is trying to kill her. "She insists on confronting the person herself. I convinced her to let me come, but only if we don't track her."

"Houston, don't worry, we'll track you from here," Cosby said.

"No, you can't, I gave her my word, I won't break it. Give me your assurance you won't track us." Houston turned, "Matt, Sissy, promise me you won't let them track us."

"Alright, Houston, if you're sure," Matt said.

"I am." He turned to Cosby, "don't worry. If Sophie has a plan, you know it's better than anything we could come up with."

Cosby relented, "she has proven that many times over. But we are still going to continue our investigation."

"Of course, sir." Houston and Fons headed to the house so they could pack for the trip.

Houston packed several suitcases, not knowing how long they were going to be gone. Then he collected all their documents and headed to the helipad. He was anxious to get back to his wife.

When Houston and Fons came back, Sophie was in their room. He brought in the suitcases and went over to kiss her.

"Sophie, tell me what's going on."

"Are you my husband right now or an Agent?" She asked point-blank.

"I'm always your husband first, you know that, but I know what you're asking. I won't interfere until you release me."

She told him that when he mentioned the hit man's name, it rang a bell but she didn't know why. Then when she was taking Bully for a walk, it hit her. Giovanni was Joe Morano's friend from Italy! Nikko had pointed him out once at a large Morano family reunion. They said he was the head of a very successful small business. If he's the one after her, Thomas will know who hired him.

Houston was shocked, Thomas's reaction at the police station seemed so genuine. She said she had planned on going to see him herself but relented when he asked her to wait.

"Thank you for waiting, what's your plan?" He asked as he was getting ready to slip into bed. She had already gotten under the covers.

"I plan on confronting him straight on. Then I'll be able to tell if he is lying to me."

They discussed it until he finally turned out the lights, holding her in his arms as they fell asleep.

CHAPTER FOURTEEN

They were on their way to New York. Houston had asked Sophie if Fons could come as back up. He would follow in his SUV. His dad offered the use of his new Cadillac since Houston didn't have a vehicle with him. She was alright with that but insisted he wait at the condo. Fons couldn't come to Thomas' office; she didn't want anyone to know she was talking to him. Fons agreed without asking any questions.

In less than two hours, they were in the elevator at Thomas' office building. Sophie walked right into his office, flying right by the secretary. Houston was right by her side.

Thomas stood up, startled, "Sophie, what are you doing here. I told you I never wanted to see you again." He snapped.

"I'm here to see why your family put a hit out on me."

"What are you talking about?" He plopped back down in his chair. Dismissing his secretary who followed her in, with a wave of his hand. "Of course you'd accuse my family, haven't you done enough."

"No! You listen to me, Thomas. You need to stop acting like a victim. I am the victim here! A victim of the Morano family. Nikko nearly beat me to death, while he was stalking me with cameras in my own home. Then he kidnapped me and brutalized me some more.

"On top of that, you put such a guilt trip on me; I went into a deep depression. Without Houston, I don't know how I would have gotten out of it. So, who is the real victim? Yes, you lost your brother, but it was his own doing. I tried to save him. Now your family has put a hit on me. You need a dose of reality." Houston had never seen her so angry.

Thomas got up and moved toward her, resting on the edge of the desk. "Sit down, Sophie. I don't know what you're talking about." His caustic tone changed to a more civilized one. She sat in front of him.

"Giovanni Brusco, your father's best friend, he's the one who's contracted to kill me. It's too much of a coincidence for it not to be coming from your family."

"Yes, he knows my family, but I promise you I know nothing about this." He was genuine.

Sophie thought for a moment, then it hit her, "your mother. It's your mother."

Throwing up his hands, he said, "don't be ridiculous, why would she do that?" Thomas stood up.

"Because you told her I killed her son."

He thought about it for a moment. It was beginning to sink in.

Sophie told him exactly what she wanted him to do. "You have until 5 pm to get into her finances and find the payment. When you do, you're going to confront her and tell her this for me. I want her to give up Giovanni and give me pictures and names of the others in his Murder for Hire Company." She took a deep breath choosing her words carefully, "if she does that, I can get her an immunity deal. The alternative is years in prison for attempted murder and murder for hire charges.

"I will have no regret calling up NYPD and having her arrested." She turned to Houston, "call Fons, have him sit on the Morano home. If Carmella attempts to leave, have him call the authorities." She was Sophie's only leverage.

The impact on Thomas showed, "Sophie, you wouldn't put my mother in jail."

"She's put a hit out on me, Thomas; you bet I will!" She snapped back.

Thomas took a few deep breaths. "You can get her immunity?"

"If I can give them something they want more, and that's Giovanni's organization. And I want proof of at least one murder because without it he won't go to jail. We can use how much jail time he gets as leverage for him to cancel the contract. Otherwise as long as he's alive the contract is still active."

"How am I supposed to do that?"

"I'm sure through the years you've heard him talking to your father about his business. Or at least your mother has. But that's not my problem. Get me what I need, or I can't get her immunity."

"Ok, just don't call the police," he said. Thomas needed time to prove to Sophie his mother didn't do this.

She stood up, "you have until 5 pm, Thomas. I will call you then."

She turned and walked out of the office. Houston had his arm around her waist. When they got in the elevator, he turned her to face him and kissed her.

"You are amazing!" Houston said with enthusiasm, "you are brilliant and amazing." He kissed her again.

She started laughing, "stop it, Houston, someone will see."

"I don't care. You are the toughest, smartest woman I've ever met."

She giggled a little, "and don't you forget it."

Prosecutor Martin was in her office when Sophie called. She asked that everything she was about to say, be held in confidence. Trindi agreed. Sophie asked for an immunity letter for Carmella Morano. Then she went on to explain what happened. Immunity would have to cover the crimes of murder for hire and attempted murder against her.

"Are you telling me you know who put the contract out, and you don't want them prosecuted, Sophie!? I can't go along with that," Trindi said indignantly.

"Trindi, listen to what we're getting in exchange. She will hand over Giovanni Brusco, along with names and pictures of the other assassins in his firm. I also insisted she provides a location on one of the buried bodies. If she doesn't come through or if she ever puts another hit out on me, this deal becomes void, and her immunity gone." Sophie waited for Trindi's response.

"She'll have to wave statute of limitations," Trindi said.

Sophie could understand Ms. Martin's hesitance. If there was no actual murder, the crime of hiring was only prosecutable for five years.

"You know how many agencies have been trying to shut Giovanni Brusco's company down. And to capture the one who started it all would be a coup for sure. But are you willing to let Mrs. Morano walk after what you've been through?" Trindi responded.

"I am. Carmella was grieving when she did this. Shutting down murderers for hire outweighs my need for revenge by putting her in jail. But there is one more thing. It won't be a collar for the Task Force. I'm giving the collar to Captain Cartwright. When the time comes, I'm going to give the go-ahead to him. His Swat Team will be lead on the takedown. The Task Force will get the kudos for coming up with the pictures and names of the rest of his hitmen. That's pretty significant in itself."

"Well, I guess you have the right to give it to whomever you choose since it was your doing. Alright, I'll write it up as long as we get everything you've committed Mrs. Morano to."

Houston had heard her tell Ms. Martin she was giving Captain Cartwright the collar.

"Sophie, this should go to the team, they may take it as a slight if you don't." Houston admonished her.

"It's my call, so stay out of it." She wasn't kidding. He backed off.

Sophie's next call was to Captain Cartwright. She asked if he would keep what she said confidential until it was time to take Brusco down. When he agreed, she told him the whole story.

"Can you back up Fons, Captain? He's watching the house, so Carmella doesn't try to run."

"Yes, I'll do whatever you need," he responded.

"And Don, I want you to take him down when we're ready, it will be your collar."

"Sophie, you don't have to do that. You did the work you need the credit."

"It's not about that for me. I know how the police department works. Promotions come from high profile collars. A collar like this should do you some good," she said.

"I would say it would. Everyone wants Giovanni. Thanks, Sophie." Her gesture moved him. They hung up, and he left to backup Fons.

Houston knew the team wouldn't understand Sophie's need to handle this on her terms. She was loyal to a fault because Thomas had saved her life and taken care of her when she had no one else. She would never forget that, even though he had mistreated her after Nikko's death. Houston would get

191

some grief over this, but he didn't care. He would back up his wife.

Houston called Fons and told him Cartwright was coming to back him up. He also mentioned that the Captain would be getting the collar on this one. Fons was not happy, but Houston shut him down. He reiterated the fact that this was his wife's operation, and she had complete say over it.

"She has a soft spot for that guy. Doesn't it make you jealous?" Fons was still annoyed.

"No, I know the history there, and when I get a chance, I'll tell you about it. It will help you to see why she's doing this." They ended their conversation.

Thomas searched all his mom's accounts on his computer. He had authorization; he wasn't invading her privacy. Although in this case, Thomas would do it anyway. He thought they had dodged a bullet when he didn't find any large transfers to Giovanni's account.

Then he remembered a secret account his mother told him about years ago. Carmella had insisted before she and Joe married that he give her a dowry of two hundred thousand dollars a year. It went into her account; one his dad couldn't access. His mother explained it was her insurance in case Joe ever abused her or committed adultery. She saw too many of her friends stuck in a bad marriage because they had no money to leave. She wasn't planning on being one of them.

Thomas remembered thinking his mother was way ahead of her times. She said his dad never failed to pay it every year. Even in the lean times, he would get a loan if necessary to keep his promise.

He started searching for that account. There it was. Two hundred thousand dollars transferred to an account in Italy. He recognized the date; it was the day Sophie married Houston. Thomas headed out to confront his mother.

When he came to the family home, he heard his mother in the kitchen.

Carmella turned when he came in, "you're early, what a nice surprise." She went over and kissed him on both cheeks, which was her custom. "Sit down. You can visit with me until our company comes."

"Company?"

"Don't you remember? I told you Giovanni is in town; he's coming for dinner."

Any hope she hadn't done this was now gone. "Mama, why did you take a contract out on Sophie?" Thomas deflated and sat down in a kitchen chair.

His mom stilled. She stood there shocked by the accusation, or more so by the fact Thomas knew what she had done. She turned, moved from the stove, and sat down beside him at the table.

"Nikko needed Sophie. She could've anchored him, kept him from going too far. They were going to give me beautiful grandbabies. But instead, Nikko was dead, and she was marrying someone else. You said it yourself; she killed Nikko. I couldn't let it go. I lost my husband and my firstborn in less than a year. Someone had to pay; she had to pay." She breathed out the explanation in a sad, weary voice. She had regretted it after the fact, but her anger and grief at the time had spurred it on.

Thomas took her hands; she was twisting them incessantly. It took him a moment to come up with words to say.

"Mom, it's my fault. I kept telling you everything that happened to Nikko was Sophie's fault. That isn't true. You need to hear the truth about what happened."

Thomas went on to tell her about Nikko putting cameras in her apartment. About the beating that almost killed her.

"He's the one who murdered Jimmy, mama." He lifted her chin to look in her eyes. "Nikko kidnapped Sophie and was taking her out of the country when the police caught up to him." He wasn't sure she believed him.

"I knew of his obsession with her. When she disappeared, I saw the pain he went through, but I never guessed he would go that far." Carmella bowed her head in disbelief.

"Mama, I'm the one who sent her away. Nikko was so jealous and out of control, he would have killed her, in time.

His mother stood up, angry. "You put your brother through that torture."

"Listen to yourself, mama. After what I told you what he did to her, you're still defending him."

She sat back down, knowing he was right. Nikko had been out of control.

"He was so much like his father; he loved walking on the edge next to a cliff. I'm the one who anchored your father. He didn't stray because he loved me so much. I knew that and used it to keep him from going too far into the darkness.

"Your father and I realized as we got older that no part of the criminal life was good. But we had grown up with it; it's what we knew. That's why your dad leaned toward your option of going legal. Criminal life will take you to places no man should go. Sophie could have kept Nikko out of the abyss."

"Mama, Sophie wasn't responsible for Nikko, we were, we should have been there to pull him off the edge. It's our fault."

"I did regret hiring Giovanni, but you know the rules. Once it's out there, there is no taking it back. I adjusted to it and moved on. How did you find out?"

"I didn't, Sophie did. She came to my office today and accused me. When she realized it wasn't me, she knew it was you."

"Is she sending the police out to get me?" His mom started crying and trembling.

"No, she gave me a way to protect you." He told her what Sophie wanted in exchange for an immunity deal.

She stood up, "I can't do that; he's like family."

"No, mama, we're family—you and me. We need to separate ourselves from our criminal past. We both need to move on. I've been pining away for someone that doesn't love me. But no more. I'll find someone to love, we will give you grandchildren, and I don't want them to know any part of our past."

"I'll never say anything bad about your father or Nikko, Thomas." She was adamant about that.

"Of course not, mama, neither will I, but we won't romanticize the life either."

Thomas asked her if she knew the other men in Giovanni's company. She said she had met them all and had pictures of some of them too. She was always taking photos when company came.

"Mama, we need proof of one of Giovanni's murders. A body location, or something."

She didn't have any idea where to get that information.

"He'll be here at 7, Thomas. I'm not an actor; he'll know something is wrong." She knew she couldn't do this.

"Don't worry, finish making dinner. I'll tell Giovanni you became ill."

She came over to him and kissed his cheeks again, "it's you and me now, Thomas."

He gave her a big hug and headed to the den. He needed to figure out how to get the information from Giovanni and wait for Sophie's call.

She called right on time. "Hello."

"It's me, Thomas, can you get what I need?" She asked.

"Mama knows all Giovanni's associates up until last year when Papa died. Many of them were at the funeral. We have those pictures and some others from family reunions. But she

195

has no idea how to get proof of one of his murders." Thomas was hoping Sophie would be satisfied with that and relent.

"I'm sorry, Thomas, that won't do. I won't get her immunity unless she gets me enough to put him away, or he'll keep coming after me." He knew that was true.

"He's coming over to dinner tonight at 7 pm. He always liked to tell stories. I'll be able to get him talking."

"Well, the immunity deal is in my hand, but the Prosecutor told me it's only valid if she meets all the conditions. I had a hard time convincing the authorities to go along with it. They don't exactly like me. But since I'm the victim here, they can't prosecute without my statement. I offered them someone they wanted more." Sophie had to keep her cover intact.

"I'll get you what you need, give me more time." Thomas' tone was a little bitter.

"Record whatever conversation you have with him. You have until midnight. Then I go a different route." Sophie had to stay firm. If Thomas thought she would back off; he would never do it.

"Alright, call me back at midnight." The idea of his mother going to prison made him physically ill. There had to be another way. The problem was there wasn't enough time to figure one out, and he knew someone was watching the house.

Sophie called Don and asked him to hop in Fons's SUV.

"Am I on speaker?" She asked.

"Yes, go ahead, Sophie," Fons answered for them both.

"I talked to Thomas; Giovanni is coming over tonight at 7 pm for dinner with the Morano's."

"What a break, we can take him down here." Fons was up for that.

"No, Fons, we can't. Word can't get out they had anything to do with it, or they'll be dead in a few days," she answered.

"Fons, do you still have some trackers in your go-bag?" Houston interrupted.

"You know I do." He turned his head to make sure the duffle was in the back.

"We need you two to wait until Giovanni is in the house, then take a tracker and put it on his car," Houston said.

"That shouldn't be too difficult," Fons responded.

"Cartwright will take the receiver with him and follow Giovanni. I need you to stay at the Morano house, Fons."

"10-4. I'll be here until you replace me or call me off."

"Thanks." They hung up. Detective Cartwright decided to wait with Rodriguez in his SUV for Giovanni.

Fons thought this was his chance to find out whether Cartwright was any threat to Houston. "Sophie has a soft spot for you," Rodriguez blurted out. "I asked Houston if it made him jealous. He told me if I understood the history, it would make sense."

"Are you asking me a question, Agent Rodriguez?" Cartwright asked with a smirk.

"I guess I am. I love those two; I want to make sure there are no flies in the ointment."

"Meaning?"

"I don't want anyone taking advantage of Sophie's generous nature or trying to get between them."

Cartwright let out a half-laugh. "That's amusing. If you want to know, ask."

"Ok, I'm asking."

Cartwright told him the story from the beginning. Rodriguez knew what was in the file. But hearing it first hand from Cartwright was much more disturbing.

"Houston told me about her nightmares and flashbacks. He said they terrify him."

"It was brutal Rodriguez, but still she forgave him and tried to save his life. She is a remarkable person."

"Yes, she is." They saw some lights coming down the street and scooted down in the seat.

They watched Giovanni knock on the door and walk in when Thomas answered it. The two men got out of the SUV. Cartwright drew his weapon to cover Rodriguez as he placed the tracker on Giovanni's car. When they got back to the car, Fons gave him the receiver. Cartwright got in his vehicle and waited for Giovanni to leave.

"Hello, Giovanni, welcome. Come in and have a drink while we wait for dinner."

Giovanni hugged him and kissed him on each cheek. "Thank you for the invitation. Where is Carmella?"

"She wasn't feeling well, so she went to her room. It's you and me tonight. Mother has dinner in the oven for us. Come in the den until the timer goes off." He poured him a drink and took his coat to hang in the closet.

About thirty minutes later, Thomas heard the timer go off. "Let's take our drinks in here so we can eat."

As they ate their meal, Thomas kept the conversation light. After he cleared the table, he led Giovanni back to the den and poured him another drink.

"I miss the stories dad used to tell us. The hair-raising experiences the family got involved in back in Sicily. I remember he told us your Papa killed a Russian for raping his sister. Is that true?"

"Yes, when we were growing up, he would tell us, 'when you kill someone, even for a good reason, it changes you.' He never got over it."

"What made you get into this business?"

"It wasn't planned. I was 18 when I finished school. I hadn't gotten a job yet. Jobs in Sicily were scarce back then if you weren't a farmer or a factory worker. One day I was in a bar, and a 'made man' came in and started hassling me for no reason. I began to defend myself, but the bar owner didn't want trouble with the mafia, so he kicked me out. I went and got a tire iron out of my car. I waited until the man came outside by himself and I hit him in the back of the head. Then I ran to my car and drove home as fast as I could.

"Days later, no one came for me, and I still had no remorse about it. It didn't change me a bit. I knew then I had a gift. I heard the stories about Murder Inc., but it no longer existed. I read all the stories in the papers from America about those men. Even the 'dons' deferred to them. They never had to pay for a meal, and they were rich."

"How did you get your first contract?"

"I knew some of the *wise guys* in the local mafia and told them I was a gun for hire. It worked. I got my first job. A man who had stolen from a protected grocery store. They wanted to make an example of him, so I disfigured him after the kill so people would get the point. They paid me one thousand dollars. That was more than most men made in three months back then. After that, jobs kept coming in. When my name traveled, I got referrals from other cities and countries. I decided to resurrect the Murder Inc. idea."

Thomas noticed Giovanni's drink was empty again and went to refresh it.

"When was your first job here in the US?" He asked, subconsciously touching his pocket where his cell phone was on record.

"It took me a long time before I was comfortable moving in these circles. Every country has corrupt police, but here I didn't have any connections in the departments — no way of bribing one of my associates or me out of prison. Finally, someone offered me enough money to make it worth a try. The contract's name was Frank Ansaid. He was having an affair, and his wife found out he was going to divorce her for a younger woman. Annette had a prenuptial agreement; she was going to lose her lifestyle in a big way. She was the first one to pay the two hundred thousand price tag." He downed his drink in one swallow.

Thomas filled it again. "How did you hide the body."

"I don't bury them anymore, it's too risky, but back then, I did. In Ansaid's case, there was a cemetery about one mile down the road from the kill site. I had perused the area ahead of time and found an open grave, ready for a funeral the next day. I went to the cemetery and dug down a few feet further, placing his body in the grave. I covered it with enough dirt no one would notice when they lowered the casket the next day. I have to say it was a perfect hiding place." Giovanni smiled at the memory.

"Do you have a signature, as some do?"

"Yes, at the beginning. No one has ever noticed it since none of the bodies I buried were ever found. I took a nail and hammered it into the heal of the victim then removed it. Even if found, no one would be able to explain it. I can't even tell you why I did it."

"What brings you to New York?" Thomas was fishing.

"A young woman who seems to have nine lives. I have made two attempts on her. Three if you count the love tap I gave her," he laughed. "That has never happened to me before. It's a matter of pride now."

"You mean you have tried to kill her twice?"

"Yes, the first time was on her honeymoon in Paris. I sent a bottle of poisoned Champagne to their room, compliments of the house. Apparently, they don't drink and don't approve of drinking; they poured it down the sink." He didn't tell him about the love tap at the park. "I made my last attempt yesterday at her office in DC. I had a head shot; she was standing still. Then out of nowhere, someone comes in the door; she turned. By the time I got another shot off, her husband had tackled her to the ground. She won't get away from me again, I plan on doing it up close and personal this time."

Thomas could tell Giovanni was beginning to feel the effects of the whiskey he'd been drinking. Hearing the attempts on Sophie's life from the killer's perspective was alarming.

Giovanni stood up, realizing he wouldn't be able to drive if he kept drinking.

"Thank you for dinner, Thomas. Your family has always been gracious to me when I'm in New York. Tell your mother I'll see her next time I'm in town.

Did I ever tell you I was in love with your mother back in Sicily when we were young? Your father made her an offer of marriage before I had the opportunity. She was and still is a beautiful woman."

Thomas didn't respond to his disclosure; it made him a little concerned. He got Giovanni's coat from the closet and handed it to him.

"It was good to see you again. Will you be in town much longer?"

"No, I plan on completing my contract in the next 24 hours and leave the country."

Thomas said goodbye, and Giovanni left in his car. It was 10 pm.

CHAPTER FIFTEEN

Thomas didn't wait for Sophie to call; he called her. She answered and put it on speaker.

"Sophie, he just left. You're in danger, he plans on getting to you in the next 24 hours, and he said it would be up close and personal. He's already tried twice."

"Twice?" Houston figured it was the Park incident and then at Ivanov's.

"Yes, he said the first attempt was on your honeymoon, he sent you Champagne on the house to your suite. He poisoned it."

That shocked Sophie and Houston. They remembered the bottle coming, but since they don't drink, they dumped it. Sophie knew that bottle of Champagne was suspicious.

"Did you get what we need to put him away?" She asked after a moment.

Thomas told her all he found out. The Prosecutor should be able to track the body to the cemetery by the date of Ansaid's death and the hole in his heel. "I taped the conversation on my phone. He never noticed. Can you bring over the immunity deal, I want this settled tonight," he insisted.

"We'll come right over," Houston answered him. Pleased they had a taped confession.

Sophie called Captain Cartwright to see where Giovanni was heading. "It's too soon to tell," he responded. Vigilant not to get too far behind him in traffic and lose the signal.

"As soon as I get the immunity deal signed, we'll catch up with you," she told him.

The Captain said the tracker worked fine. He expected Giovanni reserved a room somewhere and would let them know when he got to his location. Houston asked him if he could get an unmarked car to take Rodriguez's place.

"We still have to keep this quiet until we are ready to take Giovanni down. We can't afford to lose him," Houston warned.

"Houston, I have to give my SWAT team a heads up so that the response time won't drag."

"I understand, put them on standby, don't tell them any more than that."

They finished their conversation and headed to the Morano home.

Thomas opened the door for Houston and Sophie, ushering them into the dining room. His mother was waiting with the names and pictures. Sophie asked Thomas to write a detailed summary of his conversation with Giovanni. She also wanted him to send her the taped confession. They were all sitting at the table.

When Carmella saw Sophie, she broke down and started crying.

"Sophie, I'm sorry. I was so angry when you got married. You were meant to be Nikko's wife; give me grandbabies. But he was dead, and you were alive and going on with your life, marrying someone else." She looked over to Houston, put her face in her hands and sobbed.

Sophie went to sit next to her, "Carmella, you put a contract out on me!"

"When I realized what I had done, it was too late to change my mind." She said through her sobs.

Sophie took her hand from her face and held it. "I couldn't marry Nikko; you would never have stayed with Joe if he abused you. But I want you to know he repented and turned his life over to Jesus before he died."

"I didn't know what Nikko did to you, Sophie. Thomas only told me tonight. Please don't send me to jail," she pleaded.

"If you can help the Prosecutor stop Giovanni and his associates, she is willing to give you immunity. I explained it to Thomas." She turned to Houston, "please go over it with them; she needs to understand every word."

Houston read over the immunity deal with Carmella and Thomas. Sophie answered a call from Cartwright.

"Sophie, Giovanni isn't going to his hotel, he's heading for Trenton. He could be making his move on you tonight."

"Hold on, I'll get Houston, you can tell him."

Sophie interrupted Houston and told him he had an emergency phone call; he took the phone. Thomas showed Carmella where to sign the immunity agreement. The Special Prosecutor already signed it. He went and made a copy in his father's office for his mother to keep. Houston was still on the phone, and she took the time to say more to Carmella.

"Carmella, I don't have much time. But I must tell you, if you ever want to see Nikko again, you must repent and turn your life over to Christ."

"I go to Mass every Sunday and go to confession at least once a month." Carmella didn't understand what Sophie was trying to explain to her.

"There is so much more to it than going to Mass. You must have a personal relationship with Jesus. Believe he died on the Cross as the ultimate sacrifice for sin." She saw no response.

"You have to ask forgiveness and put your sins under the blood covering. Turn your life over to Him; be born again."

"I do believe Christ died for us, but I don't understand what it means to be born again."

"We were all born into sin. Dead spiritually because of Adam and Eve's disobedience in the Garden. When we ask for forgiveness, we become spiritually alive again. Our spirit reconnects with the Creator, renews our relationship with God. You must first believe Jesus is the Son of God and that He died in our place, so we could live. Then when you ask to be forgiven, He covers our sins with his blood. Jesus said, 'I tell you the truth, no one can see the kingdom of God unless he is born again.' John 3:3."

"Can I do that now? Here?" She asked.

"Yes, Carmella you can do it right now, would you like me to pray with you?"

"Yes, what do I say."

She explained the simple sinner's prayer and heard her repeat it.

"It's like the weight of the world has fallen off my shoulders," Carmella said, tears running down her cheeks.

Sophie hugged her and kissed her cheek, "it only gets better from here. Find a church that teaches the undiluted Word of God, and your life will never be the same." Thomas listened but never responded.

Houston came in and said, "we have to go, Sophie." She saw his distress. But Thomas took her arm and moved her away from his mother to talk to her privately.

"I'm sorry for how I treated you, Sophie, I was so angry Nikko died. I loved him so much. I was mad at myself for not getting him out of his aberrant lifestyle. I took it out on you. He's dead because of me. And now your married, and I've lost you too."

"Thomas, Nikko's death was no one's fault but his. Neither of us is to blame." She put her hand on his arm, "as for a future for us, that was never going to happen. When I came back from Lake View, I was different. I did love you once, Thomas. But when I came back, I knew it was not *that* kind of love anymore. I will always be grateful to you. And care for you deeply, for saving my life and taking care of me. But there was no longer a romantic connection that was going to develop. You will find a woman who will love you with her whole heart, and I know you'll be happy."

Houston came to her and motioned they needed to leave. Thomas walked them to the door and thanked them for not putting his mother in jail. He shook Houston's hand and hugged Sophie.

Fons was waiting for them by the Cadillac. After Houston opened the door for Sophie, he turned to Fons.

"I need you to follow us back to Trenton. Cartwright says Giovanni's on his way there. Giovanni won't make a move until he has confirmed we're there, so we're going in. I need you to wait with the SRT team, outside. Cartwright's Swat team will be hiding inside." He slapped Fons on the back. "I need you to have our backs, Fons."

"You know I will, Houston." The relief car that Cartwright ordered to watch the Morano home, showed up as they were talking. Fons got in his car and followed Houston.

"Sophie, you have to release me from my promise now. I need to take control of this situation. Giovanni is on the way to the ranch."

"Thank you for keeping your word to me. Do what you need to."

Houston talked with Cartwright for a long time. He filled
Sophie in on their plans. "SWAT is on their way to Trenton in
a helicopter. They are taking the lead. The SRT, already there
will be back up. They will watch the perimeter of the house
outside. The SWAT team will hide inside. SRT will wait until
Giovanni enters the house, then follow him in. They'll take
Giovanni into custody, hopefully without a shot being fired."

Houston called Cartwright to give the *go-ahead* on the
plan. His mother was escorted to Sam's house, but Jack
wouldn't leave.

Houston needed this to work. They may never get another
chance to take Giovanni down, and he would keep coming for
Sophie. They made it to Trenton in less than an hour; the late
hour and minimal traffic helped.

Houston was sure Giovanni would be watching the house,
waiting to make sure his target was there before he made a
move. He didn't want Sophie involved, but there was no choice.
They pulled up to the house and headed to the stairs.

It was a strange sensation. Sophie knew there were law
enforcement crawling all over the place. But it was so still
outside she could hear the crickets. The light was on in the
kitchen and the bedroom upstairs. She couldn't hear Bully; her
guess was they sent him with Lily, so he wouldn't bark and give
them away.

When they entered the house, the Captain gave Houston
an earpiece so he could hear what was going on. His dad was
there with his rifle. He went with them to their bedroom
upstairs. Houston and Jack were the last line of defense if
Giovanni got past the men downstairs.

Giovanni parked his vehicle on a dirt road about a half a mile away. Grabbing his Browning 9 mm, he checked the clip and chamber before putting it in its leather holster and slipping it on his belt. The duffle with his sniper rifle and other tools of the trade were in the back seat. Putting on his jacket and gloves, he grabbed the duffle and headed out. Giovanni wanted to get close enough to her to look her in the eyes. But he was smart enough to take the safe shot from a distance if it presented itself. Giovanni used the moon's light to traverse the land between him and the Townsend home.

Fons was in the barn with the SRT team waiting. He had his concerns about this plan. Why were they convinced Giovanni would come through one of the doors? They were underestimating him. The man was smart enough not to have been caught for thirty years. Fons had a gut feeling this was a mistake.

Giovanni pulled out his binoculars and scoped out the area around the house. He saw Houston and Sophie walking in. Giovanni could have used his rifle if he'd gotten there a few minutes earlier. Now he would have to go in, that was his first choice anyway. The kitchen light soon went off. He was scanning the house for a good entry point.

He could only see the back and east side of the house from his vantage point. As he moved his binoculars around, he stopped.

Giovanni spotted climbing roses under an upstairs window. He knew there had to be a trellis. The question was whether it could hold up under his weight.

He stayed where he was until the light in the bedroom had been out for some time. Then he removed some items from the duffel, leaving it on the ground as he walked to the trellis. Giovanni tested it and found it could hold his weight. Looking at the window on the second floor, he continued up.

When he reached the window, he found it locked. He pulled the glass cutter from his pocket and went to work on the glass.

Fons decided to listen to his gut. He moved out of the barn and into the dark, keeping cover where he could. He remembered the story Houston told him.

His father had made a trellis for Lily's favorite climbing roses. It was right under Spring's bedroom window. He had made it so sturdy that Spring had used it to sneak out of the house as a teenager. After getting caught a few times, her father threatened to tear it down. Spring knew how much her mother loved those roses, so she finally stopped doing it.

Fons wanted to keep an eye on it in case Giovanni decided to use it to enter the house. He made it around the corner as he saw a man's leg going in through the window. Fons quietly followed and entered the house. He was afraid to use his mic for fear the hitman would hear. But he did click it a few times hoping Houston would be alerted.

"Mitchell, did you hear that?" Houston heard Cartwright ask the SWAT team leader. He stood up on alert.

"Yes sir, who signaled?" Mitchell responded.

"I don't know, but I'm going to move some men upstairs. Someone saw something none of the rest of us did."

The Captain met two of his men at the bottom of the stairs and quietly started up.

The SRT moved in around the house to secure all exits.

Giovanni had seen the light go out upstairs. So he had a pretty good idea where they were. It didn't matter since no witnesses could be left anyway. It made sense to start at the end of the hall. He screwed on the silencer before he entered the room. He moved slowly to the bed. The only light was from the moon coming through the window. He had to get close to see that no one was in bed. The door to the bathroom was open; he moved toward it. He saw it connected to the other bedroom.

Fons met up with the men coming up the stairs and pointed to the first bedroom. Fons and the Captain quietly entered the bedroom where Houston was. The others went to the first bedroom. With hand motions, Fons let Houston know what was happening. All four men aimed their weapons at the connecting bathroom door. Houston motioned to Sophie to move to the walk-in closet.

Down the hall, the two SWAT team members entered the room. They quickly scanned it, finding it empty, checking the closet to be safe. They moved to the open bathroom door.

Giovanni focused on the door in front of him, placing his hand on the doorknob, believing his target was behind the door. He didn't hear the men come up behind him.

"STOP RIGHT THERE! DROP THE GUN AND PUT YOUR HANDS ON YOUR HEAD!...GET DOWN ON YOUR KNEES!"

Giovanni stood still deciding what to do as the SWAT team kept hollering the same orders over and over to him. He stood there, facing the door as it opened. In front of him were men standing with Sophie's husband, pointing their guns at his chest. He hesitated, knowing he was trapped. His only decision was whether he wanted to go quietly or take someone with him. Giovanni knew himself well enough to know he wouldn't do well in prison. With that in mind, he decided to kill Sophie's husband. He lifted his gun and fired. Houston went down. He tried to get another shot off before the others opened fire on him. To prevent crossfire, only the ones facing him responded. That was the standing rule in their squad.

Giovanni went down, but he was still conscious. An officer grabbed his gun. He had fallen face down. To treat his wounds, they turned him on his back and handcuffed him in front.

Sophie ran over to Houston when she heard 'all clear' and saw he was on the ground. He was stunned, but the vest took the bullet. He would have a bruise, maybe a cracked rib, but he would be alright. Fons helped his partner up. Sophie moved over to where the Captain was.

"I'd like to talk to him, Don," Sophie requested.

"It's pretty messy, Sophie, I don't think SWAT will let you contaminate the scene."

"Please, Don, I need to ask him some questions," she pleaded.

Cartwright looked at Houston; he knew the man couldn't hurt her now. He understood why she would want to talk to him.

"I'll go with her, Captain." Houston volunteered.

"Alright," he spoke to the men who were all waiting for the paramedics they had on standby a few miles away.

"Make room for Ms. Star. She needs information from the assailant. Let her in." They made room for her.

Sophie moved to where Giovanni was lying and knelt beside him, careful not to step in his blood. It was the widest spot in the room. One of the men had packed his chest with gauze to control the bleeding, then stayed by him, putting pressure on it.

"Giovanni, I know you have a contract to kill me, and I know this lifestyle was a choice you made many years ago. You need to know your wounds are serious, and there is a chance you won't make it. Has anyone ever told you about salvation? That Jesus died that you may have life."

He tried to laugh, but it was difficult to breathe. "All you *Christians* are the same," he gasped, blood still soaking the gauze from the holes in his chest. "You're so naive, Ms. Star. I know all about your God. I don't believe it. Religion is for the weak..." He couldn't finish the sentence, losing the strength to go on.

"I'm not talking about religion; I'm asking if you would like to have a relationship with the one who created you?"

"My mother and father created me. Not some imaginary God." His voice, barely audible now.

"But what if you're wrong and you spend eternity separated from Him. In Hell."

"I will die as I lived. We are born..." Giovanni violently coughed. Blood drops instead of saliva came out with his words. Struggling to get a breath, he continued, "we die, and we become part of the cosmos. A speck of dust."

"Your wrong, there is a God, and he's giving you a chance to ask for forgiveness, even now He will forgive you."

"I don't need forgiveness. I lived the way I wanted, and I won't apologize for it." His body started to convulse.

Houston heard the paramedics were here through the earpiece. "Sophie, we have to make way for the medics." He went to help her up. As he did, Giovanni, grabbed her wrist.

"You are a hard woman to kill," he said, seeming to draw on the last bit of strength in his body.

"That same God, you don't believe in protects me."

"My only regret is this contract dies with me," he coughed out with disdain in his voice. Likely the last words he would ever speak.

Houston peeled Giovanni's fingers from her wrist and moved her away. Before she left, she looked down and said, "I forgive you." She heard him scoff at her as she walked away. The paramedics came in, and Houston and Sophie moved to the bedroom to get out of the way.

"Are you alright, Sophie?" Houston put his arm around her.

"I knew there were people in this world who didn't want God. But to make that choice on your death bed..." She took a deep breath, "it's hard to accept."

"Some men's hearts are seared by the choices they make. So hardened that God gives them up to a delusion. The Bible says, 'They perish because they refused to love the truth and so be saved. For this reason God sends them a powerful delusion. So that they will believe the lie and so that all will be condemned who have not believed the truth. But have delighted in wickedness.'" (2 Thessalonians 2:9-12).

Jack made his way over to them to make sure they were alright. He stepped to the bathroom and saw the remains of the shootout.

"Lilly never sees any of this, Houston," Jack said bluntly.

"Of course, Dad, as soon as the crime scene investigators finish, you, Teddy, Sam, and I will redo the bathroom. Mom will never see it." Jack went to sit with them on the edge of the bed. Fons was working the crime scene with the Captain.

"We need to get Sophie somewhere to rest. She's exhausted. You two stay at Spring's tonight. She will want you there," Jack insisted. Houston put their things in his father's car but was adamant that his father take her. He had to stay and give statements and work with his team. Sophie didn't argue. Houston kissed her and then went to work.

It was 1:30 am when he and Fons called Deputy Director Cosby to give him the final rundown of the scene. The cell was on speaker. Houston passed on the news that Giovanni died on the way to the hospital. He told him Fons would come back with the names and photos of the other associates in Brusco's Murder for Hire. Fons added he planned on staying at his place in New York tonight and go back to DC tomorrow afternoon.

"Rodriguez, take pictures of what you have and text them to headquarters. I've got pressure on me to get those pictures distributed to other agencies. Getting pictures of Giovanni's associates is a nice collar; our stock shot up again. Too bad, Ms. Star insisted on giving NYPD the collar for Giovanni."

"Not my call, sir, this wasn't one of our operations, we're lucky she gave us any of the credit," Houston interjected.

"I'm painfully aware of that. I'm getting requests from other agencies to loan Ms. Star out to blueprint their tough operations. I explained she's not mine to loan, but an independent contractor. Nice call, by the way, Agent Townsend." Houston was too tired to go into the details on why she insisted on being an independent contractor. "When can I get you and Ms. Star on a plane to Hong Kong?"

"I don't know, sir, she needs some time. She's been in one dangerous situation after another, and I can see it's taking a toll on her. If she's still willing, it won't be until the end of the week."

"I can give you until Saturday, but we have to get those plates from Yon. We can't let this opportunity pass us by," Cosby ordered.

Houston didn't want to be disrespectful, so he listened. But he would back up his wife whatever her decision. They finished the call, and Fons sent photos of the pictures to Command.

"What are your plans, Houston?" Fons asked.

"I have to help my father redo that bathroom tomorrow; then I'm not sure. I need to talk to Sophie." Fons could see how the stress of these attempts on his wife's life had aged him.

Fons said goodbye and headed to New York.

When Houston got to his sister's house, Sophie was in bed, he changed and got into bed without disturbing her. He leaned in and kissed her cheek and patted Bully on his head when he came over to his side. He was asleep in seconds.

CHAPTER SIXTEEN

When Houston woke up, Sophie was out of bed. Houston slipped on some sweats and headed to the kitchen for coffee. He saw Bully was laying in front of the bathroom. Sophie was in there taking a shower.

"Good morning, Houston, you ready for breakfast?" Spring asked as she saw him come out of his room.

"No, just coffee for now. I've got to get dressed. Teddy and Sam took the day off so we could help dad redo mom's guest bathroom. Will you keep an eye on Sophie while I'm gone?"

"Do you think she's still in danger?" Spring's face showed her worry, moving closer to Houston to speak softly.

"No, Sis, but she needs time to sort through it," putting his arm around her, he kissed her cheek.

Houston headed back to the guest room. Sophie was in there dressing when he got back. He walked over to her, kissed her, and held her for a long time.

"I have to go help dad redo that bathroom, will you be alright until I come back? We have a lot to talk about." He was still holding her close.

"I would like to go riding today." She moved away to finish dressing.

"I'm sure Spring would love to ride with you, I'll ask her." He headed for the shower.

Houston, his dad, and brothers had gotten back from Home Depot when he saw Spring's car by the barn. He walked over to see if he could help them with the saddles.

Houston suggested Bully stay with him at the house. He wasn't trained around horses. He didn't want Bully to get underfoot and cause an accident. Bully was hesitant to let the horses go without him, but he listened to Houston's command.

They worked on the house all day, only stopping to eat the lunch his mom brought over and let the paint dry. They would put the toilet in now that the new floor was down, but they would put the sinks in tomorrow. They wanted to get it done in time for dinner and get ready for a mid-week service. Sophie and Spring had finished their horseback ride, and left hours earlier.

Sophie was glad to be in Church. After the worship service, the Pastor started his sermon.

"Edmund Burke said, 'the only thing necessary for the triumph of evil is for good men to do nothing.' Christians put it this way. 'Neither do men light a candle and put it under a bushel. But on a candlestick; and it giveth light unto all that are in the house.' Matt. 5:15.

"So many of us think only Pastors, Evangelists, and Church leaders have a calling. But that's not so. 'Ye are the salt of the earth: but if the salt have lost his savor, wherewith shall it be salted? it is thenceforth good for nothing, but to be cast out, and to be trodden under foot of men.' Matt. 5:13. The salt and the light are the same if we don't make use of it, it's useless.

"We are all called to push back the darkness and shed light in whatever field God puts us. First responders, for instance, literally push back the darkness. They stand between evil and those who can't protect themselves. We want to leave the hard work and sacrifices for others to do. But we are all called 'to take up our cross and follow Him,' according to the Word. We have the answers for the lost, but there will be some that reject the truth. Someone must stop those men, or women, from harming others."

His sermon went on for about ten more minutes, but Sophie had already felt the conviction in her heart. She spent the rest of the time repenting.

Sophie had planned to quit the Task Force but hadn't told Houston yet. She wanted to say it was more than she could take, but now realized it was selfish to expect others to make sacrifices she wasn't willing to make. What made her so special that she didn't have to take up her cross. His words were such a revelation to her; God had changed her thinking. Tears started rolling down her cheeks. Before she realized it, the Church service was over, but the sermon remained on her mind.

When they left the Church, Sophie whispered to Houston, "I'd like to go home."

He knew she meant New York, which was always home to her. "I'll get our things together."

Houston went to his dad and told him he needed to take Sophie home. He hated that he was leaving his father before the job's completion. He also apologized for the danger he brought to the ranch.

"Son, you know we're always glad to be here for you. As far as the work, Teddy will help me put the sinks in when he gets off work tomorrow."

"I'll need someone to drive us. I don't have a car here."

"Take my car. I'll have Spring and John take us up there this weekend. It will be a treat for your mom. I'll take her to a live performance and dinner; we'll stay overnight. Just leave the keys locked in the car, I have an extra set.

"You have the key to the condo in case we're gone. Stay there, dad, that extra room is made up for you and mom anytime."

"Ok, Son, better let your mom know you're leaving, she'll be disappointed."

They said their goodbyes to everyone and headed back to New York. Sophie hadn't spoken much. Bully was on a blanket asleep in the back seat. He got plenty of exercise whenever he came to the ranch. For a long time, they rode in silence.

"Houston, I had decided to quit the Task Force after what happened last night. I planned on telling you that, but God has changed my mind."

She went on and explained all the Lord revealed to her through the Pastor's sermon. He hadn't known Cosby had called her last night to make sure she was alright. He told her that the other agencies were wanting her to do the same thing for them. It overwhelmed her. Law enforcement wasn't what she had planned for her life. But now she realized it might not be her choice, but God's. God had given he a gift. She was able to take complex objectives and transform them into a workable mission. She could foresee what people would do in reaction to what she set before them. Sophie couldn't explain it, she just knew it. It was her light; she couldn't put it under a bushel because it required sacrifice on her part.

"But I can't do it without you. I need to know that you're ok if I decide I need a break or don't want to take on a case. And I don't want it to interfere with your career pursuits. I won't do this without you."

"Princess, your mind is a gift." He took her hand and kissed her palm, "I must say I was hoping you would tell me you were done with the Task Force. The sermon hit me too. I've been concerned this life is too dangerous, but our lives are not our own but God's. I can make things as safe as possible. We can decide which agency cases we want to take. When we need a break, we'll take one." He saw her body relax with his response. Sophie scooted closer and put her head on his shoulder.

"What do you want to do about Yon?"

"We need to get those plates," she said, lifting her head.

"I'll let Cosby know tomorrow." He took his eyes off the road for a second to look over at her. "In the meantime, we have a few days off."

They dropped the subject, talking about more personal things the rest of the way home.

Houston woke up when he heard a soft voice. He opened his eyes and saw his wife praying at the edge of her bed. He rolled out of bed and prayed with her. When the burden lifted they slipped back in bed.

It was late morning when they finally woke.

"Houston, I'm going to take Bully for a walk and grab some groceries from the corner market."

"Wait while I get ready, I'll go with you."

Sophie went over to the bed and put her hand on his face and kissed him. "No, I'm no longer in danger, and I like having a little freedom." He smiled at her and nodded his head.

Later in the day, Houston and Sophie took a cab to Time Square. They held hands as they walked down the street, looking in windows. They went to Macy's and did some early Christmas shopping. She wanted to go off on her own, so he went and picked up perfume for the women in his life. Then hunted the jewelry counter for some beautiful things for Sophie's stocking.

Houston packed their purchases, deciding to walk instead of taking a taxi. They decided to hunt for a restaurant they had never been to before. After enjoying the food at a Thai restaurant, they snagged a taxi and headed home.

Gail Turner was interviewing Captain Cartwright on a local station. Houston called out for Sophie to come watch. She was happy he was getting the attention he deserved.

Bully missed being home. He loved the balcony, and they all ended up there until it started getting chilly. They spent the rest of the evening watching movies.

The next day was more of the same, except Houston surprised her with tickets to a live performance. It was so much fun sitting in the general seating section, feeling part of the performance, enjoying the reactions. They went home and spent the rest of the night together. They knew tomorrow they would be on a plane to Hong Kong.

Saturday morning, Houston checked in with Command to confirm the accommodations. He also needed to confirm Cosby approved Rodriguez and Timms coming as backup. They would travel on different airlines. Houston knew the Hong Kong's Ministry of State Security did not back this operation. They were never eager to cooperate with other law enforcement agencies. That made the risk level higher. They had no local backup. Fons and Timms would stay close enough to them to pick up the mic's they would be wearing. DOJ wanted everything recorded for the prosecution. Cosby insisted they also wear trackers to be safe. Anything could go wrong when you're on foreign soil.

Sophie was fast asleep in first-class, curled up against his arm; he liked the feel of her head resting on him. He didn't know how she could sleep. It was always so difficult for him to sleep on a plane. Houston pulled down his table and started working on his computer. He went over the plan they had worked out, reassessing the details.

Sophie made her first contact with Yon the next morning, asking him to meet them in their hotel room.

Yon came around noon Sunday.

Houston opened the door for him and shook his hand. Sophie came over and welcomed him.

"Please come sit down, let me get you some coffee or tea," she said.

"Tea would be nice." Yon moved over to the table Houston was directing him to.

Sophie brought over the teapot and cups along with an assortment of teas, cookies, sugar, and honey on a platter. "Min-ji, I do believe I can help you set up a business that would be next to impossible to penetrate by law enforcement. But my husband wants to know what you are willing to offer in exchange for our contribution."

Yon turned to Houston, "I've been thinking about your proposal. I do believe with your and your wife's expertise, a partnership would be beneficial to me. I would like to offer you 25% of the business."

Houston thought for a moment. "If you are willing to give up 30%, that would be acceptable to me."

Yon agreed without hesitation. Sophie explained the things she planned on doing to get his business on the right track.

"Have you found a location yet?" Sophie asked.

"Yes, and I have ordered the first ream of paper with the security strips."

"You haven't paid for anything yet, have you?" She got up to get more hot water for the teapot.

"No, you told me to wait." Yon responded, adding more honey to his tea.

"Good, I want to be sure from the start we're protected. I won't put my husband or myself in jeopardy."

They discussed business for several more hours, then ordered dinner. At 8 pm Yon finally suggested they meet again in the morning.

Before he left, Houston asked, "Do you have the plates here?"

Yon hesitated, "Yes, they are safe." It was apparent he still didn't trust them.

"Before we go any further, we would like to see them. We need to know the plates exist. I don't think that is too much to ask. We barely know each other, and it would go a long way to building trust." Sophie said, deciding she needed to push him a little.

At first, Sophie thought Yon took offense that his word wasn't good enough. But after a moment, he agreed to meet them tomorrow at the Bank and show them the plates. They ended their night and planned to meet at 10 am at the Hong Kong and Shanghai Banking Corporation Limited. (HSBC)

Rodriguez and Timms followed Yon to see where he went and who he talked to. They didn't want to be blindsided or set up.

Houston talked to Fons about getting a tracker into the container holding the plates. They were afraid Yon might move the plates after showing them. Timms had gotten ahold of the local asset and procured an assortment of technology. He suggested a small tracker made of reflective material. It was almost invisible once attached, taking on the look of whatever surrounded it. Houston agreed.

Sophie wasn't feeling well, so they stayed in, and she went to bed early.

Houston and Sophie met Yon on time. A bank officer led them into the safe deposit room. Once they unlocked the box, the bank officer directed them into a private room to view their items. Yon opened the box and removed a velvet bag. Inside the bag were the plates in bubble wrap. Unwrapping them, he handed the plates to Houston, setting the bag down in front of Sophie. Houston slipped the tracker to Sophie. Yon focused on Houston while he inspected the plates.

"Do these plates have any flaws?" He asked, keeping Yon's attention on him. Sophie peeled off the backing and attached the tracker to the inside seam at the bottom of the bag.

"Yes, but no one has ever found them. Even if the US Treasury makes changes on the hundred-dollar bills, these will be usable for at least thirty more years."

"How many bills did your father make per year?"

"He made at least 100 million, but on occasion double that."

"What do you want to do, Min-ji?" Sophie interjected.

"I would like your input on that, Ms. Star."

"If we want to take the long view, we can't threaten the economy too much, or we will have every agency after us. I suggest we stay at fifty million. My off the cuff projection of profit on that would be more than thirty-five million a year. In ten years we will have more money than we can spend in two lifetimes. The key to staying off the radar is not to be greedy," Sophie said.

"It's in man's nature to get all they can get up front, but I agree with your point of view. I believe Alex Ivanov got arrested because he was in a hurry to get rich. He took chances he shouldn't have," Yon said.

"My husband and I plan on taking our thirty percent and investing in legal businesses. We don't want the law after us when we start having children. How much money can a person spend in their lifetime?" Sophie added.

"You have a refreshing take on it, Ms. Star. I may follow your lead." Yon seemed impressed.

"I do have a few more questions, but we need to leave the Bank. Can we treat you to lunch, Min-ji?" Houston wanted to plant some more seeds to make their plan work.

"Yes, there is a wonderful restaurant not too far from here. We can walk if you like."

The hostess seated them without a wait; they ordered what Yon suggested. Houston asked Yon if Alex knew much about his business. Anything Alex might trade for leniency that could compromise them.

"His father's attorneys will pump him for information they can use to get Alex a minimal sentence by giving you up. There are a lot of agencies that would like to get their hands on the plates and put you in jail," Houston said.

"I only stayed with Alex for a few days. He did pick me up at my private jet. But I doubt he will see the value in that. I can't think of anything else. He never knew I had the plates." Yon explained.

Sophie and Yon agreed she should go back to the suite and start working on the company's structure. She said she would also write up the contract between them. "Min-ji, what do we want to use as a front for the store?"

"I hadn't thought about it. What do you suggest?"

Sophie suggested using Alex's idea of money exchange and check cashing business. That way, they could distribute a small portion of their merchandise and make a higher profit. It would also make having large amounts of money on hand less suspicious. Yon liked the idea.

Yon and Houston walked Sophie back to her suite and went to the potential site. They walked the perimeter. The upstairs was perfect for the money exchange business.

The printing press and the rest of the operation would fit in the basement. It was a perfect setup with a downtown location. Houston was playing his part, feigning excitement to get started. They started redesigning the place on paper then decided to call it a night.

When Houston got back to the suite, he noticed Sophie was in bed. He decided to wake her, "Sweetheart, are you feeling alright?"

"No, I have bad cramps, can you get me some Tylenol?"

He went to the small hotel gift shop and brought them back to her.

Houston let her sleep and went to work out some details with Command.

The next morning Sophie felt better, so she started working on contracts. She had finished the new shell corporation yesterday, completing the agreement on the facility and the contract between them. Sophie made it a 5-year lease with a $5,000 payoff if breached. She would insist the Taskforce honor that payout. Yon needed to believe his company was taking shape. Houston met him at the facility.

Yon and Houston discussed how they would get the printer in the basement. Then they worked more on the design for the money exchange and check cashing business. Houston told him he didn't notice a serial number on the plate, so he asked how he planned on doing that.

"That was the secret to our success. We designed computer software. It allowed us to add sequential serial numbers on each sheet of money while they printed it. It's what makes them so difficult to detect. Most counterfeit money has one serial number etched on the plates." Yon explained.

"That's brilliant, do you have the software for that?" Houston asked.

"Yes, it's on a flash drive in the safe deposit box."

"The next thing we have to do is decide where we want a floor safe so we can get those plates out of the Bank. It's too risky not having them where we can get our hands on them. If you have to run, you won't have time to go to the Bank and retrieve them." Houston wanted the plates within reaching distance if the plan went awry.

They decided where the safe would go and started looking online for the one they wanted. Houston and Yon also looked for a high-end security system. They would have another visible safe, so if a thief did come in, they wouldn't look for the other one. Yon was buying it. They needed to get the plates on the premises as soon as possible. Houston ordered the safe and the security system since it was on Yon's dime. They would be there in a few days.

The next few days, Yon worked hand in hand with Houston. They spent a whole day putting in the safe themselves, putting it where the built-in cabinets were going. In order for someone to find it, they would have to open the cabinet door and remove the bottom shelf to get to it. Yon was very impressed. They laid the floor then put a bigger Sentry safe in for the business front. They spent the rest of the week putting in the cameras while the security company put in the new high-tech system.

Houston convinced Yon that it was time to get the plates and the flash drive from the Bank's safe deposit box.

CHAPTER SEVENTEEN

Sophie talked to Prosecutor Martin about an idea she had early that morning. If they offer Alex a few years off for information on Yon, they could point their finger at him when Yon gets picked up. Sophie was concerned about retribution on her and Houston if Yon ever found out they set him up. Ms. Martin wasn't crazy about it but relented.

The Prosecutor knew the US Treasury and Secret Service wanted those plates, and Deputy Director Cosby needed to keep the Townsends cover intact. Sophie asked that Ms. Martin get all the necessary approvals so they could move to the next step. She said to wait for her call to make the offer.

After Yon picked the plates and flash drive up from the bank, he met Houston at the property. They programmed the safe, securing the plates and flash drive.

"I was going to go by Aqua Tokyo for takeout, want to come over and eat with us?" Houston asked.

"I would love to, but I have a date." Yon smiled while Houston raised his eyebrows in a teasing gesture.

"Have a good time; I'll talk to you tomorrow."

Houston headed home after turning on the security. Then he gave Fons a call, "make sure you stay on Yon tonight. We can't afford to have him get hinky and take those plates back."

"We're on him. How's Sophie feeling?"

"Not good, as soon as we're done here and get home, I'm insisting she sees her doctor."

"How much longer before we close in on those plates? I get calls from Cosby every day. He has a ton of pressure on him to get our hands on them."

"I'll ask Sophie tonight, but we're ready."

They finished their conversation, and he headed to pick up dinner.

Houston woke to Sophie in the bathroom, throwing up. He knew something wasn't right, but she insisted they needed to put the final leg of the plan in play today. Then she would address whatever was going on with her body. She called Ms. Martin and told her it was time to get ahold of the Ivanov attorneys.

Yon, Houston, and Sophie met at the storefront and were discussing the next steps. Houston could see Sophie was trying to hide the pain. As she sat down, her phone pinged a text.

"Min-ji, tell me again what Alex Ivanov knows that could hurt you?" She asked, concerned.

"He knows my family is dead, and we ran the counterfeit business, but other than that, not anything that could hurt me. He doesn't know I have the plates."

"Did he know where you were going?" Houston interrupted.

"No, I told no one. What's going on?" Yon started rubbing his neck. A nervous habit Houston had noticed early on.

"I have a contact in the prosecutor's office. He said the Prosecutor is offering Ivanov a deal for information on you." Sophie went on to say, "he might just be trying to see if he knows anything. My contact will get back to me if the prosecution gives him a deal, which will mean he gave them something."

"Min-ji, we need to have a contingency plan." Houston moved away from the cabinet he was fixing.

"What do you suggest?"

"If the worst happens and he gives up the info on your plane, which he may not. Then we will have to do some miss direction. They can track you here from the airport logs that day. So you'll have to take the plates with you and take your jet somewhere like Japan. I can have a rented jet waiting in the name of one of my shell companies, you can go anywhere you'd like to visit for a while. Where would you like to vacation for a few weeks?" She winced as her cramps kept getting worse.

"I've always wanted to spend time in Hawaii. I have a friend there, but my Appa never let me go." Yon said.

He could have chosen anywhere in the world, and he chose US soil, it didn't get any better than that. It would have been much more challenging to run the operation on foreign territory.

"That's doable, Min-ji," Sophie said.

"What would you do?" He asked.

"They're not after us. We'll stay here and keep our progress going forward," Houston replied.

"Why send the plates with me then, why not leave them here?" Yon asked.

"I appreciate the fact you want to show you trust us, but I don't want you to have any doubts about our partnership. At this point, you can only trust yourself; in time, our loyalty will be clear to you." Yon had to have the plates on him when they captured him. Yon looked comfortable with that explanation.

They moved on to the business again, so it didn't appear to be their only focus. Yon seemed excited about the possibility of going to Hawaii.

Even though they ordered the printing press, Command put a hold on all but the computer at the dock. They didn't want to be responsible for someone else getting their hands on it once the mission was over. This way, it would go back to the shipper.

Sophie stepped outside and called the Special Prosecutor. It was time to make a deal of some kind with Alex.

Yon and Houston had the computer downstairs on the desk, setting it up. They came back upstairs to wait for the printing press. Houston feigned a call to the dock to see when it would arrive.

He was told faulty paperwork delayed the delivery. He passed on the news to Yon and Sophie.

"I will go into the government offices tomorrow and get a business license. It doesn't matter how many hoops or red tape they make us go through; it gives us legitimacy to be here. We can work on the press regardless."

Sophie received a text. "I just got word they dropped five years off Alex Ivanov's sentence. He gave information on your whereabouts." She got up and started pacing.

"We better put our diversion plan in motion. The US won't get much help from the locals. You can probably come back in four months. By then, we should have this place running like a real business," Houston said.

"Four months? What do I do for that length of time?" Yon asked.

"Enjoy yourself. We're all in this for the long haul. Four months gives us time to make sure we've got everything functioning. Do we need to hire a print master for the machine?"

"No, my father trained me. He didn't trust anyone, and he treated me like the help anyway." Sophie could hear grief and bitterness in Yon's tone.

"How long will it take you to go pack your things and get in the air?" Houston asked.

"I can be wheels up in an hour."

"I'd say the sooner the better. Have your pilot file a flight plan for Narita Airport on Honshu Island. We will have a charter plane waiting to take you to Hilo, Hawaii, the big island. The Island is quiet; no one can find you there. Come back here to get the plates, and the reservation information, we'll wait for you. Do you have an alias?" Sophie asked.

"Yes."

"Do you have a passport with that name on it? If so, write it down, and I'll make the reservation in that name."

He wrote down the name, and she got on the computer to make a reservation for him. Yon left, and Houston contacted Fons and told them the last leg was in play.

Timms had already reached Command and set up the charter to take Yon from Japan to Hawaii. Once on the ground, the FBI would pick him up and arrest him and the crew. If all goes well, we should have the plates, the flash drive, and Yon Min-ji wrapped up in a bow in about 10 hours.

Yon was back in forty-five minutes for the plates and flash drive. He said the plane was fueled and waiting. Sophie gave him his reservation information at the Hilo Hawaiian Hotel.

"Once your plane lands in Japan, send it to Mexico. Have it stored there and make arrangements for your pilot to go on vacation somewhere remote," Sophie suggested.

"I'm sorry this puts a kink in our plans, Ms. Star." He looked down at his hands. He was creasing the paper she gave him.

"We have time, Min-ji. These things happen in our business, you know that. As long as you have the plates, we're still in business," Sophie added. She got up to give him a sideways hug goodbye. She sat back down; the pain was getting worse.

Yon took the plates, shook Houston's hand, and headed out the door.

Houston turned to Sophie, "we need to pray this goes off without a hitch."

She stood up, her blood pressure dropped, and she yelled, "Houston!"

He was only a few feet away and was able to catch her when she fainted. He looked down on the floor. There was blood. He took his coat off and wrapped the arms around her waist while holding her up. Then he picked her up and ran to the car. He laid her in the back seat and drove to the nearest hospital.

"Fons, I know you can hear me, Sophie fainted, she's losing blood, I'm taking her to the hospital. This operation is on you, now."

Fons heard Houston's frantic voice; he had no idea what could have happened. Fons desperately wanted to go to the hospital to be there for them. He knew he couldn't. Houston was counting on him to make sure the final stages of this operation materialized.

Timms called Command and gave them an update on Yon and Sophie. They followed Yon to the airstrip and saw the plane take off. The tracker was still sending a signal, so they knew it was on the plane with him. He relayed that message and gave them the tracker frequency. This way, the team in Tokyo could be sure Yon didn't hide the plates on his private plane when he got on the charter.

Houston reached the Evangel Hospital pulling up to the emergency room. He carried Sophie to the nurse on duty. She saw the blood on Sophie's pant leg and grabbed a wheelchair. The nurse pushed her into an examining room and went to get a doctor. Houston's cell rang.

"Where are you? I'm coming to meet you," Fons said when Houston answered.

"I'm at Evangel Hospital in the emergency room. Thanks, Fons." Houston was pacing a few feet away from the bed. A nurse helped a barely conscious Sophie into a hospital gown.

Fons had Timms let him off at the hospital. Someone had to close out the operation and collect their things from the hotel. Timms volunteered so that Fons could be with Houston.

Fons ran to the receptionist at the entrance asking where Sophie Townsend was. They wouldn't let Fons go back to her room, but they let Houston know he was in the waiting room. Houston walked back to the waiting area to fill him in on what he knew so far, which wasn't much.

"You go be with her, I'm here when you need me," Fons said.

Houston gave him a man hug and nodded his head. He went back to sit with his wife.

Finally, the doctor came in. He did a pelvic exam and had the nurse type and match her blood for a transfusion. He tried to rouse her.

"Mrs. Townsend," he rubbed his knuckles on her breastbone. She came around.

"Hi, I'm Doctor Lok Chi. It appears you are having a miscarriage, Mrs. Townsend. Do you know how far along you are?"

She had trouble getting her words out, "I didn't know I was pregnant." She looked at Houston, distressed, bringing her hands to her face.

"You didn't notice you missed your cycle?"

"My cycles aren't regular, but I did notice it was off even for me, I thought nothing of it."

"That's understandable. We'll register you in a room. I have some tests ordered, and I'll get the surgeon on call to come and talk to you. You will need a D&A if you're in your first trimester, which is my estimation." He went out to make the call.

Houston told Fons what happened. They sat together for a while, not saying much. Fons could see the pain in Houston's eyes, grief for the loss, and worry for his wife compounding it.

"Maybe doing this operation contributed to her losing the baby. I knew she was under a great deal of stress. Maybe getting her to the doctor the minute she got sick, could've changed things." Houston confided in Fons. His mind was running non-stop with guilt.

Fons did his best to comfort him but had no idea what to say.

When Houston went back to her room, the Doctor and his nurse scribe were in there. Houston sat down by her bed and waited for the doctor to explain what was going to happen.

"Mr. and Mrs. Townsend, my name is Dr. Eto Ren. I will be doing the D&A. It's a less invasive procedure than a D&C. It will clean out the uterus and keep you from getting any kind of infection. I do have a few questions. Have you had an injury or accident in the last several years?"

Sophie looked at Houston, "I was injured several years ago. Why do you ask?"

"The pelvic exam showed a prolapsed uterus and fallopian tube. This pregnancy wasn't viable." He gave them a moment for them to soak in what he was telling them. "You have several options. After the D&A, I can use an applicator to place an anchor within the ligaments. It will leave two degradable sutures in the vagina. Then I would take button-like securing elements threading them along these sutures. Fixing them in place along each side of the vaginal wall, this would support the Uterus. Or I can remove the uterus if you do not plan on having children."

"No! I don't want it removed; we want children." She took Houston's hand. "what about the fallopian tube?" Sophie asked the Doctor.

"I don't think it will prevent you from having children. It may take a little longer."

Houston needed more information. "Doctor, is there more risk to the procedure you explained than removing it?"

Sophie gasped, "Houston, I will not have my uterus removed, we want children. I don't care about the risk."

"But I do," he turned to the doctor.

"Mr. Townsend, I see no reason to believe either procedure would endanger your wife. If I find anything suspicious when I get in there, I will let you know, and then you can decide what to do. We will give you another transfusion to replace the blood you lost. The surgery shouldn't take more than an hour or so. I would like to keep you overnight."

"Thank you, Doctor." Houston was still holding her hand, concerned.

"My nurse has some papers you need to sign, and then we will prep you for surgery."

Houston and Sophie read the papers and then signed them. The Doctor's nurse took the papers and sent in the surgical prep nurse.

"Houston, I'm sorry I lost our baby." Sophie said with tears running down the side of her face and onto the pillow.

He held her close and whispered to her, "you had nothing in it, God made this decision, and I trust Him. We will meet our baby one day. In the meantime, we still have each other." Houston said, trying to hold back the water forming in his own eyes.

The nurse came. He kissed her forehead and left the room so the nurse could prep her.

Houston stepped out the door and leaned against the wall, his head tilted back touching it. *'Lord, I do trust you, but I would have loved this baby.'* Fons was down the hall. He was told he could come back now that she was in a room.

"Houston, are you alright?" Picking up his pace, seeing Houston in distress.

"I don't know, Fons. We talked about having kids, but it was in the abstract. We didn't set a date. We figured it would eventually happen. But now that she had a miscarriage, it brings up a sense of sadness in me, I can't explain. The thought of a possible little Sophie in my arms makes my heart melt. I would have loved her so much. But she's lost to me now."

"You know you'll see her again..." Fons copied Houston's stance against the wall. "But that doesn't stop the pain you're feeling now."

Houston nodded. "The Doctor who's doing the procedure says there is little to no risk; they're prepping her now." Fons told him he would be in the waiting room.

Houston went back into Sophie's room. They waited and prayed together until they wheeled her away.

Yon was sitting on his plush private jet. He felt comfortable with his new partners. Particularly, Houston, he never had a friend growing up. Yon liked fixing the store up with him. He had no intention of leaving the plates. But the fact they were the ones who insisted he take them set well with him. Yon lifted the plates from his briefcase and pulled them out of the bag; he considered them a work of art. When he emptied the bag, a small disk fell on the table. He inspected it and realized what it was. *Who could have put it there?* He hadn't noticed it before. When he took Houston and Sophie to the Bank, he was with them the whole time. *Can I trust my partners?* His mind was spinning, sitting there looking at the tracker. He decided to call Houston. One way or another, he would know when he spoke with him.

Houston was in the waiting room with Fons when his phone rang. He saw the caller ID, so he motioned Fons to follow him into one of the conference rooms by the waiting area.

"Hello?"

"Houston, I found a tracker in the bag with the plates. What should I do?"

Yon finding the tracker wasn't good. Houston ran his hands through his hair, trying to think of the right answer.

"It can't be the Americans because it would've had to happen while the plates were at the Bank. The US doesn't have enough clout with the Hong Kong judicial system to get a warrant. Do you think your father could have done it in case anyone stole them? And would your family have known that and be tracking you?

"My uncle's family would. They never trusted anyone, not even each other. But they are all dead unless one of my cousins knows about it. The Supreme Leader won't want the flow of money my family contributed to his coffers stifled for long. What should I do?"

"Drop it into some liquid. That should destroy it. NO wait! I have a better idea."

He gave him the plan. He was to put the counterfeit plates in his briefcase without the velvet bag. He needed to put the tracker back in the bag, and then after he lands in Tokyo, he is to send the velvet bag with the jet to Mexico.

"Do you know anyone you can leak that you plan to sell the plates to a Mexican Cartel; someone who will pass it on to your family in North Korea.

"Yes, I have a few men in Hong Kong who would love to sell that information. That's a good idea. I don't think they would tangle with the cartel in Mexico, but since they won't have them anyway, it doesn't matter."

"I will send you a couple of bodyguards to escort you from your plane to the one we have waiting to take you to Hilo. Make sure your pilot goes to Mexico City as planned. Don't tell him where you're going."

"Thanks, Houston, I was afraid it might have been you, but that made no sense. You could have gotten to them anytime while they were in the store."

"Do you think your uncle's family knows we are involved with you?"

"I don't see how, but it's possible. Maybe you better leave for a while too."

"You're right. I'll take Sophie on a short vacation. We'll call you in Hilo when it's safe. Take care, Min-ji."

"Fons, call Command, we have a change in plans. We need to protect our cover a little better."

He discussed with Fons his idea. "When the plane lands in Tokyo, two men can escort Yon to the other jet. Once it gets to Hilo, the airport can instruct all pilots there has been a terrorist threat. All planes and passengers with their baggage will be detained and inspected. Our men disguised as TSA can do the inspection. This way, they can find the plates by accident and call in the Secret Service."

CHAPTER EIGHTEEN

Sophie was in recovery, but the Doctor had come and talked to Houston. Everything went well, and he felt there should be no further problem. Houston walked to her room down a hall that now felt endless.

Fons heard from Command that Yon had landed in Tokyo and was now on the charter to Hilo; everything was 'go'.

Fons met Timms and they went to Yon's store and gathered anything that might be evidence. Cosby was aware there would be a penalty for breaching the lease. He wasn't happy, but Sophie had insisted the owner not suffer for a US operation.

Timms came to the hospital as soon as he closed down the operation. "They want us on the next flight home in the morning," Timms announced. "I'll pick you up when Sophie's released."

Houston decided to charter a private jet to take them home. He wanted his wife to be as comfortable as possible. He planned on getting off in New York, then send the plane on to DC with Fons and Timms.

The Doctor told Sophie he would release her at the end of the day. Houston and Sophie ordered lunch from the hospital kitchen and waited for the call that Yon was in custody.

Sophie slept most of the flight home. The seat laid back comfortably. Houston was reclining in the seat next to her. His eyes were closed, but he wasn't sleeping; guilt still plagued him. If he had done things differently, she might not have lost their baby. It was a hard pill to swallow, and it was eating him up. The guilt of bringing her on this operation after being hunted by an assassin. The remorse for not getting her to a doctor immediately. The thoughts kept playing a loop in his mind.

The plane landed late, New York time. He had called ahead for a town car, and after loading their things, went straight home. Sophie changed and went straight to bed. Houston called Max and let him know they were back, and he would pick up Bully Jr. in the morning. Max offered to bring him on his way to work, so they settled on that.

Houston stayed up unpacking and putting clothes in the washer. His mind wouldn't let him sleep, and he didn't want to wake Sophie by his tossing and turning. He needed to talk to his dad, he knew it was late, but his father never complained.

"Dad?" Houston sat on the couch with his elbows on his knees.

"Houston, your back, is everything alright, son?"

"No," Houston stalled as his voice got lost by the tightness in his throat. He rubbed his face with his free hand, trying to stop the tears.

His father let his son cry for a bit. "What is it son, tell me."

"Sophie had a miscarriage while we were in Hong Kong. We didn't even know she was pregnant..." Houston sighed, taking a deep breath. "I guess I'm surprised by my reaction to the loss."

His father was quiet for a long time, weighing up his words. "We never spoke to any of you about this. It was too personal. But your mother miscarried her first pregnancy too. She was in her first trimester, and one day, she started cramping. I rushed her to the hospital, but she still miscarried.

"The Doctor said the body knows there's a problem. Most often, chromosomal abnormalities. It makes the pregnancy non-viable, and the body rejects it. He told us that as many as 25% of first pregnancies end up in a miscarriage. There is nothing either of you did wrong son, nothing you could have done to prevent it. I know that's what you think because that's what hounded me."

"I keep thinking if I had done this or that, or if she were in the US, it would have turned out different." Houston leaned back on the couch.

"It wouldn't have made any difference. God knows all things, and he is in control of your life. You have to keep trusting him," Jack's voice cracked. "He gave us four wonderful children. He'll do the same for you."

"I believe that dad, it's just..." he faltered, "the thought of that baby in my arms brought something out in me. I didn't realize how much I wanted to have a child."

"And your wife will be having the same feelings. You make sure she doesn't get caught in some false guilt; that she could have prevented it. Let her know how you feel. Keep encouraging one another and love each other. That's what marriage is all about; going through sorrows together."

"Thanks, Dad, I needed to hear this. I'm sorry I didn't wait until morning."

"I'm not. If I thought you waited to call it would have meant I didn't show you that nothing matters to me more than my family."

245

Houston and his dad said their goodbyes. He put the last load of laundry in the dryer and headed for bed. His Dad's testimony of his own experience helped him.

Sophie and Houston sat on the patio, eating breakfast. They liked the feel of the early morning, that slight chill even on a warm day. He told her all his father had said the night before, and he explained to her how he felt. Sophie was having a hard time expressing her feelings about the loss. But after hearing what Houston's dad told him, she was able to verbalize her feelings a little better. Knowing Houston didn't blame her, was a weight off her shoulders. He held his wife while she cried. Then they talked about when they would like to try to have children and how many. They decided to wait a few years.

All through the day, flowers showed up at the door. They came from their team, Houston's family, friends, and even the President and First Lady. It was all very touching. Sophie had a lot of 'Thank You' cards to write. Lily and Jack came by later in the afternoon to see how they were doing.

Houston had to go to DC to finish his reports and debrief. Sophie decided to stay in New York and Skype hers. Bully could sense her sadness and kept close by her side.

When he came back, Houston stopped to pick up groceries. They had cleaned out most of the fresh food when they headed for Hong Kong. Opening the door to the complex, he saw Secret Service agents in the lobby. He instantly thought something happened to Sophie. He rushed over to one of the Agents and asked what was going on.

"Don't be alarmed Mr. Townsend, FLOTUS came to visit your wife, that's all."

Relieved, he headed to the condo. He knew Sissy and Carol had visited earlier. He nodded to the Secret Service men at the door. Houston walked in and noticed the ladies sitting on the patio having tea. He didn't want to disturb them, but he felt it would be disrespectful not to acknowledge the First Lady.

He opened the patio door, "Mrs. Madden, it's an honor to have you in our home."

"Houston, I wanted to come by and make sure you were both alright."

"Thank you, ma'am."

"It's good to have you back in the country. By all reports, we now have our hands on those plates because of your team. I hope it didn't play a part in your loss. Sophie assures me it did not."

"No, ma'am, it didn't. But thank you for your concern." She got up to leave. Sophie got up, thanked her for coming, and walk her to the door. The First Lady hugged Sophie and headed to her other commitments.

Yon had been brought to DC so the Special Prosecutor could interrogate him. Ms. Martin couldn't let on how much she knew about him, without blowing the team's cover.

Ms. Martin walked into the interrogation room, paused, looked at him, then took a seat across the table. She opened his passport and read his name, then laid it on the table.

"Mr. Ma, is it? My name is Special Prosecutor Martin, did the TSA agents read you your rights when they arrested you?"

"Yes." Yon was handcuffed to a metal ring attached to the table.

"It seems they found a unique item, in your possession. What do you have to say about that?"

"Nothing." Yon sat up a little straighter in defiance.

"Well, the bad news is, possessing those plates will cost you 25 years. The really bad news is if we find any murders committed in the distribution of the phony money you printed; you might as well consider America your home for life. We are scanning the plates now to see if we've confiscated any of it in the United States." She watched the expression on his face barely change.

"You can't prove I printed the money because the plates are in my possession." Yon looked her straight in the eye.

"Are you saying you have partners?"

"No." Yon dropped his eyes and focused on his hands.

"Do you?" She leaned forward, acting like the information would be worth something.

"If I did, why would I tell you?"

Ms. Martin settled back in her chair, "it's a possibility I would let your partners take some of your sentence. You may be young enough to get married and have kids when you get out of prison."

"What if I had information better than a partner." Yon leaned back, mirroring her action to show her he was confident in his statement.

"Like your real name, for instance."

"I may know some people with counterfeit bills that you won't want to enter the country."

Ms. Martin slammed her hand on the table, "that is way too vague, Mr. Ma." Her action startled Yon.

He looked her in the eye, trying to decide if he could trust her. "If I give you information, what kind of deal will you make with me?"

"Before I decide that. I need you to tell me the truth about who you are and your country of origin. Something I can verify, so I can tell if your information would even be worth investigating."

Yon relented and told her his real name and how he came to have the plates after his family's massacre. He didn't give up Houston and Sophie's names.

"Alright, Mr. Yon, I'm going to verify what you've told me. If it checks out, I'm going to see what kind of a deal my office would be willing to make." She left the room to let him stew for a while.

Trindi contacted Houston to see if he had any idea what information Yon might be giving her. Houston put the phone on speaker so Sophie could hear. They were at the kitchen table having coffee.

"I don't have a clue what it could be," Houston replied, looking at Sophie.

"I don't either. Yon never alluded to anything I can recall," Sophie added, taking another sip.

Trindi thanked them, then headed back to the interrogation room.

"Mr. Yon, I have the authorization to whittle off up to 10 years based on the value of your information."

The plates were in DOJ's possession and out of North Korea. One of the biggest threats to the US economy and security. So Yon's threat index went down significantly. It was his father who they would have liked to get their hands on to prosecute.

"My father sold 10 million in 100-dollar bills to Al-Qaeda. They plan on using it to fund their cell groups in the US."

"That's interesting but not new information, Mr. Yon. You'll have to do better than that."

"There's more, they plan on putting a deadly strain of anthrax virus on one million dollars of it. Then circulate it into the population. They expect that half a million people will die."

Ms. Martin couldn't show how startled she was. "How do you know this?" She placed her hands on her lap so her nerves wouldn't give her away.

"I was in my father's office. His phone was on speaker when he was making a deal with the leader of one of the Al-Qaeda groups in Iran. He told my father about his plans."

"Why would he tell your father?"

"To get a better deal. Everyone knows North Korea hates the United States. 'The enemy of my enemy is my friend.' Do you know that saying, Ms. Martin?" He waited, leaning the top of his body over the table as if he was waiting to hear a secret.

"I do. Winston Churchill said it. But giving me this information does nothing to stop it, so what do we gain by it." She needed more than accusations.

Yon explained that the Iranian told his father how they plan to get the money and the virus into the United States. They were going to send out the tainted money on the anniversary of some event. Yon couldn't remember which one, or the routes and times. But his father had recorded the conversation, as was his custom. He assumed it was for leverage of some kind.

Ms. Martin tried to keep her voice calm, "and where are these recordings?"

"My father had a secret hiding place in our home. I only know about it because he didn't see me behind him when he got into it. When I saw what he was doing, I hid."

"If all this checks out, I would be willing to give you a lighter sentence, Mr. Yon, but I have one more question. How do we get our hands on them?"

"There is only one couple I know who could make that happen. My partners, but I won't tell you who they are unless I'm certain you won't prosecute them." Yon was adamant about it.

"I can't promise you that. If there are warrants from other agencies, I may not be able to give them immunity."

"Then you'll have to figure it out yourself." Yon leaned back in his chair, not wanting to show his disappointment.

"What if you give me one of their names without a location so I can check to see if there are any warrants."

"His name is Houston Townsend."

She wanted to be sure it was them. Yon could've had other partners.

"Let me check him out. I'll be right back."

Prosecutor Martin went into her AG's office and told him the whole story. He immediately contacted Deputy Director Cosby, the HSC Terrorism Unit, and the CDC. They set up a conference call. The money wasn't the crisis; the anthrax was.

"He mentioned his 'partners' could come up with a way to get their hands on the recordings." Ms. Martin spoke to them all through the speakerphone.

"That could work for us. The Townsend's would be my choice to lead this operation anyway," Cosby added.

Cosby decided to call Houston and Sophie to see how they wanted to handle this. They ended the conference call, and he and Ms. Martin walked to command and made the call on the secure video feed.

"Hello?" Houston answered on his secure network.

His face appeared on the big screen in Command. "Houston is Sophie with you?"

He walked out of his office and called for Sophie.

"Yon's in the interview room, he has given us information that needs to be analyzed." He told them the whole story. Cosby said Yon suggested his partners were the best choice to come up with a plan to recover the recordings. Deputy Director Cosby wasn't sure if Sophie would be willing to come back so soon after her miscarriage.

"It never fails; these operations lead us to places we never planned on going. But if it means taking down some terrorists and keeping our citizens safe, it's worth it," Cosby said. The fatigued evident on his face. "We have to get ahold of that anthrax. If we lose the cash, I can live with that, but I can't live with the kind of death toll anthrax can bring," he added.

"He never gave us any indication he was sitting on that kind of information," Sophie responded, sitting down next to Houston.

"Can I get back to you in a few minutes, Sir?" Houston asked.

"Yes, but you know time is of the essence here."

"Yes Sir."

When they cut the communication, he turned to her. "Sophie, you just got out of the Hospital. I'm not sure putting more stress on you would be a good idea right now."

She took his hand and leaned toward him. "I appreciate your concern, but this isn't fieldwork. I'll be in the Command Center, and you'll be with me. There is a bed in my office if I get too tired. But this needs immediate attention. I don't see how we can refuse. Do you?"

"Our Task Force is the best chance they have to get that threat off the table. So, if you're sure you feel up to it." He looked her in the eyes to see if there was any kind of trepidation about it.

They called Cosby back and gave him their decision. Sophie suggested Ms. Martin get Yon to contact them and convince them to help. Yon would then feel obligated. That will help to get him to co-operate. Cosby was sending a plane in the morning.

Ms. Martin went back into the interview room and told Yon she would give his partners immunity if they would help. Ms. Martin handed him a phone, and he made the call.

"Hello?" Sophie answered. They were waiting for the call in their home office.

"Sophie?"

"Min-ji, is that you? Where did you go? You never checked into the Hilo Hawaiian; we thought your family caught up to you." She spoke fast as if she had been worried about him.

"No, when I arrived at Hilo International Airport, there was a terror threat. They grounded all the planes coming and going to check for explosives. The TSA came to our charter and checked my baggage; they found the plates. Secret Service has me in custody."

"Then how are you calling us Yon, did you give us up?" She said, feigning anger.

"No, of course not. I have information that I can trade to get my sentence reduced, but I need your help to make it happen."

"You want us to turn ourselves in?" Sophie blurted.

"No, you would have immunity. I need to get my hands on some information in North Korea. You are the only ones I could think of that could make it happen. They will take years off my sentence if I can get it to them right away." He was pleading his case, sitting straight up in the chair.

"You said they would give us immunity?"

"Yes."

Sophie explained it all to Houston so Yon could hear their conversation. Houston acted as if he wasn't sure he could trust the prosecutor for immunity. Yon insisted he could talk to her himself and make her put it in writing. Houston agreed. Yon handed Ms. Martin the phone, and they continued the conversation about immunity. When she hung up with Houston, she let Yon know they decided to come tomorrow. When they did, he could explain everything to them in person.

CHAPTER NINETEEN

Since they weren't going commercial and Bully had a service vest, he traveled in the cabin with them. The trip was short, and as soon as they landed, Houston and Sophie went straight into the Command center. After each member of the team spoke of sadness for their loss and welcomed them back, they got to work. Sophie settled Bully in her office, then met the others in the conference room.

"If what Yon is telling us is true, we have little time to waste. We need that information," Cosby said as they all took their seats.

"Do you have any idea how to get our hands on those recordings, Ms. Star?" Ms. Martin asked. Tenting her hands and placing them up to lips in thought.

"I need to talk to Yon before any plan can develop." Sophie had an idea but needed to keep it to herself for now.

Yon was in the FBI holding the night before; they brought him to an interrogation room not far from the Command Center a few hours earlier. Ms. Martin accompanied them to the interview room.

She opened the door. "Mr. Yon, your partners have arrived and signed their immunity agreements." Yon stood to greet them as best he could with his handcuffs attached to the metal ring on the table.

"Houston and I would like to talk to Mr. Yon alone, and that means the cameras and mics off." Sophie insisted, looking Ms. Martin right in the eye.

"I'm sorry that isn't going to happen." Ms. Martin replied.

"Then we have all wasted our time." Sophie turned to leave.

Ms. Martin stopped her, "don't push me too far, Ms. Star." Then Ms. Martin left. It was all pre-arranged to give Yon more incentive to speak freely.

She never said she would turn off the cameras and mics, also predetermined. Then she headed with the other interested parties to watch the interview.

"Yon, what is it you think we can do to help you get your sentenced reduced?" Houston started the conversation holding the chair for his wife before seating himself.

Yon told them the whole story, including how he found where his father hid the recordings.

"Thank you for not giving us up to the DOJ." Sophie interjected, "I'll need more information to see if there's anything we can do."

"I'll tell you everything I know."

"You spoke to us about your father, but very little about your mother, is she still in North Korea?"

"Yes, my mother's name is Yon Moon. I am so ashamed, I left her there when I ran the night of the massacre. I was too afraid to go back to the house to get her. Afraid someone would ask questions, I ran and left her there to take the fallout." His voice faltered at the end of his explanation. Yon's head bowed in shame.

"Is she in good health?"

"Yes, she is strong at 55 years old." He answered, looking up again.

"Does she speak English as well as you?"

"No, my mother was from a poor family who could not pay for school. When she married my father, she was able to get educated. One could learn English in elite schools. But my father wanted to be able to talk to his clients without his wife understanding, so he forbade it. I tried to teach her when I was young, but my father found out and beat me with a stick. My mother threw her body over mine and took most of the beating. After that, she wouldn't let me teach her."

"Does she still have strong family ties to North Korea? If there was a way for us to get her out, would she come?" Sophie moved closer, speaking almost in a whisper.

Yon lowered his head for a moment. "My mother is a Christian, Sophie. She has prayed God would deliver us from that miserable country from the day she knew what prayer was."

Yon's answer visibly shook Sophie. Now the idea God had given her started to make sense.

"Do you think the United States would give her asylum?"

"I don't know, but if we had enough to offer them, maybe. Is there anything else on those recordings that would make them want to do it?" Sophie's voice was starting to sound hopeful.

"There were a lot of clients that wanted to hurt the US. I remember one Russian client. He wanted to use the money to pay computer experts to hack into the Pentagon computers. My father had the name of the hacker. Several terrorists from Iran and Iraq wanted to bomb certain Iconic buildings in the US. But some of this information is old by now. I do remember hearing the plan for the Boston Marathon bombing. I was quite a bit younger. The names of his clients are on the recordings and where the money was delivered. Others could be delivering money to those same clients."

"Do you know of any way we can contact your mother?"

"I once bought her a cell phone, the disposable kind, I never told my father, he would have taken it. Very few nationals have them, but my father and I did because of the business. She knows how to use it, but I have no idea if it's charged or turned on. The electricity in North Korea is sporadic, as is the cell tower coverage. It did work in our region when I left."

"Is there a landline in your home?"

"No."

"Is there a landline anywhere your mother may be or go in the next 24 hours?" Sophie knew there had to be a way to reach her.

"She worked at the hospital administration office three days a week. That was before my father died, and I became a defector. I'm afraid my mother may be in prison unless she knew where my father kept his money and could buy her way out of it." Yon's hope was now faltering with the knowledge of the consequences to her for his actions.

"If the prosecutor will bring in someone who speaks Korean, can we reach your mother by phone at the hospital? Would you have that number?" Sophie stopped to think if there was anything else that might help. "Is there anything we can tell her that would make her understand you want to call her?"

Yon lowered his head to meet his hands and wipe away his tears. His mind was running through everything he could remember about the Hospital. Were there any phones near her office? He tried to remember the hours she worked and the number he used to get ahold of her. He asked for a pen and paper and wrote down all he could remember.

"As far as some code to let her know to turn on her phone, I don't know what it would be," Yon finally said.

Houston had an idea. "If we were able to send her a message by drone, where would we tell her to look?"

"When my mother became a Christian, she would read the bible to me outside behind the storage shed. If someone told her to check her favorite reading spot, she would understand."

They talked through some more details then Houston and Sophie left the room. Yon was still in interrogation, cuffed to the table.

Sophie stopped Houston before they went into the Command Center. She told him she wanted to find a way to get Yon's mother out of North Korea. On the plane that morning, a plan had come to her that included Yon's mother, now she knew why. God was going to answer Yon's mother's prayers.

"Sophie, do you have any idea how difficult that will be. Can we put others in danger trying to get her out?"

"I trust if I do as the Lord directs me, he will protect everyone involved. Besides, we need that information, and she's our best access to it." Sophie reminded him of the story of Paul's shipwreck. How the angel of the Lord promised him that if they did what he instructed; no life would be lost. Houston agreed and told her he would back her up.

Entering the Command Center, they went directly to Deputy Director Cosby and requested Sergeant Abbott, the Seal Team Three leader, and Vice Admiral Rossen come to the conference room at Command to be read into the plan. As head of the Naval submarine fleet, they would need Vice Admiral Rossen's collaboration on this plan.

While they were waiting for everyone to arrive, she asked to speak with Ms. Martin alone in her office.

Sophie directed her to the couch. As they were sitting, Sophie asked, "Ms. Martin, how far are you willing to go to get this information?"

Trindi squeezed her eyebrows together, forming a line between her eyes. "Ms. Star, if you are asking if I understand how critical this intel is, I assure you I do."

"I'm not trying to be confrontational, Trindi. I have a plan, and I need to know how much leeway you have to negotiate." Sophie had turned her body so she could look Trindi in the eyes.

Trindi squirmed a little. She didn't want to reveal to Sophie that the brass had already told her to give Sophie carte blanche.

"I have a plan to get the recordings, but I need you to approve asylum for Yon and his mother. If we give her asylum, he will help us retrieve the recordings. And you know they would execute Yon if we deported him back to North Korea after he's released from prison." Ms. Martin considered Sophie's statement beginning to understand how her mind worked. She wasn't crazy about giving away asylum to anyone who asked for it. But she had her directive and agreed to start the procedure.

The ladies left the office and entered the conference room where the others had arrived. The Vice Admiral brought his aide Petty Officer Ebby.

Cosby opened the meeting.

"Ms. Star, I take it you have a plan to get those recordings, can you lay it out for us?"

"I do, Sir. It's entirely dependent on details that need to be followed to the letter. For that reason, I need to have total autonomy in the supervision of this mission. When the mission is live, I need to be in full control. You know what I'm asking for, Sir, without it, I'm out."

Vice Admiral Rossen stood to his feet and slapped his hand on the table. "That is completely out of the question, young lady. No one orders my men but me or those above me." His face had turned red.

Sophie looked at Deputy Director Cosby, startled. She had never worked with Vice Admiral Rossen before. His vitriolic response surprised her. Sophie turned to Cosby, "sir, you know me, I wouldn't ask this if it weren't necessary."

"May I speak with Vice Admiral Rossen alone." It was an order, not a request.

Everyone left the conference room. It was apparent Petty Officer Ebby was as upset at the request as his boss. He went to sit in front of the big plasmas. Smith was sitting next to him.

"How can you tolerate working with *'that pushy woman,'*" PO Ebby snarled.

"*'That woman'* has given this team an unprecedented success rate. And she has *earned* the respect of everyone on this team, including me. So, if you have something negative to say, I suggest you take it somewhere else." Smith had turned to face the obstinate assistant.

"Well, that *'little lady'* will be put in her place shortly by the Vice Admiral." His tone intended as an insult.

Smith stood up his knees hitting the chair, pushing it off balance and to the floor as he did. He grabbed the Petty Officer by the shirt, lifting him from his seat and shoved him backward into a table. The commotion brought Timms and Mathews over.

"What's going on here?" Timms shouted, pulling Smith off of the man.

Neither said anything. Smith didn't want the comments the Petty Officer made to get back to Ms. Star; he shrugged his shoulders. The Petty Officer didn't want any more trouble either, so he moved to another seat.

"Kenny, are you alright?" Mathews asked.

"Yeah, I didn't like his attitude."

While the heated discussion was going on in the conference room, Sophie told Houston what she had asked Ms. Martin.

Ten minutes later, Cosby asked everyone to come back to the conference room.

"Ms. Star, we have agreed to your terms. I'm sure you want that in writing," Cosby stated. "Yes, Sir. It needs to be assimilated to all the parties who will be working in the field. The submarine, the Seal Team, everyone has to know that they answer to my orders, Sir." Sophie was firm on the matter.

"Alright, Ms. Star, let's move on," Cosby was annoyed. He could see that Vice Admiral Rossen was still fuming.

"Ms. Martin, will you take care of that?" Sophie asked. Ms. Martin nodded.

"Sir, I am convinced the only way to get those recordings is to have Yon's mother do it for us. Putting our men deep onto North Korean soil would, I'm sure, constitute an act of war in the site of their government."

"I'm not sure the President would care what they think. He is more concerned about an Anthrax virus unleashed on his citizens," Sergeant Abbott answered.

"I understand that sir, but why chance trouble if we have another choice. What I'm suggesting is that we contact Yon's mother at her place of work. We let her know that she needs to go to a certain location that only she would know." Sophie looked down at her hands that were on the table in front of her. "The next step would be getting the drone to her. How close can a submarine get to the shores of the Gulf of North Korea?"

"International waters limit is 13.8 miles. They patrol their waters above and below. We have gotten as close as 2 miles without detection on rare occasions. Which is top secret information, that can't leave this room." Vice Admiral Rossen ordered gruffly, still annoyed.

"How far away can we launch one of our drones?" Houston questioned.

"One of our smaller stealth drones can stay airborne for up to 23 hours," The Vice Admiral informed him.

"Can we operate it from here?"

"Yes, a drone pilot from the Navy can operate it," The Vice Admiral replied.

Sophie asked how soon a drone could be on a submarine in the yellow sea. Sergeant Abbott interjected he could send one with Seal Team 3, who can be in the air shortly to meet up with the sub. She gave him a list of what the drone needed to carry to Yon's mother.

"Agent Rodriguez, can you take a satellite image and a map into Yon. See if he could pinpoint his home as near as possible." She asked Sergeant Abbott if he could get one of his Korean speaking officers here as soon as possible. They had to wait for the translator, so Cosby dismissed the meeting. Everyone moved out of the conference room.

"Ms. Martin, I do need that in writing and signed by everyone that was in this room." Sophie had waited for everyone to leave before stopping her.

"I'll have it for you," she responded.

Sophie headed to her office. Houston went to make sure Yon had a bathroom break and some lunch.

Ms. Martin had circulated the letter of autonomy Sophie had requested. Smith read the letter, and a smile came across his face as he gave a glance at PO Ebby, who was still there reading it. Mathews transmitted the message to every agency that had a part in this operation. Verification of receipt with signatures requested.

The team had orders to take their breaks whenever possible. Once this mission started, it would require all hands on deck. Houston brought his and Sophie's lunch to her office.

"Houston, I would like to buy a fourplex in Trenton." She said, opening the Styrofoam container holding her lunch, keeping her eyes on it.

Houston stalled for a moment to look at her, puzzled at this statement. "That was random. What are you up to, sweetheart?"

"What makes you think I'm up to something?" She got up and wrapped her arms around his neck, where he was seated.

He laughed, "that," referring to the hug. He stood up and kissed Sophie's forehead, "when you get around to telling me the whole story, we'll talk about it."

After they ate, she gave him a list of things that needed to be done before they could bring Yon's mother out. He left to check on the team's progress.

The officer who spoke Korean had arrived. Sophie invited him into her office. He introduced himself as SPC Park.

"Specialist Park, thank you for helping us." She rose from her seat and greeted him.

"It's my pleasure, ma'am. What is it you need?" He and Houston moved to sit in the chairs across from her.

She explained the situation. A message needed to get to Yon Moon at the Hospital. Then she requested he stay with the team until the mission was over since he had Top Secret clearance.

After meeting with Sophie, Houston directed him to a chair next to Agent Smith. He introduced them, explaining what SPC Park's orders were.

Fons took the map where Yon had pinpointed his home to Smith. It was approximately five miles from the Gulf of North Korea. They had studied the terrain and found where the Sub needed to surface. The Combat Rubber Reconnaissance Craft carrying Seal Team 3 would launch from there, rendezvousing with Yon Moon at the shore. Yon had told Sophie that his mother was in good physical condition and would be able to walk five miles. She worked from 7 am to 3 pm North Korean time. It was 8:30 pm in DC; time to make the call. They all met back in the conference room.

"The initial phone call has been successful. I want to lay out the entire plan for you." Sophie began, standing behind her chair, resting her hands on the back of it.

"A US Navy Sub is heading to the rendezvous spot off the Gulf of North Korea. Seal Team 3 will arrive on the Sub in a few hours and will be the ones extracting Yon Moon and the recordings. At approximately 6:45 pm their time the Sub will surface in international waters. From there, the drone will take Yon Moon, a satellite phone, a GPS locator, and some instructions in Korean.

At approximately 7 pm her time, Yon Min-ji will call his mother and tell her where the recordings are. She is to get them and anything else in the hiding spot. Then she will walk to the rendezvous location already programmed into a hand-held GPS. The drone will follow her from a height that will keep it from view and off the radar. The seal team will leave the Sub waiting at the international water line. They will Take a CRRC from there and go in stealthily the last few miles. Once the recordings and Yon Moon are with Seal Team 3, they will return to the Sub. Are there any questions?" She moved her hands from the back of the chair, interlacing them, waiting for a response.

After seeing no one had questions, Cosby spoke up. "The plan seems pretty straight forward, Ms. Star. If you're comfortable letting your team go home, we can meet back here a 5 am. Everything that needs doing tonight is being done off-site."

"Sir, can the Navy pilot be here in the morning?" Houston asked.

"Yes, I'll see he gets the message to be here at 5 am."

"Who is in charge of the prisoner tonight, sir?" Houston asked.

"The FBI will put him back in holding at our facility and bring him here by 5 am."

"Thank you, sir." Houston went back to helping close the Command Center down for the night.

The team finished what they were doing and headed out the door. Before Sophie left, Deputy Director Cosby stopped her.

"Ms. Star, Vice Admiral Rossen was against your taking over this operation. He didn't appreciate your threat," Cosby said.

"I'm sorry, Sir. But I have a specific direction this plan has to follow. I'm afraid if anyone interferes or tries to take over, it will cost us the recordings or someone's life," she defended herself.

"I shut him down but only because the President gave me an order to give you whatever you asked. He wants those recordings. The threat of Anthrax has him walking the floor. What I'm saying is you need to watch your back with the Vice Admiral."

"Thank you. I trust my team to do that." She finished saying her goodbyes and headed home with Houston and Bully.

Houston drove through a fast food place on the way home. Rodriguez had sent for some government vehicles for their use. Houston grabbed their luggage; Sophie grabbed the meal and opened the back door to let Bully out. She was getting to appreciate her home here in DC as much as their condo in New York.

Sophie fed Bully and let him roam outside while they ate their dinner. It was still early, so they decided to get comfortable in bed and put on a movie. He set the alarm for 4 am. She snuggled up close to him, and before the movie was half over, she was sound asleep.

CHAPTER TWENTY

Sophie was out of the shower when the alarm went off. Houston could hear her praying when she was drying her hair. He made some eggs and bacon while she was dressing, then he got dressed and ate with her. They hurried with Bully to the car and made it to Command on time.

The team was prepped and ready for the missions. The first major hurdle was the Navy drone pilot getting the drone to Yon Moon without being shot down. They were doing the preflight exercise now. The pilot had eyes on the drone sitting on the surfaced sub. It was a 'go' whenever the order came through.

Houston and Sophie went into the interview room where Yon was waiting. Houston had the phone Min-ji was to use to contact his mother. The room mics and cameras were on. Houston and Sophie had comms so that they could hear the interpreted conversation in real-time.

"Houston, where have you been. No one is telling me anything." The fear of not knowing what's going on was driving Yon's emotions.

"We've been trying to work a plan the agencies would agree too," Houston explained.

Sophie told Yon what was going to happen. It surprised him; how simple it sounded. But he knew it was anything but that. Getting her to the rendezvous at the shore undetected was a significant obstacle.

"Sophie, those shores are patrolled by air and on foot. It's a big risk."

"Is it a risk your mother would be willing to take to get out of North Korea?"

Yon thought for a moment. "Yes, she would do anything to get out of that place."

"Are you willing to make the call."

"Yes. What is it you need me to say?"

"We need her to get a secure bag and put everything from the hiding place into it. Then she needs to put on several layers of clothes and a heavy jacket and get on the road. Is there anything she will fight to bring along with her?"

"Only her Bible; she loves it."

"That shouldn't be a problem, but she has a long, rugged walk ahead of her. She won't be able to make it if she's packing too much. There will be a drone meeting her at her reading place. It will have a satellite phone and a GPS locator. Do you think she will be able to work them if you explain it?"

"Yes, she is very smart."

They heard through their comms that Command was ready and it was time. Sophie left Yon to give the 'go-ahead' to the pilot.

"Ms. Star, luck is on our side tonight. The electricity is out in that entire vicinity. Not only the lights, but the security barriers are down in that sector," Lt. Murphy said.

"Lieutenant, it's not luck. God is in control. He did this." She noted the strange look on his face. "The mission is a 'go'."

She watched as the pilot maneuvered the drone to the location behind Yon's home. Lt. Murphy landed the drone and worked it into the bushes to hide it. He kept the camera on so they would know when Yon Moon came.

Ten minutes later, they saw her come around the edge of the building. She was a small woman, 5'2", couldn't weigh more than 120 pounds. She found the drone and moved it around, trying to locate a pocket of some sort with a phone in it. She finally found it and held it in her hands, waiting for the phone call.

Sophie headed back to the interview room. This time with the iPad Matt gave her so she could see what was happening.

"Alright, Yon, your mother is waiting for your phone call."

Sophie dialed the number for him and put it on speaker. The interpreter was translating into the comms so they could be sure he was doing as agreed.

"Yes?" Yon Moon answered on the first ring.

"Eomma," was all he could say because of the lump in his throat.

"Min-ji, is that you?" She said, crying.

Yon tried to compose himself, "Eomma, I'm so sorry I left you behind. Please forgive me."

"Min-ji, I only care that you are alright. I thought you were dead, like your father."

"I am fine, but the Americans have me in custody. I need your help."

"What can I do?" Her eyes were darting to and fro on alert in case she heard someone.

"Appa had a hiding place in the house. He has some recordings and other things in it. If I give them to the American's, they will reduce my sentence."

"Even if I find them, how will I get them to you?"

"They have someone waiting for you at the shore. They will take you away from there and bring you to America."

Yon Moon gasped, "they will take me to America?"

"Yes, if we help them."

Yon Moon explained to him what happened after the massacre. When they found out Yon defected, his uncle's

271

youngest son, Yon Won-Shik's family took over her home. She tried to get them out, but she no longer had any standing, and no one would help her. They let her stay, but Yon Moon became their servant.

Yon asked if she would be able to get to the hiding place without them seeing her. She said that Won-Shik's mother got very ill a few hours ago. He and the family went to the hospital to check on her.

Min-ji told her she needed a very secure bag to place the items in and then told her where to find them. She kept him on the line while she went to the hiding place.

"Eomma, is there anything else in there besides the recordings?" Yon asked.

"Yes, there's a stack of papers bound by rubber bands."

"Take everything, then go put on layers of clothing, a heavy coat and take a flashlight that has a narrow beam. When you're done, go back to the drone. You can't take anything else, Eomma. You will have to walk five miles on rough terrain."

"Can I take my Bible?" She pleaded.

He looked at Sophie, who nodded.

"Yes, Eomma, take your Bible and get out of there in a hurry."

Yon told her to bring the phone he had bought her, too. It only took her a few minutes to get back to the drone. It had reached pitch blackness in the time she was in the house. He told her to take the GPS from the drone and explained which buttons to push. He then called her on the cell and told her to keep it on in her pocket; they wanted to hear if anything went wrong.

"All you have to do is follow the arrow, turn when it turns and go straight when it goes straight."

Yon Moon headed in the direction indicated and started walking. The pilot got the drone back in the air. The darkness outside was so thick even her little flashlight appeared as a beacon. Murphy used the night vision camera.

"You did good, Yon. I'm sure your mom will make it here safe." Sophie knew it wasn't smart to promise something like that, but she trusted God's leading.

Sophie and Houston took the phone back to Command. They needed to hear everything that went on. They watched as she progressed.

"Agent Smith, how fast is she moving?" Sophie asked.

"She's walking at about three miles per hour right now, but she's on flat ground. I expect her to slow down to about a mile and a half shortly."

"I need a time frame for the Seal Team."

Smith figured it out and told her. "I'd say about three hours."

"Sergeant Abbott, can you hear me," Sophie spoke into the mic.

"Yes, Ms. Star. What do you have for me?"

"She is heading your way. We expect it to take her about three hours."

"Understood. It will take my team over an hour to row to the rendezvous point. I will have my team there at least forty-five minutes ahead of Yon Moon in case of trouble," Sergeant Abbott said.

"We should go for an hour ahead, Sergeant, in case she's faster than we predict."

"Understood."

Everything was in motion; all they could do now was wait and pray. Sophie went to her office, watching the infrared satellite images on the plasmas from there.

She was two and a half hours in, Yon Moon's pace had steadily slowed down. She was still almost thirty minutes away from the rendezvous point.

Houston got closer to the plasmas, "What is that." He pointed to a red figure moving in the direction of Yon Moon. Sophie left her office to get closer to the plasmas.

Mathew started zooming in on the picture.

"It's most likely one of the patrols," Rossen suggested.

"She's heading right in his path," Timms added.

"Agent Mathews, can you make some sort of noise through that cell to get her attention?"

"I'll try, but if it's too loud, the patrol might pick it up."

He sent a low-frequency tone to the cell. No response. Trying different tactics still got no results, the figure was getting closer. Suddenly Yon Moon was tumbling down a small ditch. The noise brought the soldier down on top of her. When the soldier saw her, he hollered at her in Korean. She stood wiping herself off.

"Stop where you are, or I will shoot."

Yon Moon stopped still in her tracks; the bundle remained on her back. The soldier told her to turn around and climb back up.

The Seal Team waiting at the shore was also tracking her by the satellite feed. They could see what Command was seeing. They were only about a ten minute run from her location.

When the soldier saw her face, he said, "Yon Moon? What are you doing here?" His voice was familiar to her.

"Seal Team, get ready to eliminate the soldier and grab the subject!" Rossen ordered.

"Belay that order, Team 3; this is Ms. Star, your directive says you only take orders from me. Stay where you are."

"Understood," came the response.

The tension in the room was palpable. Sophie didn't like her team working with this added stress.

"Your lack of experience is going to put this mission in jeopardy, Ms. Star." Rossen had moved right up to her, his face red.

"Sir listen to his voice, he knows her, there's no hostility, she's in no danger right now. What do you suppose will happen if the Seal Team shows up? I don't want a death if we can prevent it." She answered him with a calmness she didn't know she possessed.

"Han Kang-Dae this is not your patrol route, what are you doing here?"

"The schedule changed; no one knows why. I will have to arrest you. What are you doing out here alone in the dark?"

"I'm leaving Han; God has answered my prayers."

"What on earth is she doing. He'll call for backup." The Vice Admiral was incensed.

Sophie ignored him. She had a peace about what was going on.

"How is that possible?" The soldier asked.

"I can't tell you. Please let me go," she begged.

To her surprise and everyone else's he threw down his rifle pleading with her, "please, Yon Moon, please take me with you."

"What about your family, Han, you will never see them again."

He told her how his family hated him now that he was a Christian. Han tried to testify to them of the power of the Cross. But his family was brainwashed by the propaganda the Supreme Leader forced fed them. They were blind to the truth. His father told him if he didn't deny Christ, they would turn him in.

"I cannot stay, Yon Moon. You know what will happen to me if they turn me in."

"Alright, come with me."

"Team 3 expect a second passenger, a soldier, he is a defector and seeking asylum," Sophie ordered.

Houston went to Ms. Martin and asked her to make up papers for asylum for Han Kang-Dae.

"I can't give out asylum like it's candy, Agent Townsend." It was clear she was annoyed.

"His knowledge of the North Korean military and their defenses will be firsthand. We have no idea if our intel is accurate," Houston replied. She hesitantly agreed that it would be valuable information.

"Ms. Star, you do not have the authority to go off-script. I'm going to take over this mission," Vice Admiral Rossen demanded.

"Not so, Admiral. Ms. Star has the Commander in Chief's approval to make any changes she needs, to ensure this mission is successful. Now please move aside." Cosby stepped in to back up Sophie.

The drone and satellite continued to follow them. It was evident when the Seals spotted them. Several figures surrounded the two and double-timed them over to the waiting CCRC. The pilot landed the drone next to the Seals, who put it in the boat with them. You could see the vessel move into the water and away from shore. They gave a whoop and holler, but Sophie was still concerned.

"We are not out of the woods until they are on that sub, gentlemen," she admonished them.

They watched as the small vessel seem to struggle to gain any ground against the currents.

"Command we are fighting strong currents. It's taking us too long. Permission to put our small motor on?" Sergeant Abbott requested.

"Not yet, hold your position, keep from drifting, but otherwise, don't stir the waters."

"Understood, ma'am."

"Sophie, what is it?" Houston asked.

"I can't explain it. Can you get Agent Mathews to see if the satellite camera can widen the view of the waters surrounding them?"

Houston went to Mathews to relay the request. On the screen came a broader view of the gulf surrounding the boat.

"What's this red image here?" She pointed to something moving on the water.

"It appears to be a boat moving pretty fast. That's the heat of the engine; it doesn't have its running lights on. They must be smugglers, but they are coming right into the path of our men."

"Sergeant, you must paddle back toward shore. There is an unauthorized vessel coming into your path, move, move now!" Rodriguez ordered.

You could see the mat boat struggle to get out of the way of the speed boat.

"Do you have a visual yet?"

"No, it's pitch black out here, you can't see one foot in front of your face. But I can hear something faintly."

"They're almost on top of you, keep paddling out of the way toward shore."

When the boat passed them, they were so close they could have reached out and touched it as it went by. The CCRC boat was rocking in the wash.

"Agent Smith, how far away does that speedboat have to be not to hear CCRC's motor."

"If they use the small motor, they're far enough away now," Agent Smith informed her.

"Permission to use the small motor now, Sergeant," Sophie relayed.

The Seal Team let the Sub know when they were close and watched it surface. After everyone was on board and the sub re-submerged, a call came in from the sub's Commander.

"Command, we have your cargo and are on our way to rendezvous with the Naval Aircraft Carrier, who will transport it to DC by jet. Any more instructions?"

Agent Smith looked to Sophie for direction. She shook her head.

"No, all's well. Thank you for your assist," Agent Smith extended.

When the transmission was over, Deputy Director Cosby got their attention.

"This was a job well done. I will inform the President the recordings will be in our hands shortly. You're all relieved until we have them to assess. Congratulations."

This time the team looked at Sophie before they started celebrating. The smile on her face gave them the permission they needed.

It would be hours until they knew what was on those tapes. They were getting ready to leave when Sophie asked Houston if he would make sure Yon went back to his cell. She didn't want him sitting in the interview room, handcuffed, and missing his meals. She also wanted him to know his mother was safe, Houston told her he already took care of it.

Once home, Sophie went in to take a nap. Houston asked Fons to come down to watch the recorded football game they missed. He dug snacks from the fridge, and they enjoyed the afternoon.

Houston grilled steaks for dinner, and Fons stayed and ate with them.

After Fons left, Sophie turned to Houston on the couch and started explaining the plan she had in mind.

"If Ms. Martin will consider the great service Yon provided to the US, I'm hoping she will give him a light sentence. Recommending a minimum-security prison in Trenton."

Sophie laid out her plan. "If we bought a fourplex in Trenton, it would house Yon Moon and Han Kang-Dae. Han could work his rent off by helping to get the place remodeled. Then we can give him half off for managing the apartments. Han could be close to Yon Moon to help her if she needs it, and she won't feel so alone. And I would like to pay for English lessons for them.

"Do you think our Church in Trenton could find a Korean speaking Church for them? They could help them get assimilated into the community. Yon Moon would have free rent until she can get a job and she would be close to the prison her son's in," Sophie said.

"You know my mom would take care of everything and love doing it. But are you sure you want to take those kinds of funds out of your account?"

"I like my money working for me, besides God gave me money for a reason, not to sit on it. The increase in property value will give me better returns than leaving my cash in the bank. The profit from the rented apartments can go into our household account."

He wasn't crazy about the idea of her profits not going back to her account, but he let it go. She asked if he would manage the remodel once they find a place.

"I don't want to spend more than $800,000, and I trust you to help me find the best property," she finished.

He liked her plan, and remodeling was something he would enjoy doing again. The more they talked, the more excited they became.

They called his parents to tell them the idea without going into too much detail of who Yon Moon and Han Kang-Dae were. They were all on speaker, so everyone was engaged in the conversation.

"As soon as Yon Moon and Han Kang-Dae can get their driver's license, I want to buy them cars. Dad, can you handle finding them cars?"

"Yes, but I insist on purchasing them, I want to be a part too."

"I know the Church will want to furnish their apartments; I can oversee that. And I want them to stay here until their apartments are ready," Lily added. Jack staunchly agreed.

They went on discussing it for another half hour, then said their goodbyes.

"I told you they would love doing this." Houston grinned as he hung up.

Deputy Director Cosby called at 10:30 pm, telling them the recordings were in his custody. He was disseminating them to the appropriate departments. He asked to have the team meet at 6 am. Sophie asked where Yon Moon and Han Kang-Dae were. Cosby told her that they were at the temporary housing complex on base and they had an interpreter with them. Sophie felt comfortable with that. Houston asked Fons to call the team to meet in the morning.

CHAPTER TWENTY-ONE

Yon Moon couldn't quit shivering. She wasn't cold but scared. Being unable to speak with anyone in a foreign place; is a horrible, lonely feeling. The very air had an alien atmosphere to it. Yon Moon had never seen another country even on TV or the internet. She felt an aloneness she couldn't put into words. Yon Moon thanked God for getting her and Han out of North Korea, but this was all strange and frightening. She didn't know where her son was or what would happen to her now.

The interpreter told her she would be given asylum, but she didn't know what that meant. They gave her and Han a good meal and sent them to their rooms for the evening. The Seal team that met her in North Korea took everything in her bag but her Bible. All she knew to do was to read God's word and trust He would make a better life for her. One where she could serve God openly.

The conference room filled at 6 am with Directors, Deputy Directors, Admirals, and administrators. Their assistants were lining the back wall behind their bosses. The team was surprised; they had no idea what was going on.

Sophie asked Houston to get Yon, his mother, and Han Kang-Dae here. She wanted Yon Moon to be able to see her son, and she also wanted to speak with them.

Deputy Director Cosby opened the meeting. "Ms. Star, although a lot of the information was outdated. It appears your team has uncovered a gold mine of valuable information for the US. Among the papers are locations of imminent terrorist activity in Europe. Those were taken by armed guards directly to the President. He will contact the authorities in those countries. We have a list of all the clients Yon Se-bin sold to over the years. Plus, a list of his suppliers of money grade paper and magnetic strips.

"We also have intel we sent to our counterparts in England about a bombing planned in a few weeks. We've offered to help any way we can." Cosby stopped to take a drink of water. "We have the tapes that belonged to Yon Se-bin's. It appears the counterfeit money we're concerned about traveled through Mexico and entered the country yesterday. The final destination is a storage unit in Dallas, Texas. We have the times and day the cell leaders are to pick up their funds. Each cell is to pick up a million in the next few days.

"The Anthrax is being flown into a private field in two days. A terrorist cell member is supposed to pick it up at the airport."

The Director of the Secret Service spoke up. "We have agencies handling these issues, Ms. Star. We want your team to stand by as back up if something goes awry. All of our teams will be stretched to their limit, and we may need your help." He said while gesturing his hand to the others in the room.

Before she could reply, Lance Sterling, the Under Secretary of Homeland Security, interrupted.

"Rather than take all the cell leaders into custody, I would like the opportunity to follow some. Maybe capture others in their cell group. I don't know that we would have another opportunity like this to do it. Although they tend to work independently, they must have a way to communicate. Getting more insight into their behaviors would be beneficial." The Director of the Secret Service Adam Bean, answered before Cosby could reply.

"I agree. Even with all the HUMINT we have, there are few details on how cells disseminate information and funds."

Deputy Director Cosby waited to see if any of the others wanted to say anything before he responded. Putting his palms on the table, using them to push him to his feet, he said, "if we all agree this information would be useful, let's decide on four of the ten leaders to surveil. The rest we'll take down immediately. Is that agreeable?" He asked and looked to each person sitting at the table for a response.

As each person nodded when he directed his eyes to them, he added. "Done. The FBI, HS CTU, the US CBPU, and the SS will be running this operation. They should decide who they want to follow. Is that acceptable?" He waited again for a response; everyone agreeing, he moved on. "I will have my task force following your missions in real-time. They will be ready if you need their backup."

He looked to Sophie, "Ms. Star, do you have anything to add?"

"Yes sir, may I make a suggestion?" She waited for his response.

"You have the floor, Ms. Star." Cosby seated himself, gesturing for her to stand.

"Sir, we used a spray tagging agent on the counterfeit funds in Alex Ivanov's condo. I recommend that the counterfeit money in the storage unit be tagged. Since we don't know which cell leader will take which stack, we will have to tag it all." She took a breath looking to those around the table. "This would be precautionary in case we lose sight of one of those we are trying to surveil."

"Ms. Star, do you have any idea how much time that will take?" The Under Secretary of Homeland Security replied. Not bothering to look at her but looking at Cosby.

It was Houston who stood and backed her plan. "We do, sir, but the alternative is unacceptable. As good as your teams are, it is too risky not to take precautions. None of us want that much money in the hands of men who want to do great harm to this country."

Cosby gestured for Houston and Sophie to sit down and said. "Under Secretary Sterling, I understand that the extra time and effort of doing this is a major factor. But Agent Townsend is correct. If these funds get away from us, are you going to be the one to tell President Madden that it was too much work to take precautions?"

The room went silent at the rebuke to the Under Secretary. No one moved. Finally, Sterling nodded his head in agreement.

US Custom and Border Protection Commissioner Maddie McDonald spoke up. "Sir, it would be beneficial to have one of your team on-site with us. Everyone here knows how successful your team is at operations as big as this one. Their instinct could be the difference between success and failure."

Cosby looked over to Houston. "Agent Townsend, who can you send?"

Houston looked to Fons, who nodded agreement. "Sir, I would recommend Agent Rodriguez. He has been with us on every operation and knows how we work."

"Ok, Agent Rodriguez will go with you to Dallas," Cosby said to Ms. McDonald.

After discussing a few more details, Cosby closed the meeting.

The crowd slowly dispersed, several of the men staying to ask questions of other team members. Agent Rodriguez informed Commissioner McDonald he could leave with their team anytime.

When all the big wigs were gone, Deputy Director Cosby called the group together.

"The President wants to give each member of this team the Presidential Gold Medal. It will be a private ceremony in the Oval Office, due to the covertness of the Task Force." Adding that it was an honor for the team and how pleased he was, their work was recognized; then he left.

The guards escorted Yon from the FBI holding. About a half-hour later, the door opened, and Yon's mother and Han Kang-Dae were allowed in to see him. Yon had only one hand cuffed to the table, so he was able to stand and hold her when she came rushing over to him. They cried on each other's shoulders for a long time. Han stood there, reverently with his head down; he was praying for Yon.

"Eomma, you are here safe. I'm so sorry I left you behind." They were speaking Korean.

"Yon, do you see now, that the God I pray to is real? How else could I have gotten out of that awful place."

"Yes, Eomma, He answered your prayers."

Yon Moon took this time to preach to her son the truth about the Gospel. She unraveled the lies he was taught his whole life by the Supreme Leader and his father. Moon didn't know if another opportunity would ever come up. She poured out her heart to him. Han Kang-Dae added his testimony to it, and together they led Yon in the sinner's prayer.

Sophie had asked Ms. Martin to meet her in her office before she left. Houston went in with her; they all sat down.

"Ms. Martin, let me tell you upfront my husband does not see these things the way I do; he is a law and order man. I try to look at the actors and their motives. Are they unredeemable? Or were the actions taken by them more circumstance and opportunity?" She took a breath, considering her words carefully. "Is our goal justice with mercy, or on what will play well in the news?"

Ms. Martin felt Sophie was questioning her integrity. "Just get to it, Ms. Star."

"What I'm asking you is done in your office every day. I want to know based on the enormous value of the information Yon gave us, if you will give Yon a light sentence. Also, I would like him placed in a minimum-security prison in Trenton."

"Wow, you've been thinking about this a lot." Trindi responded.

"Yes, I have. I know prosecutors have given hit men lighter sentences if they turn on their employer. I don't see how this is any different."

"Ms. Star, we have a lot of evidence against Mr. Yon. Thanks to your team. Yet, you're right, this is something we often do, and I'm not opposed to it."

"What kind of deal would you be willing to make?"

"He needs to do some jail time. At least three years with parole available in 18 months."

Sophie turned to her husband, "Houston, I'd like your opinion."

"Prosecutors make deals all the time I don't like. But, considering the information he gave us, it's appropriate in this case. I do agree he needs to spend some time in jail. We don't know what kind of crimes he committed before we met him. But we can't judge him on things we can't prove, so three years seems reasonable."

"Thank you, Houston." She looked at Ms. Martin, "If you can get that approved, I would be grateful, Trindi."

"Why do you care so much about this man?" She asked.

"He has a praying mother." She replied, knowing Ms. Martin wouldn't understand.

Ms. Martin began to stand, but Sophie said she had another request.

"As I mentioned before, I would like to make sure the three of them get on the path to citizenship even though Yon will have a criminal record. He did the US a great service, and there is no way he can return to North Korea. He would immediately be put in prison and tortured."

Sophie took a breath, "and I would like Yon Moon to get a stipend while her son is in prison. It will take her a while to get a job. She'll likely need to learn English first. Also, Han Kang-Dae will need a stipend for at least six months."

"Ms. Star, that is unorthodox," letting out an annoyed grumble. "I don't know if I could sell that idea to my boss." She was upset by the number of requests asked.

"Please try, consider it a debt I will owe you; you may want my help on something one day," Sophie bartered.

"I want to move Yon Moon and Han Kang-Dae out of the base right away. Houston's parents in Trenton offered to house them until they have other accommodations."

Ms. Martin told her she would try but made no promises.

"Are Vice Admiral Rossen's men finished with Han Kang-Dae? I know he wanted a thorough briefing into North Korea's military condition," Ms. Martin asked.

"I believe they finished last night. But we can make sure Han Kang-Dae is available to come whenever needed," Houston responded.

They left the office, and the team decided to take a two-hour lunch.

Houston and Sophie went into the interview room. Yon, his mother, and Han Kang-Dae were waiting. The reunion had been emotional; they were chatting away in Korean. When Houston and Sophie came in, the others stood.

"Please sit, Min-ji, can you interpret for us? I have information she needs to understand." Nodding toward his mother.

Han offered Sophie his chair, and Houston leaned against the door frame. She told Yon the recordings and papers were of value to the US. Because of that, they were willing to give him a light sentence. He would go to a minimum-security prison in Trenton. His sentence would be for three years, with parole available in 18 months. She told him he must be on his best behavior so that he might get out early.

Yon asked what was going to happen to his mother while he was incarcerated. Sophie told him the plan to get her an apartment in Trenton so she could be close to him for visits. She would have a stipend from the government while he was in prison.

As he was translating all this to Yon Moon, you could see her tears of relief to know God had her future planned. Yon Moon asked what would happen to Han Kang-Dae. Sophie explained he would have an apartment and a stipend also until he could get work. He would have to continue to cooperate with the government. Give them whatever information he had.

Yon Moon stood up and came to Sophie and hugged her. She wished she could tell her they were Christians too, but she had to maintain her cover.

Houston told them they would stay where they are until his parents came to drive them to Trenton. Then the guard took Yon back to FBI holding. And ordered transport for Yon Moon and Han Kang-Dae.

The team decided that Matt should accompany Fons to Dallas. SRT was heading down with them. They would be the ones that would follow the target for the FBI. The Homeland Security office in Dallas agreed to handle the tracking. The Secret Service would tag the money. Houston sent everyone home to rest until the action started.

Bully was glad they were home and demanded attention. Sophie put one of Carol's dinners in the oven and sat with Houston. They needed to call his folks.

"Mom, can you get dad on the line too." She called for Jack to come to the phone.

"We're here, Houston."

"We're ready to send Yon Moon and Han Kang-Dae to Trenton. They're in a temporary housing unit on base now, but they have nothing, no clothes, no money. I hate to ask, we planned on making the trip to take them to you, but we can't leave right now."

"We are more than happy to come, we can be there tomorrow night," Jack said.

"Your father has been getting things ready here so that they will be comfortable. I've contacted the Korean community center in town to see if they could send a translator. We'll need help to communicate once they get here," Lily added.

"Sophie negotiated a stipend for them. They will have money coming, but I don't know how soon it will start."

"You know that's not a problem. I can supply clothes and food until they get it," Jack insisted.

"Dad, there's one more thing. No one can tell that Sophie and I are part of law enforcement. I don't know how to get that message to everyone involved. I'm a bodyguard, and Sophie is an accountant. It's vital, Dad."

"We'll tell the Pastor he'll make sure everyone knows."

They visited for a while and then said their goodbyes.

After dinner, they watched some TV and then went to get some much-needed sleep.

Sophie asked Ms. Martin to meet with her in her office. She wanted to know if she got the approval on all her requests. While Sophie waited for her, she talked with Sissy about yesterday's events.

Ms. Martin came in, dressed more casually. Usually outfitted in a power suit. Today she had on a straight skirt and silk top. Her hair was down, and she had makeup on. Sophie couldn't help but wonder what was going on. She gave Trindi that quizzical look every woman understands when they went to her office.

"I have a dinner date after work. If that's what you're wondering?" Sophie half laughed at Trindi's response.

"Is it Lieutenant Murphy? I saw him eyeing you the other day." Sophie had a big smile on her face.

"You are way too observant, Ms. Star." She waved her off.

"It is him." All Sophie got was a sly smile in response. "Well, you look great."

"I know that's not why you called me in here. If you are wondering about your requests," she gave a disparaging look to Sophie. "It appears that no one wants to say no to you right now. It's a good place to be, but it doesn't last forever. Don't think I can pull this off again. And I will call on that favor you owe me some time. Your results have gotten you a free pass, Ms. Star. Even though I don't particularly agree with what you're doing."

"Thank you, Trindi. I know you disagree." Sophie was so pleased she stepped forward to hug her; then thought better of it. If Trindi noticed she hid it well.

Ms. Martin left Command, and Sophie headed back to work with the team. They heard from Matt that the only security cameras on the storage unit belonged to the business. US Border Enforcement and Protection was in control of hacking into them to set up a loop. Then Secret Service could get in unseen and tag the money. It was going to take a while.

The spray they were using would attach to the surface of the bills when applied, keeping its potency for a couple of months. Ten agents were working on it. Fons was at the Command Center at Homeland Security headquarters in Dallas. The agencies involved would have to decide who they would follow on the fly. Until they could do face recognition, they had no idea who the targets were.

Sophie knew it would be hours before any of the action started and suggested the team take a break. She wanted to talk to Yon before he got transported to Trenton. She was waiting for him in an interrogation room when the guard escorted him in. The guard took one cuff and attached it to the bar on the table.

"Ms. Star, is everything alright? Is my mother ok?" Yon was asking while he sat. The guard stayed in the room.

"Yes Min-ji, everything is fine. I wanted to talk to you. We may not have access to you after this." She moved her hands from her lap and put them on the table between them. Interlacing her fingers. "Min-ji, I want you to know Houston, and I will make sure your mother's taken care of until you get out of prison."

He reached for her hand to thank her, but a guard gave him a warning.

"I can't thank you enough for what you have done for her," he hesitated, "for both of us."

"I was curious about what you're going to do when you get out of prison." She wanted to make sure he had made a real change in his life.

"I don't know, I no longer have the plates, but Ms. Star...I have to tell you I don't plan on doing anything illegal. My mother has been praying for my salvation for many years, and yesterday, I turned my life over to Christ." Yon bowed his head. Sophie saw a tear when he looked back up at her. "I know I promised I'd be in business with you, but I don't want that kind of life anymore. I'm sorry."

"No Min-ji, it's the right thing to do. In prison, you can get permission to continue your education. Would you like that?"

"Yes, I would. Will the DOJ confiscate my four million dollars in the Hong Kong bank?"

"I wouldn't know that." Sophie did know but felt that was information she couldn't reveal. Ms. Martin was going to try to confiscate it. She knew it would be next to impossible getting it released from a bank in Hong Kong. Yon was Korean and not an American citizen; the US had no grounds to request its confiscation. There was a good chance he would still have access to it when he got out.

"What will you and Houston do now?"

"We've always wanted to open a CPA and consulting firm; we'll likely do that. What kind of field would you want to study?"

"I'm intrigued with your laws, can a criminal become a lawyer in the US?"

"It's happened. That's a great idea. I know you'll get a waiver to allow you to become an American citizen. The information you provided with those documents will go a long way in our war on terrorism. Do you think you'll stay in the US?"

"Yes, my mother has wanted to live here since she became a Christian. I would never move her away."

They chatted for a few more minutes, and then she headed back to the Command Center. She was certain Yon was going to do what he said. She couldn't wait to tell Houston.

Fons had called to let the team know everything was a 'go' on their end. The agencies involved added drones and pilots for backup and had them on standby. Now it was a waiting game.

Houston and Sophie had nothing urgent at the Command Center, so they headed home to meet his parents. They wanted to be the ones to introduce them to Yon Moon and Han Kang-Dae.

Sophie had preordered a nice dinner from Carol. She wanted them to have a meal before they went over to the temporary housing on base. In the middle of setting the table, they showed up.

Jack didn't look at all tired from the trip and was excited to meet his soon to be houseguests. Lily was equally as excited. During the meal, they discussed all the preparations made with the help of the Church. They all want Yon Moon and Han Kang-Dae to have success assimilating into their new life. As soon as the meal was over, they were anxious to pick up their new guests.

The interpreter introduced Jack and Lily. He explained Jack and Lily were there to take them to Trenton. They conversed through the interpreter for a while. When they could see Yon Moon and Han were comfortable, they packed up what little they had. Said their goodbyes and got on the road.

CHAPTER TWENTY-TWO

Everyone made it into the Command Center early to make sure the communications were set up. It was time for the first cell leader to show up. Deputy Director Cosby and the Under Secretary of HS Lance Stirling were waiting with them in DC. Commander Devlon Corrigan was running the active Task Force operation in Dallas. As Commander of the HS Counter Terrorism Unit, he was the most senior official on-site.

Matt was in Dallas with Fons running media. He put the cameras inside and out of the storage units, up on the plasmas. DC linked to Dallas in real-time.

"Someone's approaching." Everyone stopped what they were doing to watch.

The chatter filtered in from the teams on site. All eyes were on the man approaching the storage unit. He looked around to see if anyone was watching and then proceeded to work the combination lock. He came into view inside the unit. He went to one of the duffle bags filled with money, opened it, did a quick overview of the bundles then zipped it up again. His face was in full view of the camera. Sissy started running it through the facial recognition software Homeland Security provided.

The US Customs operations manager spoke, "team one, do you have eyes on the subject?"

"Yes sir, we will take over from here." Their SRT lead reported.

HS designated a Global Positioning System Satellite for this operation. The four teams following cell leaders were fitted for visual and sound.

Sissy got a hit on the first target, "he's an Iranian with a Saudi passport. A college student who came into the country on a student visa. He attends Western Michigan University in Kalamazoo. His name is Navid Rafati; he's not on any watch list; age 26." Sissy was handling facial recognition, passing what she learned on to Dallas.

"We need all the personal information you can get, Ms. Corban," Sophie replied.

The second subject approached and did precisely the same thing. Team one of the Secret Service took that one. Sissy processed facial recognition and found a match. It came up as Jihan Shafael. He was not here legally and was on a watch list; his last known location was Sudan.

It was like clockwork from there every two hours; they had names to match all but two faces of the ten suspects, of which six were immediately taken into custody. The respective teams had all the information known for three of the four targets that were being surveilled. Two subjects were driving. Two were taking the train. They couldn't go by plane with the amount of money in their possession. The FBI and US Customs had the addresses of the two on the trains. Dallas Command would have SUV's and drones available for the Agents when the suspects they were following got off the train.

The other two teams would tail the men driving, so the terrorist and the money never left their site. The small stealth military drones the teams were using could stay up for 23 hours. The drones allowed the surveillance teams some distance. They were using the Ion Tiger that runs on a Protonex hydrogen fuel cell, one of the newer drones in use.

FBI techs had addresses for three of the targets and put cameras and mics in their homes. It was reasonable to assume that's where they were going. If not, it was still the best plan they had. It would take the first subject 18 hours to get home.

Now it was time to turn their attention to the critical operation; how to capture the Anthrax. The plane was landing in 45 minutes. The FBI, US Customs, and Hazmat teams surrounded the field, out of sight. They had to wait for the plane to shut down its engines so it couldn't rev up and take off again. The teams had spent hours deciding the best time to advance. Since US Customs had a Hazmat unit, they were designated to go onboard and take out the Anthrax; after the terrorists were in custody. They had Hazmat respirator face masks and full Hazmat-suits.

The plane was coming down in Oklahoma City, on a remote field, belonging to an abandoned ranch. Someone had kept the airstrip in good condition, no doubt being used by smugglers. US Customs would put it on their watch list.

"The plane is in our field of vision." One of the teams was narrating the scene. The plane circled the area checking for intruders and then lined up to land.

The touchdown was smooth, and the aircraft taxied close to a hangar. The team moved in, still out of sight. The minute the door opened, stairs down, FBI agents aimed their Colt M4 Carbine machine guns at the pilot. The pilot knew the window would be no match for the bullets and immediately put his hands in the air. A three-man US Customs team wearing Level B Hazmat masks and bodysuits stormed up the stairs and boarded. The narrow quarters of the small plane made this the most dangerous part. They could hear the shouted commands through the speakers. Fuzzy images were coming from inside the plane. There was some gunfire, and then the all-clear was heard. One terrorist was dead, the other wounded. They were taken from the aircraft along with the pilot.

There were three men of Persian descent in custody. One being the pilot, after being checked for contamination by the Hazmat Team, they put him in cuffs. The man in the body bag was also tested and taken to a waiting van. The wounded man was tested and taken to the hospital with the FBI guarding him.

Others in full Level A Hazmat outfits boarded the plane. They had on body cams so the teams could follow. After a thorough check of the plane, inside and out, they found only one metal cylinder in the bathroom. The team used their meters to check for leakage. Convinced it was secure and there was only one container, Hazmat hauled it off in a sealed containment unit. The FBI confiscated the plane, and that ended the successful operation.

In the morning, not much had changed. All teams were on point, and the subjects were still heading in the directions of their homes.

By 1 pm the CBP team followed Navid Rafati into his parking spot at his off-campus apartment, in Kalamazoo, MI. Sissy put the transmissions from his residence on one of the plasmas.

They saw him enter the apartment and put the duffle bag on the floor next to the couch and lock the door. He rubbed his hands down his face as he walked into the bathroom. He was exhausted after driving straight through in heavy rain. He grabbed the duffle and headed to the bedroom to get some sleep. There was a loose board on the floor under his bed. He took the money out of the bag and placed it under the floorboards, then moved the bed back over it. Team one could see the same things on their computer. They landed the drone, replaced the fuel cell, and slept in shifts while things were quiet.

The Dallas CTU Team was getting off the train in Silicon Valley. The California CTU met them with a vehicle and a drone. The team thanked them and took off. Silicon Valley would have the least cell members if it were the cyber cell.

They caught up to Jihan Shafael on the road to his home address. Jihan had slept on the train; he was ready to distribute the money. He made his first phone call.

"As-salamu 'alaykum," came the voice on the other end.

"Wa 'alaykumu s-salam," was Jihan's response.

They continued their conversation in English.

"Sa´id, we have it; the money to buy more time on the Supercomputer," Jihan related.

"That's great. I'll be right over."

Sa´id showed up about thirty minutes later. Once in the room, Sissy started running facial recognition. Jihan gave him half of the money, which was a surprise to the teams. Could this team only have the two members? If so, they could take them down now.

"Jihan, we need to work together."

"No, you know that's not allowed."

"If they want us to take down the entire east coast electrical grid on Thanksgiving Day, then we have no choice. We need to collaborate."

You could hear the chatter pick up over the speaker. This operation was paying off in a big way. The team on Jihan called in for direction.

The lead CTU agent in Dallas ordered a takedown.

"Wait," Sissy stood addressing Sophie. "if we can wait to see if they talk about how they intend to do this, we can work on countermeasures for the future."

"She's right, and we can get more incriminating evidence against them." Matt interrupted through the speaker.

Sophie agreed, she got on the line with Commander Corrigan. She requested they hold on the takedown, explaining the reasoning behind it.

The Commander paused for a moment, then got on the comms and said, "Cancel that last order. We are holding position for more information. Stand down until further notice."

Fortunately, the two agents were not spotted by the suspects and moved back to their vehicle to wait for more instructions.

Sissy's computer came up with the name of the second cell member while she listened intently to the technical conversation going on between the men.

His name is Sa´id Arbab; he was born in the US. His parents were Muslim refugees who love this country. Sa´id met Jihan while working in Silicon Valley and took up the cause. They gleaned the information from bits of social media.

The men talked for two hours while the CTU Agents waited for the word to breach. Finally, the order came to breach with a no-knock warrant. You could hear the standard orders shouted. It was all on bodycams so the teams could see it go down. They took out the men in cuffs and transported them to HS headquarters for later transport to DC. All the suspects would transfer to DC for interrogation. The CTU team stayed and collected everything of interest in the apartment then sealed it.

"Excellent job, that attack is off the table, at least for now." The Commander congratulated the teams.

Surveillance is a slow and tedious process. It would be hours before the subject heading for DC would get home. They still had no idea where the fourth cell leader was heading.

The DC cell leader made it home; the Secret Service team pulled across the street to park. Facial recognition brought up the name Mark Taylor. He had been recruited online and had changed his name to Muhsin Rafiq. The small house he rented had cameras and mics.

As the Secret Service team waited outside, they watched on the SUV's installed computer. Muhsin went straight to the phone and made his first call.

The phone rang three times before someone picked it up and said, "Hello?"

"As 'salamu 'alaykum," Muhsin replied.

"Wa 'alaykumu s-salam," came the hesitant response. No names were spoken; no camaraderie detected. "Be here in one hour."

That was the entire conversation. Muhsin did the same thing five more times staggering their arrival.

The SS Tier One team leader in Dallas spoke to the men in the field, trying to come up with a workable plan.

"Can we take them down one at a time without Muhsin seeing?" The team leader queried.

"Sir, only if we have more help. We could follow each one as they leave the area and then take him down out of sight of the house."

"How much help will you need," came the quick response.

"If we have two agents in an unmarked van close by, we could take down the suspect, and the van could hold them. Then we would be free to arrest the next one. Muhsin has staggered them in such a way we could make it work." The team in the field responded.

"So you are requesting an unmarked van with a two-member team parked close to function as a holding cell." The team leader repeated the request.

"Yes sir."

You could hear the Dallas command center in the background making arrangements. "That's a go. The driver will alert you to their location once they are in place."

"Understood."

The Command Center was all focused on the DC team when Timms got their attention.

"Ma'am, we have a situation."

Houston and Sophie moved over to where Timms was on the computer putting up an accident on the plasma.

"What is this Timms?" Houston asked, looking at the screen.

"Sir, the FBI SRT following the fourth cell leader, got caught up in that accident. It's a twenty-car pileup. They were ten cars behind their target using the tagged money as a beacon, so they didn't get spotted. The target got through before a semi jackknifed. The driver overcompensated when a motorcycle cut in front of him."

Before Timms could go on, they heard Fons voice come over the speakers. "Agent Townsend, Ms. Star, are you seeing this?"

"Yes, Agent Rodriguez," Houston replied.

"The men in our follow car are seriously injured." The timbre of his voice changed. "It's Denison and Jacobs, ma'am."

They could hear her gasp over the line. "How bad is it?"

"We haven't heard yet, ma'am, but they had to Life Flight Jacobs to the nearest Trauma unit." Fons could hear Cosby in the background ordering his assistant to get the hospital information.

Cosby was the one who had sent Denison's SRT unit to Dallas for the FBI's part in this operation, his best team. Sophie knew Cosby had worked with Denison and Jacobs for many years. She could see the worry on his face.

Getting back to urgent business, Fons spoke up. "We are going to need help on this right away. We have the target's name from face recognition, Ali Akhtar, an Iranian; he was the only one for which they had no address. We have no idea where he's headed, and everyone in the loop are all too far away to do anything about it."

"Do you want us to back up the FBI team?" Sophie asked her voice a little unsteady.

"Yes, ma'am. The route he drove gives us reason to believe he was heading for New York. We can continue to track the money, but we need you to get there ahead of this guy." Fons continued. "Houston, can you take over?"

"Yes, I'll be on the first flight." The Task Force had already agreed to be backup for whoever needed them.

"You need a partner with you, Houston." Sophie turned to Agent Timms. "Agent Timms, can you partner with Houston on this?"

"Yes, of course, ma'am." Timms responded while keeping his eye on the computers."

"Ms. Corban, can you arrange it for them? They need to get to New York in a hurry. They'll also need a vehicle, firepower, and a way to listen and watch the target once he gets home."

"That's not a problem, ma'am," Sissy answered. Grabbing her laptop and phone, she moved to the conference room to close out the ambient noise.

Smith was still monitoring the DC team, while all this was happening. They had arrested one of the targets and was now following the second. It appeared that situation was well in hand.

Houston and Denny Timms arrived at JFK at 3 pm. Meeting them at the gate was Agent Reddy. He took them to the SUV, waiting with the supplies they needed.

"Agent Reddy, thank you," Houston offered his hand to him, Reddy reciprocated.

Once Houston was behind the wheel, Timms got on the computer. He linked into Dallas command and the GPS following the money.

"The car is traveling on the New Jersey Pike right now. They can go anywhere from there. What do you want to do, Houston?"

Timms looked over to Houston, who was maneuvering to get free of the airport traffic.

Houston had his eyes on the road, his mind trying to figure where this guy was headed. There was no way to know, so he said. "Let's head to Manhattan. I don't want to cross the Hudson River right now in this traffic unless we need to."

"Yeah, and for sure, we don't want to deal with the Lincoln Tunnel," Timms agreed.

Houston got off the I-678 and got on I-495 crossing the East River. He snaked through the city, getting off on Dryer Avenue, deciding to head to Capizzi's Restaurant's parking lot to wait for their target to get closer.

Houston and Denny watched as the dot got closer and closer. He was on the I-95 expressway, "It looks like he's heading for the George Washington Bridge." Fons relayed over the comms.

"That's our guess too," Timms responded as Houston started the SUV and headed that direction.

The target turned off the bridge and got on Broadway headed toward Manhattan. Houston and Denny got behind him as he crossed W 97th St.

"It looks like he's heading to Hell's Kitchen, Houston," Fons speculated.

"We're about five cars behind. We won't lose him." Timms informed him. The target turned off onto Columbus Ave.

"He's turning on W 47th," Timms gave a running account for the benefit of the Dallas Command. "He's turning into an alley behind the Sullivan Street Bakery." Houston stopped so Timms could follow on foot. There was no way he wouldn't be compromised if he followed in the SUV.

"He's parking. I see stairs leading to an upstairs apartment." Timms reported from behind a dumpster in the alley.

"Timms, do you see anywhere we can set up to watch without being seen?" Houston asked.

"I'm behind a dumpster, but there is a fire escape on the next building that leads to the roof. We should be able to see into our targets apartment from there."

"Ok, head up there. I'll find a place to park and come with our gear." Houston pulled out of the no parking zone he was in and went around the corner in search of a legitimate space to park.

Even with Houston's 6'1" stature, it took him two jumps to grab the last rung of the fire escape. He wondered how Timms did it; he was at least two inches shorter. When he finally got to the roof, he asked, "what do you see, Denny?"

Timms put down his binoculars to respond. "I can see into the living room window. It appears to be a studio apartment. He's making a call. That's all so far."

"We need to get ears in there," Houston said while looking around for a way to get access. "In the meantime, let's use this directional. That will give us something." Houston pulled the directional mic from the duffle.

Timms connected the mic to his headphones and linked Dallas command to what he was hearing. Houston walked the perimeter next to the wall, trying to see some way to get to the roof above Akhtar's apartment. There wasn't any easy way, but he felt he could jump it safely.

Their team in DC was monitoring everything. "Ms. Star is Ms. Corban available?" Houston questioned as he headed back to where he left Timms.

"Yes, she is online. Go ahead." Came the response from DC.

"Ms. Corban, I need some direction here on the best way to use the mics I have."

"What do you need it to do, Agent Townsend?"

"I don't have access to his apartment, but I can access his roof, and I think I can reach his window. It's a studio apartment, so one mic might do. What do I have that will be sensitive enough to get us a clear read on what's said?"

"Let's try the obvious first. Can you see a laptop in the room?"

Houston looked through his binoculars. "Yes."

"Is it open?"

"Yes."

"I need you to use your iPhone's data to find out if he has Wi-Fi. If he has it, I need to piggyback on your iPhone to use my Firesheep App to hack into his computer. I'll use a 'man in the middle' hack."

Timms was bringing up his data as she was speaking. "Ok, do you see it, Ms. Corban?" Timms asked.

"Yes." There was silence for a while as she was working. Houston saw a young man in a pair of blue jeans and a hoody carrying a black backpack. He was walking up the stairs to Akhtar's apartment.

Houston was using the binoculars and Timms the directional while Ms. Corban worked on hacking his computer. Command couldn't see what was happening, so Houston was giving them a play by play of what he saw.

"As-salamu 'alaykum," Ali Akhtar greeted his guest.

"Wa 'alaykumu s-salam," came the response, with the traditional hug and kissed cheeks. They spoke in Farsi; the interpreter entered the translation on the plasmas.

"Is everything a go on the commuter train today? Will Nasser place the bomb on the bridge?" Ali Akhtar asked. The voices started to fade, "Ms. Corban, they are moving away from our direct line of sight, we are going to lose sound! We need to hear this!" Houston was still looking through the binoculars.

"I know Houston, let me work! Firesheep didn't work on his computer. I'm using another App. Give me a minute," came her response.

They could hear parts of the conversation as the young man and Ali were walking in and out of range.

"Yes, Nasser will...the bomb...But no sooner than... the train leaves at 5:42...kill 300. All Praise...

"Good, that will... another year... If we don't get... they will..." Ali Akhtar said.

"I got it," came over the comm. "Switch to my feed." It only took seconds for the Command Centers and Timms to switch over. Houston put down his binoculars as Timms had his laptop open and connected to the feed.

The new subjects picture went through facial recognition software. Fons said, it came back as Sadik Farazn, who has a green card to work for one of the high-end software companies.

The shock of what they heard set in, the chatter was coming from every direction on the speaker.

"Keep listening. We need to know what Station the train is leaving," Smith stated. "There are five train stations out of New York, and that's assuming it's the originating site.

"Agent Mathews, Ms. Corban, I need you hunting for any trains from the five stations that leave at 5:42 am or pm," Smith requested.

"We are going to need help, Command. Timms has to stay here while I follow Sadik. We don't dare take either of them into custody until we have that bomb." Houston rattled off while he was climbing down the fire escape heading to his SUV. Timms would relay to him when Sadik left the building.

"Understood." Came Sophie's reply. She directed her next words to Fons in Dallas. "Agent Rodriguez, I need you to get a team on Akhtar's house to relieve Agent Timms. Agent Townsend is going to follow Farazn. We'll need another team to stay on Akhtar, and someone to take Agent Timms to meet back up with Agent Townsend. They'll stay on Farazn when Nassar shows up. Our team will follow Nasser and the Bomb." She took a moment to think. She was standing facing the plasmas at Smith's side, watching every move on the screens. "We better get a drone on standby in case we lose him?"

"Drones are already on standby, ma'am. I'll take care of the rest ASAP," Fons relayed.

Agent Timms's voice broke through, "Houston Farazn is leaving the apartment." He watched to see which way he was turning. "He's headed to the west end of the alley."

"I'll track your GPS Houston, so Agent Timms can meet up with you when he is relieved." Smith relayed back to the team in the field.

"He's at the bus stop on the corner. I'll follow behind." Houston reported.

Deputy Director Cosby received a memo from his aide about the men in the hospital it read:

SRT team member Jacobs died from severe head
trauma. Lt. Denison is in ICU but is stable
and the outlook is positive.

Deputy Director Cosby debated whether to pass this on to Ms. Star during a live operation. She had requested updates as they came in. As the head of the Task Force, he did not want to disrespect her by hanging onto it. It would look like he felt she couldn't handle it. That might have been true when he first met her. But during the Morano takedown, she had proven herself.

Cosby now saw her as an equal and a commanding leader. The one thing he saw as a flaw was her soft heart and tender nature. He had often told her she would have to toughen up if she wanted to protect herself from heartache in this line of work. Cosby stepped up to Sophie and handed her the note. He stood close by.

When she read the note, a sob came out and over the intercom. She immediately covered her mouth and took off her headset to prevent more. Everyone in the room looked up to see what had happened. Cosby stepped next to her, put his arm around her, and pulled out a chair for her to sit.

"Stay on task." Was all Cosby said to the team.

"What's happened?" Houston, Fons, and Matt, all speaking at the same time.

"Everything is fine. Keep on task," came Cosby's response.

Nothing more was said. Sophie got up from her chair and went to her office.

Sophie knew she had to pull herself together. There would be time to morn after this operation; lives were at stake now. She knew Houston had to be on edge, wondering why she was upset.

She hurried into the bathroom, blew her nose, and put cold water on her eyes to avoid puffiness. Then she headed back to the Tactical Operations Center. After getting back on the intercom, Sophie said, "Agent Timms, have you been relieved yet?" She knew the team needed to hear her voice, strong and steady.

"Yes ma'am, I am with the second team heading to meet up with Houston."

"Farazn is still on the bus. We are heading out of Hell's Kitchen." Houston was giving a running account of the progress. Although Houston was glad to hear her, he could tell by the timbre of her voice, she had been crying. He would have to wait to find out what happened.

"He's getting off the bus, but he's not walking, he's waiting for another bus," Houston relayed.

"Understood." Came Fons's reply in Dallas.

"Agent Smith, what's happening with the DC Secret Service team?" Sophie watched as he put up the DC team on one of the plasmas.

"DC Team. We need an update?" Agent Smith requested.

"We have four of our targets now. One should be arriving in twenty minutes. We should have all six members and Muhsin Rafiq by later this evening. All the members so far have been identified." The Agent was silent for a moment. "Ma'am, we heard about the accident involving your SRT team. We're sorry. If there is anything we can do to help, just say the word."

"Thank you, Agent. All of us here appreciate your offer. Stay on task. We will contact you for an update." Dallas was the Tactical Command Center for that team. But Sophie needed to follow their progress, as their team was their backup in DC.

Agent Timms was able to catch up with Houston while he waited for Farazn to get on another bus.

He had caught a ride with two agents that introduced themselves as Agents Kono and Mallory. They would relieve Houston once Farazn landed somewhere. Houston and Timms would wait for Nasser, then follow him.

"He's getting on the bus to Gramercy Park." Houston reported to all listening.

"That's in the Flatiron District," Matt added. "Ma'am, I think we need a drone up to follow in case they lose him."

"Do it."

"The US Marshals have one within ten miles. It's a Zenmuse XT2 FLIR Thermal Camera. We'll get them to redirect it," Matt informed her.

As Sophie moved back and forth between the tactical center and Sissy's station, she asked. "Agent Smith, what have you found out about the trains?"

"Agent Mathews was able to narrow it down to five trains going over bridges out of Penn Station. Ms. Corban is working the trains schedule to see which ones fit the time criteria best." Smith answered. "Three commuter trains leave at approximately 6 pm from Penn and four from Grand Central. None leave at 5:42 am. But the ones from Grand Central don't go over bridges."

After listening to the update on the trains, Houston turned back to his task at hand as he maneuvered through heavy traffic.

"Denny, we need this bus route up on the computer in case we lose sight of it."

Agent Timms had it up in seconds. "Done," he said.

They traveled three cars behind through the heavy traffic for forty minutes.

"There. Farazn is getting off. We're on Park Ave. S and E 27th," Timms shouted out.

"I see. Follow on foot. I'll try to stay out of sight." Houston gave the order.

"Command?"

"Yes, Agent Townsend." Sophie moved behind an empty chair, resting her hands on the back of it.

"Timms is on foot following. We're keeping the SUVs out of sight. We don't want to spook him."

Timms gave a running account while the Command Centers were able to watch it on his hidden body cam. "He's crossing the grassy area and heading to a building. The number is 240 27th St." Timms hustled to bridge the gap between them, worried he'd lose him inside the building.

Command watched as he followed Farazn inside. "He's heading for the elevator. I'm going to lose him." Houston and the backup team found a place to park around the corner. Their SUVs were standing out like a sore thumb. Houston grabbed his gear bag and hustled to Timms' location. The backup team not far behind.

"Ms. Corban, can you get your hands on the names of everyone in that apartment building?" Sophie had moved over to where she was sitting—looking over her shoulder for the information.

"Yes, ma'am."

Timms's voice broke in, "the elevator stopped on the third floor." He ran as fast as he could take the stairs hoping he could see Farazn go into an apartment. He opened the stairwell door, but there was no sign of Farazn. "I've lost him, ma'am." Came Timms' statement, his breath winded from the sprint up the stairs.

"Hold tight, Agent Timms, we are trying to get a list of tenants." Sophie relayed the information while walking back to the plasmas.

Houston asked the backup team to find a place to watch the front and back doors without being seen. He was heading inside to meet up with Agent Timms.

"Hey Houston, I'm sorry man, I couldn't get up here in time to see which apartment he was going in," Timms said. Both now waiting in the stairwell for instructions from Command.

"You're the fastest runner on the team. If you couldn't, none of us could have either. No worries, we'll get him." He patted Denny on the back.

CHAPTER TWENTY-THREE

It felt like time was standing still. Matt and Sissy both worked their computer to try to locate names for each apartment on the third floor. Matt was working the electric company and Sissy, the cable company.

"I have it!' Matt shouted into his headset. He sent the list of names to the plasmas in both Command Centers. Everyone's eyes now on the screens in front of them.

Smith looked over the names. "His name isn't there," stating the obvious. "There is no way we'll be able to tell from this which room he's in."

"Maybe not. But it will help to eliminate ones." Sophie paced.

"Agent Townsend, do you have the snake camera I requested to be in your gear bag?" Matt interrupted.

"That's affirmative."

"Ms. Star, I suggest they use that to look inside each apartment. We should be able to tell who lives there by the furnishings even if he's not in view," Matt suggested.

"Agreed. Go with that Agent Townsend."

"Yes ma'am."

Timms stood as a lookout as Houston dug out the equipment and headed for the first door. The first apartment had an older woman, in the kitchen/living room, making tea.

He moved to number two of the six apartments. On the screen came a cluttered room with toys and clothes on the floor. A toddler crawling on the floor noticed the snake and crawled over to see what it was, trying to grab it. Houston quickly removed it. Room three and four were complete opposites. One was immaculate with frilly curtains on its one window: the other had dishes all over and clothes on the floor. The fifth apartment was sparse. He saw a table with takeout food containers, an old couch, and a coffee table made of concrete bricks and wood. A newer computer was sitting open on the makeshift coffee table. The camera/mic picked up a toilet flushing. Then out of a room in the back came Farazn.

"We got him. He's in apartment 305." Stating what he knew they couldn't see. "Ma'am, I have a mini mic I can attach to the under part of the door. There is enough gap that it won't get snagged when the door opens."

"Go with that, Agent Townsend," Sophie approved.

Agent Timms found the item in the gear bag and ran it out to Houston, who attached it and moved back into the stairwell.

Timms reported to the Command Centers the frequency as 375 MHz so all could pick it up off the satellite.

"Someone is approaching the back door." The team on the roof reported, looking at the drone images. They had climbed up the fire escape. Agent Mallory used his binoculars to scan the surrounding area. Everyone waited for more information.

"He's wearing jeans and a denim jacket with a hoody underneath. He has a black backpack."

"Understood." Houston and Timms moved to the second floor. Waiting just inside the hallway, in case the young man decided to take the stairs. They heard the elevator, so they ran back up to the third floor. They cracked the door just enough to peek out to see if the suspect got out on the third floor.

The elevator door opened. The man described walked to 305 and knocked on the door.

"It has to be Nasser," Timms said. "Do you want us to use the snake camera, ma'am."

"No Agent Timms. We can hear, no reason to risk exposing you." Came Sophie's reply.

"As-salamu 'alaykum," Farazn said when he opened the door—doing the traditional hug and kiss on both cheeks.

"Wa 'alaykumu s-salam," Nasser responded, taking off his jacket and heading to the couch.

Farazn stood in front of him. "I have money for you. Ali wants more bombs. After you place the bomb on the bridge, come back, and I will give you what you need. We have all the money we need now to crush the Great Satan." He raised his hands in triumph.

"Thank you for opening my eyes to the truth. I'm proud to be a part of this, Sadik."

"Our rewards will be great, my friend." Sadik went to where Nasser was sitting and patted him on the back.

Sadik brought Nasser some tea and shortbread cookies. The two talked about their plans.

A half-hour later, they got up and moved to the door.

"So Nasser is the bomb maker. We need to find out where he lives." Sophie turned and walked toward Sissy's station but directed her statement to the men in the field. "We need a good picture of his face so we can do facial recognition."

"Understood." Both teams in the field responded.

The conversation in the apartment ended, and the door opened. Nasser headed to the elevator. Houston and Timms ran down the stairs.

"I'll grab the SUV; you follow on foot." Houston directed to Timms as they hit the bottom step. "You're on your own Agents Mallory and Kono."

"Got it, sir."

They didn't dare take down Akhtar or Farazn until they had Nasser and the bomb. They didn't need Nasser going dark when they had no idea how many explosives he had or even who he was or where he lived.

"I'm right behind him. He's turning South on 2nd."

"Do we have the drone in place, Agent Mathews?" Sophie asked.

"Yes ma'am, it's following Nasser."

"Please put it up on the screen."

"Done."

"Ma'am, the backup team got a picture of Nasser as he left the apartment. It's not a full face, but it's pretty good. I'll run it." Sissy reported.

Immediately the view from the drone came up on the plasmas. Next to it, a partial view of Nasser's face came up.

"He's cutting through some sort of mall and office complex."

"It looks like he is heading to Bellevue South Park. I'm directing the drone ahead." Matt responded. There was a pause as the park came into view. "It looks like there is some sort of festival going on there. There are hundreds of people!" Sophie could hear Matt's frustration.

"Ma'am, the facial recognition came up empty." Sissy relayed.

"Try Interpol," Sophie responded.

"Agent Mathews, tell the pilot he must keep that drone on him," Sophie snapped, "we have no facial recognition."

"Yes ma'am."

Timms jogged to get up closer before Nasser got to the crowd. "Houston, I'm going to need you on foot. Can you get to the other side of the park?"

"Yes, I'm parking now." Houston parked on E 28th and Mt. Carmel Place and headed to the north side of the park, walking the length of it back and forth. "Can you send us the picture of Nasser you have, Command?" Houston asked.

"Done." Sissy sent it to both Timms and Houston's phones.

"He's in the crowd. I'm moving in to get close to him. He's heading north," Timms communicated.

Houston went on alert, trying to watch the entire north side of the park.

"Does the drone have him?" Houston asked.

"Yes. Nasser is winding his way to you, Houston. Stay where you are."

"Understood." Houston backed up a little to get a broader view of the area.

"I've lost him!" Timms hollered.

Smith checked the drones live feed. "The drone still has him. He is moving northwest."

Houston and Timms moved in that direction.

"He's gone into the bathroom on the northwest side." Timms moved faster to get there. Houston stayed in position.

The drone stayed in place as dozens of people went in and out in the next five minutes. Timms decided to take the chance and go inside and make sure he was there. He waited in the long line and watched as each man finished and walked out past the line. By the time he got to the front of the line, each stall or urinal had been turned over several times.

"He's not here. He must have left before I came in."

"No. The drone has been outside the whole time. We had eyes on what he was wearing," Matt conveyed.

"Unless he took off his jacket." Sophie responded, clasping, and unclasping her hands while watching this all play out.

"Houston, you'll have to forget about what he's wearing and look at the faces and body type."

"Understood."

Timms moved quickly to the edge of the park to help Houston. They were looking at anyone with Nasser's physique. The drone circled the park dozens of times. To no avail. An hour later, they decided they were wasting precious time.

"We've lost him, ma'am." Houston finally relented.

"That's a setback for finding where he lives, and we can't find him by the tagged money since he hasn't taken any yet. But we still know where he is going to be at approximately 5:30 pm. He will be on a train track that goes over a bridge." Sophie turned to Agent Smith and walked over to him. "Have we pinpointed which train that will be?"

"We know that there are three trains that go over a bridge at about that time out of Penn Station."

"Where do you want us?" Houston interjected, waiting for orders.

"Hold your position for now. Keep looking. I'll get back to you shortly."

"Agent Rodriguez is Commander Corrigan with you?

"Yes ma'am," came the reply.

"Please have him call me."

"Yes ma'am."

"Agent Smith, please send the call to my office when it comes in."

"Will do."

Sophie requests Deputy Director Cosby, and Under Secretary Sterling to join her. The call came in in less than a minute.

"Ms. Star, you requested a call?" Corrigan opened.

"Yes sir, I'm putting you on speaker. I'm in my office with Deputy Director Cosby and Under Secretary Sterling."

"That's fine. Go ahead."

"Sir, as I'm sure you know. We have lost Nasser. Our only chance now of finding him is in the act. But there is no way we can take the chance of losing 300 or more souls by not stopping the train." Cosby was following where she was going and continued on that thought.

"Devlon, what we need is for you to contact Penn Station and use your influence as HSCTU. We need to stop the three trains in question from leaving on time. And we need to do it without letting the passengers know what's going on."

"You're afraid they might have someone on the train watching?" Sterling interrupted.

"Yes, they would know where to get off before it hits the bomb. We also need to have one of your men on each train with the engineer making sure the order is obeyed."

"I understand. I will get right on it." Corrigan signed off.

"Thank you, sir," Sophie responded.

"We need to pinpoint the targeted train." Cosby addressed the other two in the room.

"I know, sir, but until then, we need to cover all three. HSCTU will be on the trains. But can you get some of your FBI agents in New York to head to the bridges to watch for Nasser? Houston and Timms can watch one, but we don't know yet where Nasser will be."

"Yes. That's not a problem, Ms. Star," Cosby responded.

"We need to stay out of sight. If we spook this guy, he'll just plant it somewhere else. I'm hoping we haven't already done that. His actions in the park make me wonder. Hopefully, if we did, he's convinced himself he has lost us and won't change his plans." Under Secretary Sterling said.

"It could be he's just paranoid," Sophie considered.

"We can use drones to cover the area, too," Cosby added.

"Yes, that would be helpful. That way, our Agents can stay out of sight," Sterling agreed.

"I'm going to send our team to the rail bridge going over the Harlem River. It's the only one that leaves exactly at 5:42 pm. But it's just too risky not to cover the others." Sophie told them.

"I agree." Cosby got up from the chair he had been sitting in and went to make some calls; Sterling joined him.

Sophie went back to the tactical center and put her headset back on.

"Agents Townsend and Timms I need you to find a spot close to the Park Ave. Bridge. A drone will be dispatched for you and linked to the computer in your SUV. You must stay out of sight but close enough to grab him once he places the bomb."

"Understood, ma'am." Came the response from both men.

"Agent Smith, are the two new teams online?" Sophie asked.

"Yes ma'am." She heard over the line.

"To whom am I speaking?"

"This is Agent Westin, ma'am."

"Agent Westin please have your team waiting at the Bridge that the train to Oakdale goes over."

"Same instructions as Agent Townsend, ma'am?"

"Exactly."

"Can do."

Another voice came through. "Ms. Star, I'm Agent Forks, where do you want us?"

"Please proceed to the bridge servicing Port Washington, Agent Forks. Ms. Corban will send you the location. Thank you for your help."

"You're welcome, ma'am."

Houston and Timms were in the SUV. They were about twenty yards away from the bridge. "Command?"

"Go, Agent Townsend," came Agent Smith's response.

"There is nowhere to hide. We are going to park in a lot next to the Bridge, but once the drone spots him and we get out, we will be visible. If we're lucky, he won't be too vigilant."

"Understood," Sophie replied, hearing his remarks.

They were keeping an eye on the images the drones sent from the three lines. Blue skies allowed for clear imaging.

It was 5:30 pm, Sophie had ordered that no trains travel on those three routes after 5. They claimed engine trouble or an obstruction on the track to delay their departure. Homeland Security blocked all cell transmission from the train station: concerned a lookout would send the delay information to Nasser.

Houston was watching the tracks through his binoculars when he saw someone. He hit Timms on the shoulder and pointed. Houston waited to make sure it wasn't just some random person. They didn't want to spook the real target. He tracked him to the center of the bridge. The suspect looked around. Not seeing anyone, he took something out of his backpack and attached it to the rail.

"That's our man!"

"Command, we see our target. Do you want us to try to follow him to his apartment?"

"No, it's too risky. Take Nasser down! " Sophie gave the order.

"Understood," Houston responded.

Sophie turned to Cosby to explain her decision. "The bomb maker is our highest priority. We don't dare lose him. We'll find his workspace another way." Lifting her hand to the screen showing the bomb on the rail to emphasize her point. Cosby quit second-guessing her long ago. He nodded his head in agreement.

"Ms. Star, Interpol can't make a match either," Sissy reported.

"Ok. Let's concentrate on not losing Nasser then."

Houston and Timms got out of the SUV and ran full speed to the bridge. Once on the tracks, they moved as quietly as they could to avoid detection. The bridge itself was only about 340 feet in length.

"Timms you stay with the bomb until the bomb squad gets here."

"Houston, you can't go after him alone. You have no idea if he's carrying a weapon. You need to wait for backup," Timms said.

"There's no time. Catch up with me when you're relieved."

Sophie released the men from the other bridges so the trains could run. She wanted the men to be available as backup if needed. Command was watching what was happening from the aerial view the drone was feeding them. They also had audio and visual from Houston and Timms communication devices. They watched as their team made it as far as the bomb before Nasser heard them and turned. Houston Started running full-on to catch up with Nasser, who was 50 yards ahead of him. They both had put on their FBI jackets for identification.

"Command, he's spotted us." Houston relayed as he ran.

"We have eyes on you," came back from Command.

Fons was watching from command in Dallas, "where's his backup, Command?"

"Timms is waiting for the bomb squad. We are requesting backup on the Harlem side of the bridge. They are about 10 minutes out," Smith answered. Sissy had made the call.

Smith checked to see how far the nearest agent was to Houston. Timms was still the closest. He could see the Bomb Squad was only twenty yards away.

Sophie was watching her husband run after the target alone. She took a moment to pray for him knowing he would do what's necessary to protect himself.

The Public Safety Bomb Technicians reached the bomb. They checked it out and found it was a simple explosive to go off on impact. They disarmed it and hauled it off in a Bomb containment chamber. Once the bomb was off the track, Sophie directed Homeland Security to release the last train.

"Command, you'll have to direct me to him, he's out of my visual." Timms had taken off running the minute the Bomb Squad was in sight.

"Stay on the tracks until the 138th St. overpass then go diagonally North East. Follow on Grand Concourse turn right at the Dunkin Donuts. They are running through that wooded area behind it. The drone's thermal imaging says they are about halfway through the trees." Smith was doing the directing.

"Come on Timms get to him," Fons whispered, stressing out for his partner's situation.

"How far away am I?" Timms was winded, still running at full speed to catch up.

"You're about forty yards behind." Came the response.

Houston got close enough to grab Nasser, but he pulled away and swung at him. Houston went down, giving Nasser sufficient time to get a few yards ahead. That short exchange allowed Timms to get within 20 yards of them. He could see Houston getting off the ground and running.

The target was heading into a more populated area, Houston was afraid he was going to lose him.

"Command, we're getting to a populated area, I'm going to need more help."

"Timms is a few yards behind you; we are directing FBI agents to your location to help take down your target." Smith relayed the information.

Houston still had Nasser in his sights; he was running into an alley and was getting ready to turn a corner. Houston slowed, so he didn't get blindsided going around the corner. When he peeked around the corner, he couldn't see his target.

"Where is he?"

Smith was monitoring the drone. "I see him running north about 25 yards ahead of you."

Timms had caught up when Houston slowed at the corner.

"He's heading North, Timms, let's go."

They ran and followed the directions as Smith relayed them. The problem was there were too many people around. The drone images made it difficult to locate their target from

324

the rest of the people. If Nasser hadn't been running, it would have been impossible. They needed to catch up quickly. His suspect was wearing the hood up on his hoody. Luckily, in this neighborhood, that made him stand out. They could see him ahead and ran to catch up. Nasser turned into a busy wholesale grocery outlet, and they followed. He maneuvered himself through the patrons and out the back door, they were right behind him.

Timms hollered out the streets they were on as they kept pursuing the target. The FBI was on the same channel; they heard it without delay. Command could see several Agents close to them. Houston saw him enter an abandoned house. He asks for Agents to surround it. Houston and Timms entered the empty house, guns drawn. They used hand signals to search. Smith told them he was in the house, back left corner. It looked like he was trying to get out the window. They rushed to catch him before he got away. Nasser had one leg out of the window when Houston reached the door.

Smith could see Nasser's figure as a red blob thanks to the drone's thermal imaging. He watched as the image's hand lifted toward the door.

"Gun! Gun, use caution entering the room!" Smith warned.

Houston stopped cold. He had been running headlong to the room. Standing to the side, he pushed the door open, Nasser let off two rounds their direction. Houston and Timms peeked into the room. Nasser was hanging out the window his head turned, Houston took the opportunity to run in and grab him. They struggled, but he managed to get him pulled back into the room. Timms wrestled the gun from his hand, and Houston contained him. Other Agents rushed into the room to help cuff him. They searched him for more weapons; he had a knife and a phone.

Sometime during the pursuit, Nasser had managed to call Sadik and warned him. Sophie gave the order to take down both Ali and Sadik once Nasser was in cuffs.

The Agents watching Sadik, caught him when he ran out the door and took him into custody.

"Thank you, God, for taking care of Houston and Denny." Sophie stretched her hand to heaven for a moment.

The FBI took Nasser to holding and gave Houston and Timms a ride back to their vehicle.

Most of the teams had finished their assignments, having their primary targets in custody. Now the only active operation left was the one in DC.

Sophie and the team watched them take down the last cell member, including the leader, Muhsin Rafiq.

It was a successful operation. Between the Task Force here and Dallas, all the counterfeit money was confiscated. The ten cell leaders, along with some of their cell members, were in custody.

Sophie made the announcement. "A great job was done by all. Congratulations!" She turned to Sissy. "Can you make arrangements for our team to come home?"

"Yes ma'am."

Thinking the men may want to stay where they are and get some rest. She put her mic back on and asked the teams in Dallas and New York, "unless you would like to stay the night where you are and rest up before coming home."

"No ma'am." Came the responses from all at the same time.

Sophie looked over to Cosby. He nodded his head.

"I have some information on our injured teammates." She hesitated. Her voice emotional, "Troy Denison is in ICU and expected to recover, but we lost John Jacobs to extreme head trauma." She stopped talking, unable to continue for the lump in her throat.

There was total silence in the Command center and on all speakers. There was nothing more to say, so Sophie ended. "Command out."

"Agent Smith, please disconnect from Dallas Command, and let's shut this down."

"Yes ma'am."

Sophie left the Tactical Command Center and went into her office. Cosby followed her a moment later.

"I could have announced the Jacobs death for you," he said, entering her office.

"No, it was for me to do." She sat down behind her desk. Cosby sat in the seat across from her.

"This operation went well, Sophie. It's astounding that we haven't lost anyone before this. Jacobs was a good man. He will be missed." Sophie nodded her head, interlaced her fingers on the desk. Her despair over John's death, causing her body to slouch.

"I will be contacting his family. They live in Montana. John wasn't married. They will probably want to take his body back home. I'll see if they will let us have some sort of memorial here." He was rambling; he didn't know what else to say. If Houston were here, he would know how to comfort her. He was at a loss. Cosby got up to leave.

"Thank you, sir, for trusting me with the news when you got it. I know you could have held it. Your confidence in me is acknowledged and appreciated."

Cosby looked back at her. The corners of his mouth made a small movement, then he nodded and left her alone.

Before Cosby left Command, he gave his last orders. "Ms. Corban, I need you and Agent Smith to give me your hard drives for security after you shut down your systems."

"Yes sir." They both responded.

"We will meet back here at 11 am to debrief and write up our AAR forms," Cosby added as he left. He turned to the Secret Service Agent assigned to the door whenever they were on a live operation.

"I need a car and two agents to take Ms. Star home. I want them to stay with her until Agent Townsend gets home."

"Understood, sir."

Sophie heard Cosby's instructions to be back at 11 am, so she called Carol to order brunch for the team. Before she left Command, she called Lt. Denison. He was groggy but was able to speak for a few minutes. Sophie told him they would come and see him in New York as soon as they could, if he was still in the Hospital. He asked how the operation went, and she gave him the highlights. Then he thanked her for calling.

When she hung up, her cell rang. "Hello?"

"Hi, sweetheart." Houston's voice was gentle.

She gave a big sigh and a sob. "Houston, we lost John."

"I know, sweetheart. I know. I'll be home soon. We can talk."

Houston pulled up in front of his home at about midnight. He saw two Agents protecting his home. His first thought was that there was another threat to Sophie's life. He hurried to the front door and asked the Agent what happened.

"Nothing sir, Deputy Director Cosby asked us to stay until you got home. Out of an abundance of caution."

"Thank you. I appreciate it." He grabbed his go bag and unlocked the door. He watched them get into their vehicle, then closed and locked the front door.

Sophie was sleeping on the couch in the living room. He went over and sat on the edge, stroking her hair until she woke.

She smiled at him and sat up. He held her close. "Why didn't you go to bed, sweetheart?"

"I knew you wouldn't wake me if I were in bed."

"You feel bad about John." He pulled her closer.

Houston let her cry quietly, stroking her hair. There was nothing he could say to make it better.

The entire team was back together, including the SRT, SS, and the FBI teams that worked the operation in DC. Fons and Matt had made it back about 2:30 am. Sophie spread Carol's brunch out in the conference room and called out the invitation to eat.

Cosby walked in with the Under Secretary of Homeland Security and spoke. "The President wants to congratulate the combined Taskforce for a very successful operation. The men in custody are in transport to the FBI headquarters in DC for extensive interrogation. But with all the audio and visual proof, they expect a successful prosecution."

The Under Secretary of Homeland Security, Sterling, spoke up. "We were able to identify Nasser. His real name is Trent Gorman. He's the son of professors at Columbia University; Trent was given a full ride. He was recruited by a radicalized sect of Islam right on campus and changed his name. We went through his apartment and found parts ready to assemble another bomb." He looked around at the teams present. "A great many lives were saved yesterday. Good work."

"The President wants you all in his office tonight at 8 pm for the private ceremony." Cosby directed to his team. "We probably won't be doing any other operations for a while. It will take months to sort through all we've done so far, and the prosecutors will have their hands full."

I want you to take a week off after you shut everything down here. Then report to your assigned 'day jobs.' Make sure all the remaining hard drives are in my hands so I can place them in 'top security' holding." He stood silent for a moment. "On another note. John's family will be picking up his body tomorrow. They would like to have a memorial for him at the National City Christian Church at 1 pm. This administration will be sending flowers along with his SRT team and, of course, our team." The place was quiet for a moment.

Sophie stood and asked, "sir, would you and Under Secretary Sterling like to stay and eat with us?" Sophie invited.

"No thank you, Ms. Star. The President wants an update from us. I'll see you all tonight." They said goodbye and left.

The rest of them spent the next two hours eating and enjoying each other. John's teammates told of his love for his job. His bravery in operations and then, of course, some funny stories to lighten the mood. As the visitors left, the team went to work shutting down their stations.

Houston met with Matt and Sissy to find out what was needed to make a small command center for Sophie at the New York condo. She planned on taking on some of the requests from other agencies on her time off. Houston didn't see why she couldn't do it from home. Sophie had no plans to do any fieldwork unless it was with this team.

Houston carried all Bully's things to the SUV first than came back for his and Sophie's items. Everyone said their goodbyes, most of the team had moved to DC. So after tonight's event, Sophie and Houston wouldn't be seeing them for a while. Only Fons kept his place in New York since he worked there with Houston. She helped her husband carry out the last of their things.

The ceremony in the Oval Office was formal despite being private. Most of Sophie's attention was on her husband even though she was receiving a medal too. Houston was such a patriot. The Presidential Gold Medal meant a lot to all of them. They listened to the accolades the President bestowed on the team. Houston was proud to be in law enforcement and pleased the Taskforce was being acknowledged for their hard work. This medal was a symbol of honor and achievement, recognition for a job done above and beyond. They understood its significance.

On the ride home, she rested her head on his shoulder.

"I'm so proud of you, Houston. You deserve this medal."

He grabbed her hand, kissed it, then held onto it. "Sweetheart, you deserve this medal as much as anyone. You don't realize how incredible you are at making these operations successful."

They went on to talk about how excited he was to be with the US Marshalls when not working the Taskforce.

The memorial for Agent John Jacobs was beautiful. The minister spoke of his courage and commitment to a country he loved. His teammates spoke of their personal stories involving John.

After the service, Sophie and Houston went to acknowledge his mother. Sophie told her, "I worked with John, and I will miss him terribly." She was going to step aside when his mother took her hand.

"You must be Ms. Star."

Sophie was surprised she would know her name. "Yes ma'am."

"John wasn't allowed to say much about his work, but last year he came home and spoke to me about you." She moved them aside away from the crowd and continued, still holding her hand.

"He had quit going to church when he took this job. He told me he just didn't see how Christ fit into his new life. His new job. But then he worked with you and your husband, Houston, right?"

"Yes ma'am."

"He said you both were committed to Christ, and your life showed it in every area. He wanted to be like you." Tears started to run down her cheeks. "He found a good Church and rededicated himself. I know now that he is with Jesus. It has given me peace to know that." She patted Sophie's hand, then took her hanky and wiped her eyes. "You are a light to those around you. Thank you for being that to my son." She let go of Sophie's hand, hugged her, and moved back to the line.

On the way home, Sophie told Houston what John's mother had said. He looked over to her, took her hand, and thanked God.

They had stayed in DC long enough to visit Lt. Denison, who had been transferred back to a local hospital. After that, Houston got the house ready to be empty for a few months. They took everything they needed to their condo in New York and then headed to Trenton to find a fourplex.

Being with Houston's family, Yon Moon and Han Kang-Dae, was a real pleasure. Three days they spent hunting for a property, finally finding a six-plex Houston liked. The deceased owner's son was trying to close the estate quickly. He was willing to negotiate a reasonable price. Sophie hadn't wanted to have six units, but the price was right, and it was only 10 minutes from the ranch. It was a complex built in the late nineties, so it wasn't in bad shape. It had a lovely yard and private fenced back patios for the first-floor tenants — balconies for the second. The dated insides were cosmetic work that wouldn't be too costly. She wanted to redesign the units a little; Houston was on board with it. They finally agreed on this property. The man accepted an offer, one hundred fifty thousand below market value. An all-cash offer is what sealed the deal. It would also speed up the closing.

It had been a productive week off. Now Houston was ready to be at the US Marshall office starting Monday.

EPILOGUE
SIX WEEKS LATER

Being US Marshalls was always the top of the heap as far as Houston and Fons were concerned. They loved this job. They would forget about the Task Force if it weren't for the team and the importance of the cases they got to handle. Last week, their unit was on protective detail for foreign dignitaries here in New York, attending the United Nations summit. Now they were working on the fugitive recovery team hunting high-profile criminals. It was a good fit for them.

On Saturdays, when they didn't have to work, they'd go to Trenton and work on the complex. They wanted to get at least the two apartments for Yon Moon and Han Kang-Dae ready. They needed the security of having their own home. His whole family was helping him as well as Han Kang-Dae.

Yon Moon had been able to see her son a few times after the mandatory thirty-day isolation. He seemed to be doing better than she expected. Moon and Han had English lessons twice a week. The local Korean social club was helping them assimilate into their new surroundings. They found a Korean speaking Church for them to attend, within walking distance.

Sissy and Matt had taken several days and put together a mini command center at the Townsend's New York Condo. It was functional and would do everything Sophie needed for a mission off site.

Sophie was at the condo going through the pictures from Halloween last Tuesday. They had gotten permission to go to the largest domestic violence shelter in New York. They brought gifts and candy to the children since it wasn't safe for the families to leave the premises. Houston dressed up as Eeyore, and Sophie was Winnie the Pooh. It was the best party the children and their mothers ever had at the facility. They decided to do it again next year. Houston was setting up permission for them to come back again the day before Christmas Eve.

Thanksgiving Day was coming. Sophie was on the computer, trying to find the best tickets for the football game at MetLife Stadium. She knew how excited Houston's family would be. It was going to be so much fun. Lily and Spring had agreed they could have their Thanksgiving meal on Friday. They all wanted to watch their family enjoy 50-yard line tickets up close. It would be a treat they would never forget. She was finishing up the purchase of 9 tickets, including one for Fons. It went through just as the phone rang.

"Hello?" She spoke while shutting down her computer.

"Sophie?" Captain Cartwright was calling.

"Yes, hi Captain. How are you?"

"I'm well, but I'm still working at a desk until one of the precinct Captains retires. I'm alright with that, but I do like having the rank. I'm calling to ask a favor."

"You know I'd do anything for you."

He laughed, "I know, Sophie. I have a woman at the hospital she's been roughed up. She won't talk to me. I was hoping she might open up to you." Sophie heard the concern in the Captain's voice.

"Don, I can do that, but what makes you think she'll open up to me?"

"She'll be intrigued by who you are... It's Gail Turner."

"The investigative reporter?" Sophie interrupted. "I'll come, but I can't promise anything. Which hospital?"

"Bellevue Hospital Center. She's still in emergency."

"I'll be there as soon as I can."

"Thanks, Sophie."

She called Houston to tell him where she was going; he was still in Trenton. He told her to call the town car, and when he got home, she could tell him all about it.

To

be

continued...

Thank you for reading "Unintended Consequences".

Although this book is fiction, I hope it gives you a sense

of how God can take the most horrific of circumstances and

make a path to forgiveness and salvation.

Look for Book Three "Flesh Peddlers" coming soon.